I0745591

Dead Prey

The New Order

Books by R. L. Clayton

The Evolution River Series
Sea Species
The Envoy
The Genesis

The Dead Series
Dead & Dead For Real
Dead Reckoning
Dead Again
Risen from the Dead
Dead Prey

Historical Novel
Wings of the WASP

Children's Book
with Abby Pickering
Penelope the Pooting Spider

R. L. Clayton

Dead Prey

The New Order

A Kiki and Nick Adventure

Acknowledgements

COVID 19 sequestration hit Tall Grass editing co op hard, so we haven't met since the start of this mess in March. Melinda, Larry, Damien, Tammy and Star helped me on the first part of the book. Their critiques were right on the money. Alexis Powers took over editing for me and proved to be invaluable as both an editor and a friend. DeeAnna Galbraith is my final authority on editing. She keeps the blunders down. Thanks. Steve Linebaugh continues to be an inspiration in both the cover design and promotion. Keep kicking my butt, Steve to push promotion. Visit him at www.artbygordon.com.

Thank you all. You make me better.

R. L. Clayton
www.rlclaytonbooks.com
email at rlclayton10@gmail.com

ISBN 9781948015196

Introduction

When I started formulating the story of *Dead Prey*, the cartel wars in Mexico claimed daily victims and made weekly headlines in U.S. newspapers. As a frequent traveler to Mexico, I began to worry. It was a nation wracked by lawlessness, corruption and violence. The root cause was and is the American hunger for drugs. The U.S. government pours money and men into missions to control the flow. But the battleground is Mexico, and the casualties are Mexican. We have exported the control of our narcotics problem to Mexico, and the citizens there pay. So I postulated: What if Mexico refused to fight that battle? Since I began the story, a massive shootout occurred that resulted in the authorities returning a prisoner to the Sineloa Cartel. Soon after, the Presidente of Mexico declared he will no longer fight these organizations. The cost in Mexican lives is too high.

At first I thought that deals with the cartels are a path to destruction. I no longer believe that. Mexico will legalize drugs on paper soon. Arrests and prosecutions are already not issues, putting control where it belongs, back in America. In Mexico, drugs are now a business, like any other. During Prohibition, Mexico and Canada continued to make and sell liquor to those who smuggled it into the United States. Prohibition was an American law, and gave rise to the violent gangs that smuggled, distributed and sold to the public who refused to go along with this attempt to legislate moral behavior. The decades-old War on Drugs is a Black Hole into which we've poured billions of dollars and put further billions of dollars into the hands of the worst people. So maybe it's time for something new.

Prologue

The hair on the back of Kiki's neck rose–a feeling she'd learned to respect while a sniper in Afghanistan. Somebody was trying to draw a bead on her. Without showing a sign of alarm, she wove through the busy plaza and into a group of tourists. Small with dark tanned skin and dark brown hair, she blended in with the Mexicans entering the cathedral. It was old Spanish style, with high arched ceilings, columns, hard pews and stained glass windows. She turned to the right, moving along the wall. This didn't feel like an up-close and face-to-face attempt. *He's a shooter, a sniper like me. He won't come in but wait for me to leave.*

She'd had the feeling somebody was watching her several times over the last few months, but it was a weak signal and she'd checked but seen nothing. Not this time. This was more than watching.

The mass hadn't begun and people were still finding seats.

Edging to the front, she found the exit that would take her out the back. If he, she assumed it was a he, knew her well enough, he'd have seen the signs that she'd made him. Kiki paused below the exit sign, hand on the open bar. Death could be waiting on the other side of the back door. She reversed her jacket and put on a hat and dark glasses. *That's the best I can do. I have to go now. I can't give him a chance to set up again.* With a deep breath, she pushed the door open, zigged to the right, then ran to the main street.

* * *

Raphael Sanchez's crosshairs tracked the small woman in black pants and white blouse as she moved across the town plaza through the crowd toward the cathedral. His finger tightened on the trigger. It was 600 yards, not an easy shot with all the people. She wove through the crowd, her gait uneven. Had she made him? Trees momentarily obscured his line of sight. Still, it was a makeable shot.

Katherine Russell had murdered his brother Miguel Sanchez over two years ago. In her defense, Sanchez was contracted to kill Russell and her companions. He was good, but she struck first. Luck was never a factor to believe in. She was better. Later she'd tracked down Jackson Jenkins, his boss, and killed him. Yeah, he'd been after her too. Rapha's code said he couldn't let her get away with it. She was a killer like he was. She'd dropped from sight for a year when he picked up on a series of killings. It was enough to find her. Everywhere he followed her, bodies dropped. He admired her skill.

Why is she in Mexico? I know she's not working alone. She's been around some hard case professionals. They carried themselves like hunters, eyes always watching their surroundings. They appeared to be a team, but he didn't know yet who they were working for. He'd followed them once, but lost the track. Cartel member bodies were found the next day. The obvious assumption was that they were working for a rival cartel. *If there's one thing I've learned, she's not conventional or obvious.*

For six months he'd been pursuing her across the United States and overseas. That could end now.

His finger eased off the trigger. He wasn't ready for the hunt to end.

Dead Prey

Chapter 1

Nick Sabino bent over his patient, Sol Ayub, who was stretched out on the table in the tiled kitchen at the Hacienda, their operations center. He'd seen enough GSWs, gunshot wounds while serving as a medic in Afghanistan that he recognized Sol's injury as non life-threatening. He probed the wound, causing Sol to flinch. *Didn't study too many GSWs in medical school or see many as a small town doctor.*

His phone vibrated in his pocket. He glanced at the display. It was his wife. "What's up, K? Thought you were doing some recon on the cartel."

There was a moment of silence. "I got close enough to clone his phone, but then that old sandbox tingle caused me to abandon the chase."

"What! Who was it?" Nick felt his heart speed up as he glanced down at Sol.

"I didn't hang around to find out. He may have my car staked out. Can you pick me up?"

"Of course. Where?" His voice rising with concern.

"I'll be at the Super Ley north of the plaza in twenty minutes. Call me when you're near. Get me on the fly."

"I might be little longer." He looked down at the man on his operating table. "I'm patching up the boss from the flesh wound he got last night. Like you'd said, it's a thru and thru. Some bleeding, but your compress slowed it down. It'll be thirty minutes before I can get to town."

"Call me."

"Yeah. Be careful." He turned back to Sol, seeing his puzzled expression. "Somebody's onto Kiki. She gets this feeling. In Afghanistan we learned not to ignore it. Saved our lives a couple of times."

Sol, the leader of their team of mercenaries, frowned. "I know feeling well," his voice like gravel on a washboard. "Any info?"

"Didn't ask. No time for that now. We'll find out when she's back." Nick pulled on latex gloves with a snap. Sol's muscular thigh twitched as Nick sewed up the entrance wound. "Okay, turn over." The table creaked as he shifted.

Sol grunted as Nick peeled away the blood-soaked bandage stuck to the back of his leg. Turning toward the case that held his bandages and meds, he said over his shoulder, "I'll pack this with antiseptic then dress it. Things have to heal and drain. Four millimeters to the right and he'd have nicked the femoral artery, and it would have been lights out."

"Yeah, I know. Am lucky bastard. Son of bitch looked like nice kid. Cannot trust anybody in this goddamn country. But we nail fuckers trying to expand their territory."

Nick paused for a second. "How many?"

"Fourteen, amateurs. We want leader for interrogation, but he hero, died in attack."

Nick flinched. He hated interrogations. Now they'd have to capture someone else to find out whether it was another cartel or just some bunch trying to break into the business.

Sol, ex-Mossad agent and now contractor had contacted Kiki and him four months ago about mercenary work in Mexico. He explained he was putting together a team to operate in northern Mexico to quell cartel violence. Both he and Kiki had dark brown hair and complexions that allowed them to blend into the native population.

After Sol set up the group, violence dropped off–if you didn't include the team's body count. Their employer's identification was a mystery. Instructions were only given to Sol, but they were clear: Reduce civilian causalities and stop the kidnappings. Those who violated these simple rules were hunted. No arrests, no trials. Bodies left as a message. They ignored drug business and immigrant smuggling while remaining invisible. The paychecks were generous and on time.

He finished dressing Sol's leg, and gave him an antibiotic injection. "Try to take it easy on this leg for a couple of days. We'll change the dressing tomorrow."

"Yeah, okay. Want me go with you for Kiki?"

"Sure, the company wouldn't hurt. We can debrief her on the trip back."

* * *

The rusty white van rumbled through the streets attracting nobody's attention. With their heads swiveling, Nick and Sol checked for anything unusual, but the streets were crowded with people shopping, doing business, nothing out of the ordinary. As they neared the plaza, Nick watched traffic and pedestrians while Sol scanned building roofs and windows. Nothing. Nick handed him his phone. "Call Kiki. We're two minutes out. We'll get her at the front door. It's always busy. Lots of people.

Pedestrian and car traffic increased as they approached the popular supermarket. People randomly crossed the street, oblivious to the cars, carrying bags of groceries, while street vendors waved their wares above their heads. They were at a crawl in front of the store when the side door of the van slid open, and Kiki jumped in slamming the door closed. Nick glanced back at her. Her tanned skin looked a little pale, but her brown eyes flashed. "Haven't had that feeling in a while." She wore black slacks and a white blouse with flowered embroidery that fit in with those worn by other women on the street.

"You okay?" He noticed she'd reversed her normally black jacket to the brown side.

"Yeah, let's get out of here. If anybody's on my tail, we're all targets." Her voice sounded nervous.

In this traffic, there was no speeding away. Nick turned right onto a dirt road that was clear and sped up, bouncing them on the potholed lane. Three blocks along, he returned to paved roads and headed south and out of town.

Sol faced Kiki in the back seat. "What happen?"

She wiped her brow. "I'll go through it all when we get to the Hacienda. Don't want to have to tell the story three or four times."

"Yeah, okay," he grunted. "We keep watch on your car with drone. If not staked out, we get it tonight."

"That could be a lead in finding out who this guy is," said Kiki.

"Or could be bad if he is good. We watch for while," said Sol.

Chapter 2

Years before when Nick and Kiki were assisting the CIA in hunting terrorists, they had met an ex-Mossad agent working with a team in Mexico. She was part of a Mossad unit hired by a coalition of resort and tourists businesses to stop the cartel wars that were driving their customers away. The government had proven ineffective in controlling the violence. Unlike Mexican law enforcement and the army, this Mossad team could not be bought.

This new team formed by Sol had eight members divided into small groups, staying in several houses in Nogales, Mexico, but the headquarters was an isolated ranch house fifteen miles away. The ranch was idled when the water table dropped as the city grew. There was enough water for them, but not cattle. It was their

Hacienda.

Nick turned onto the dirt road leading to several buildings half a mile away. The countryside was rolling-hill grassland with the occasional oak tree. The growl of the van echoed around them as Nick drove into the rusty equipment shed. As he shut the engine off, the only sound in the sudden silence was the ticking of the cooling motor. The smell of old oil and dust hung in the air.

The house was built in the territorial style, a box with an interior courtyard. There was an arched entrance with a car parked in the patio. It was summer and hot, but the thick adobe walls kept the ranch house cool inside where it felt dark and safe. The interior décor was old-style ranch with heavy oak furniture, patterned rugs on the walls and saltillo tiled floors. Everything looked old and traditional except the satellite dishes in the courtyard, invisible from outside. Sol led them across the cracked concrete of the patio to a room opposite.

The heavy steel door was an indication that this was different. His thumb unlocked it, and they stepped into a dim room lit mostly by an electronic kaleidoscope of monitors, screens and blinking lights. Several monitors showed views of the surrounding land, one a view from a drone 5,000 feet overhead.

The technology Sol's team used was NSA quality, better in some ways thanks to Bob and Kathy Meisenburg, the tech designers and builders Sol had brought on board at Nick's suggestion. In addition to drones, they could monitor the phone system. The high altitude drone belonged to DEA, but Ilia had tapped in and decoded their signal.

Their cell phone monitor used key words that would set off an alarm, alerting them, resulting in targeted eavesdropping, surveillance, and bugs being planted. So far, the cartels hadn't caught on, though Los Xecas were a hi-tech organization made up of ex-Mexican Special Forces, many trained in the U.S. Thus far they had stayed out of Sonora.

Sol's team had technology that allowed them to make preemptive strikes, reducing the number of attacks. As in the U.S. there were no secrets, not really. The locals labeled them the *Fantasmas*–they came from nowhere, struck unseen and left nothing but bodies behind.

Ilia Belikova and Dawn Bordowitz, their techies, were seated at a control panel and nodded at Kiki. Ilia was small and thin, with dark hair and skin. It was a casual atmosphere, both of the techies wearing shorts and tees. Ilia had worked undercover in Russia for Mossad before coming to Mexico with Sol. When angered, the only sign was his black eyes flashed.

"Heard you might have had some problems," said Ilia's sister, Sasha, as she rose from a seat in the corner. She was blonde and gorgeous. As an Olympic skier, she was beyond fit, though the loose cammies hid her figure. From an early age, she had attended school in the United States, skiing the best slopes. Though Israeli, she spoke with an American accent.

A very tall, thin woman leaned against the wall near her. Her skin was ebony, her accent heavy, her hair cut close to her scalp. "You have problem?" her voice rumbled.

"I'm fine, Zyra. I just had a feeling."

"Ja, I have those. Then somebody dies." She smiled, her white teeth in sharp contrast to her skin and the black skintight clothes she wore. Her fingers caressed the hilt of the knife in the sheath at her waist.

Kiki, along with Nick, Ilia, Sasha and Zyra had

been a team that brought smallpox vaccine from Russia to the U.S., stemming the outbreak that plagued America in a bio-attack–the bio part of the Bio-Cyber War.

Dawn had been on her sniper team several years ago when they retook California from the gangs. She had a model's willowy body, fawn-colored hair, and lively eyes that drew you in. She had been sharp, picking up things rapidly. Since that time, she'd become tech savvy.

Kiki turned to Ilia. "Did you have a drone watching me at the plaza?"

"Yeah, one of the buzzard drones."

"Let me run the footage for you," said Dawn, her slender fingers playing across a keyboard. The monitor in front of them showed the plaza from above. People strolled across it heading toward the cathedral. Some sat on benches under the trees. A few more keystrokes and the image appeared on a wide-screen mounted on the wall. A green dot indicated Kiki. A red dot indicated her target, a member of a kidnapping and human slavery ring. The green dot eased up next to the red. Suddenly she turned away and moved into a crowd of tourists.

"That's when I sensed someone watching me. Freeze it for a moment." They all began searching the crowd for anyone paying attention to her. Nothing stood out. "My feeling is that this guy is a shooter like me. I think he'll be away, not close and somewhere with a view of the plaza." She shrugged. "Just a feeling." Walking to the screen, she used her finger to trace paths, clear views from her position outward.

"These are the lines-of-sight I would pick." Dawn overlaid her paths onto the image. They saw nobody on any of the roofs of the buildings surrounding the plaza or the water tower. "Unless he's a real amateur, he won't be in a tree, too exposed," Kiki murmured. Two blocks away, an electric utility bucket truck was parked near the power lines. "Zoom in on that," she pointed. It was empty. Many of the buildings were two-story, shops and stores on the bottom floor, residences on the top. Nothing looked amiss.

Dawn started the action again. They watched people going about their business, strolling along, couples arm in arm, carts selling street food, venders sitting in front of their stores awaiting customers. Women were heading to the grocery store with bags to carry dinner fixings. Children were getting home from school.

"Fast forward," said Kiki, leaning in.

A man in mariachi garb with a guitar case over his shoulder exited one building and headed away, maybe an evening gig at a restaurant somewhere. Maybe not. Nothing stood out, except when he dropped his keys beside her car. "Zoom in." If he'd done something, the camera didn't pick it up.

"Someone was targeting me," her voice firm. "I know what I felt." She faced Sol, arms crossed.

"I am sure you did. I know feeling, but nerves come into play. We watch your six."

Nick put his hand on Kiki's shoulder. "We'll stay here tonight, just in case someone has the house staked out."

"I'm going to put a bird drone outside your house to keep an eye," said Ilia. "It'll just be another raven, nobody will notice. You want monitors inside?"

Nick shook his head. "We have a good security system. Just link it into your circuits."

"Ilia," said Sol, "put bird near Kiki's car. Must be sure it is clear before we pick it up. No surprises."

"Or we find someone to talk to," chuckled Zyra.

Sol faced Kiki. "What is sitrep on our target?"

"I got close enough to clone his cell." She handed her phone to Dawn. "What's our next move, Sol?"

Dawn plugged a cord into Kiki's phone, keyed in some instructions and looked at another monitor. "He's making a call."

In Spanish a voice said, "Rujilio, I told you not to call me here."

"I must see you. I'll come by the station."

"Don't…" the call ended. A map came up. A red dot was blinking. "Well, there's our guy on his way to the police station," Dawn pointed. "Does he seem like a good cop's buddy?"

"Not at all," snapped Kiki.

"Well, he was talking to some cop. He's making another call." Another keystroke and Rujilio's voice came up.

In Spanish he said, "Jefe, he will pick up another girl tomorrow and bring her out to the ranch."

"We will be ready," a raspy voice replied. "With her we'll have enough to ship them out tomorrow night." They talked a little more, then "I will see you at the ranch tomorrow night. Adios."

Kiki faced Dawn. "Could you tell who he talked to at the station?"

"No, but we can follow the phone."

Sol turned to Nick. "You start interrogations when we get somebody. Don't have jail cells."

Nick's chin fell to his chest.

Zyra laughed. "This sounds promising. Maybe we have fun. I watch."

Chapter 3

From inside the beat-up white van, Kiki watched the boys and girls in their school uniforms, plaid skirts or black pants, all wearing white tops as they ran out of the schoolhouse door. In the warm afternoon, they walked away in small groups, laughing and giggling. A blue and white police cruiser eased past the chatting groups of kids. It turned right at the next street. Five minutes later it reappeared.

"You on this, Ilia?" she asked, glancing at the screen in the lap of the drone operator sitting beside her. Though it was 500 feet above, and looked like a circling vulture, the image on the screen was clear. It had the best optics they could get.

"Yeah, the car circled the block. This is the phone we marked yesterday."

A red dot was on the image of the cruiser. "We can watch him on the monitor, don't have to keep him in sight."

They watched for a few minutes more but other cars just sped past the students. The red dot turned off the street further down and circled the block again. The group of students grew smaller as each child reached their home until one figure walked alone. The car drew alongside and parked. A uniformed man got out and approached the girl. She stopped.

Kiki started the van. "I'm going to get closer."

"He's put her in the car!" cried Ilia.

Shit! Kiki glanced at the screen. "We're a block away."

"The car's heading for the highway south. Our vulture can't keep up. I'll alert Sol. They can launch another drone to take over."

The van motor gave out a throaty roar as she sped up to get closer in case there was a gap before the other drone arrived on station. Though the van looked like a beater, under the hood was a first class power plant.

As open country replaced the buildings of the city, they lost their overhead visual. Ilia glanced at

Kiki. "Ten minutes before the other drone is in position."

"I've got him in sight. We're all right." She stayed back a half-a-mile. "What about the team?"

"They're thirty minutes behind." In silence they followed. Kiki shivered. *That poor girl, probably scared out of her wits.*

"Drone's on station." Ilia turned the screen so she could see it. The red dot moved down the highway, their green one behind. On the screen, the map showed a ranch road two miles ahead. The cruiser slowed. "He's going to turn off. There's a building about a mile down that road."

Kiki glanced out the windows. "This country's wide open. If we follow we'll be spotted."

"There's a side road that goes to a cattle tank coming up. Take that. We'll wait for the team there."

After bumping down the dirt road, she curved around the berm of the cattle tank. *That's out of sight from the ranch road,* They stopped under a mesquite tree as she turned off the engine. In the silence of the open countryside, they both watched the screen. The ranch house was small, maybe two or three rooms, with a rusty corrugated metal roof and weathered wood sides. A hulk of a pickup truck, weeds growing through the windows, was rusting into a heap behind it next to the outhouse.

The cruiser stopped in front of the house beside a black SUV. Dust hung in the air as the cop pulled the struggling girl from the car by her hair. He hit her. She went limp, and he dragged her inside. After twenty minutes, he came out, hitching up his pants. He turned and waved at someone in the doorway, climbed into his car and drove off.

Bastard! You'll pay for hitting that girl and anything else you did, I promise that. Kiki snarled, "Shit! We missed him,"

"It's okay," Ilia asserted. "He'll be easy to find. Got his cell phone tagged. Team's ten minutes out. You want to wait until dark? We'll be exposed if we go in now."

"Yeah. I hate to think what that poor girl's going through, but if we go in too soon, they'll kill her before we can get to her."

Ten minutes later, another beat-up van rumbled up beside them.

Zyra, dressed in her black skin-tight outfit, stepped out. Black on black, she'd be invisible in the dark. Her head swiveled as she surveyed the countryside checking for danger.

"Glad you're here," said Kiki getting out of their van. *Too bad the cop isn't here. Zyra would love to take care of him.*

Zyra's intense eyes turned. "We are waiting?"

Ilia shrugged. "The countryside is too open to assault in daylight. In an hour it will be dark. We'll go in then. We haven't seen any activity. The wide eaves hide the house. I don't even know if there's a back door."

"We do reconnaissance." Zyra picked up her rifle and nodded to Sasha. "We go for hike."

Kiki watched the deadly pair move away. Within minutes, they had disappeared into the brush and growing darkness. She was glad to see both of them here. As ex-Mossad, they and Ilia had proven deadly in Russia.

She nodded to Sol, as his stocky frame approached in a lumbering walk. "Kiki, we follow you on monitor, so looks like is kidnapping ring we suspected or part of one."

Sol's team instructions from their boss were specific: kidnapping and human trafficking were issues they had free reign to stop. That was proving difficult because there was so much money in selling young girls and boys into the sex trade.

The other issue was killing civilians, whether through inter-cartel warfare or extortion. The team was the enforcer of someone's new policy. Whoever their boss was knew this had to be secret.

The cartels had divisions–drugs and people smuggling, drug manufacture, extortion, and kidnapping. The Sonora Cartel controlled the smuggling routes into the United States from the California border to Texas. They moved other cartel products for a fee, but also their own products, mostly drugs and people.

The Xecas, mostly in eastern Mexico, were the kidnapping, extortion and protection kings in Mexico. The Sonora Cartel had kept some kidnapping and human slave trade areas for themselves, making them a target for the Xecas and the *Fantasmas*.

Sol's contract to reduce the violence against Mexican citizens was somebody's new policy to bring Mexico back to civilization. The cartels could never be wiped out. The business of drugs and immigrant smuggling was ignored becoming de facto legitimate. Those were American problems. The press was instructed to minimize reports of drug war casualties, but that was sweeping the problem under the rug. Bodies would continue to drop unless the cartels learned what was acceptable and what was not. The *Fantasmas'* job was to make the actions against Mexican citizens too expensive to continue.

Chapter 4

"There is back door." Zyra's voice coming from the darkness caused them to jump. "Nothing hard. We can go into house from two sides." Nobody had heard Sasha and her approach. She wore a thin smile.

"Another car is arriving," Ilia called from the van. They gathered around his laptop. The drone had switched to infrared as darkness fell. Two figures emerged and entered the house. Ilia brought the drone around to see the license plate. Their computer ran the plate. "Shit! It is the Chief of Police."

Zyra smiled. "Good for interrogation, I think. Lot of information. Maybe no need to talk to underlings."

Sasha laughed. "He has to stay alive for that."

Sol huddled with the team members. "Nobody leaves ranch house except those with us. Kiki, you cover from front. Where you set up?" Kiki pointed to a brushy area about three-hundred yards from the front. "Good. Sasha, you and Zyra go in back door. Ilia, stay here with drone monitor. Alert us if any interference." Ilia nodded that he understood.

"Remember, first is save hostage or hostages. Second is capture someone. Nick, stay here with Ilia in case we need medical help. When I signal, come knock out those we take with us. I disable their cars. Emilio, you and I enter front door on my signal."

Within twenty minutes the team was in position.

* * *

Zyra checked the Uzi slung around her shoulders as she and Sasha crouched on either side of the flimsy door. The soft glow of a kerosene lantern leaked through the gap around the door. She reached down and caressed the hilt of the knife at her waist. She favored it over the gun, but they had to take out the men inside fast. Without at least a day to recon, they weren't sure how many men were involved, at least four. The police chief and one other needed to be kept alive, and none of the prisoners could be hurt. *It will be tricky, but we can do it.* Sol and Emilio had tasers for the captives.

"On my count," Sol's voice came over the com unit. "Three, two, one. GO! GO! GO!"

Zyra kicked the flimsy door apart and stepped in, moving to the side, giving Sasha a clear line of fire. One man rose, knocking over a bottle on the table next to the lantern. He reached for a pistol in his waistband. Sasha shot him between the eyes, the suppressed Uzi making a sharp pop.

Screams filled the air. Zyra stepped forward and cut the throat of a man scrabbling across the dirt floor on all fours trying to get away. The fountain of blood brought a smile to her lips. *I prefer death to be close.* Against one wall was a cage with four naked girls locked inside. At the sight of the man bleeding out on the floor, they shut up in shock. Another man in uniform, a deputy, sat beside the cage. He reached for his gun. Emilio knocked him down with a taser shot.

The girls broke out of their shock. Their screams again filled the room. Sol kicked in the door to a bedroom. In the glow of a second lantern, the police chief tried to pull up his pants as he rose from the student they'd seen taken that afternoon. Sol hit him with the taser. He went down, jerking like a puppet with broken strings, soiling his clothes and dampening the floor.

A lone man stood, his hands raised. "Who else is here?" asked Emilio in Spanish.

"Nobody," he answered.

"Who is the boss?"

"I am Juan Soto."

Emilio nodded and shot him with a taser. Zyra stepped over to the deputy. She grabbed him by the hair and hauled him up. "We don't need you." She pulled his head back and cut his throat. The shock of the fountain of blood spurting onto the floor, the gurgling sound as he tried to yell shut everybody up but only for a few seconds.

Ilia's voice crackled over the comms. "We have incoming. Single vehicle, big SUV."

Sol barked, "Zyra, Sasha, out the back."

"Yah, we go around and cover the front."

"Emilio, secure chief and Soto. I gag them. We drag them into bedroom. Kiki, you got us?"

"Yeah, Freefire?"

"If you identify jefe, don't kill him. He have info for us."

"Sheesh. You don't make it easy."

Sol turned to the cage and put his finger to his lips, signaling the girls to be quiet. With their eyes the size of silver dollars, their mouths snapped shut.

In the sudden silence Ilia's voice came over the com unit. "They're in front, next to the police car."

"Yeah, I see 'em," Kiki answered. "Three guys getting out. In Mexico the boss never drives. He's the one carrying the bag. Zyra, I'll hit 'em when they get near the door. Guy lagging behind is rear guard, so you and Sasha take him out. I'll hit the other guy holding the gun. I'll wound the one with the bag."

The shots came so quickly they almost sounded like one.

"Everybody's down. Sol, you can come out. Nick, the guy I wounded will need attention.

Sol's voice broke the silence. "We're clear in here. Ilia, Nick, bring the vans. We need medical in here too. There're five girls to check out and two prisoners to sedate." He glanced around the small room now reeking with the coppery smell from the hot spattered blood. "This will send a message." He stuck a small button mic behind a Madonna statue in a hollowed-out shelf in the wall. "Conversation when these bodies are found may be interesting."

In the yard, Zyra had slashed the throats of the two guards just to send a message. The wounded man was crying and writhing on the ground, his shoulder wound leaking blood into the sand. Sasha picked up his bag from the ground near him. She opened it and held up a wad of cash. "See, crime does pay."

Ilia leaped from the van as it slid to a halt. "Roads looked clear for at least a couple of miles, but we should hurry."

Nick emerged from the other van with his medical bag. He went to the wounded man, looked at his shoulder and rolled him over, ripping his shirt off. The man screamed. "Not fatal if we stop the bleeding. What is your name?"

"Alfredo Bautista," he gasped. "You are all dead for this!"

Nick pressed a bandage to the wounds on the man. He screamed. The screaming stopped after Nick injected him. "Press here," he instructed. Picking up his medical bag, he headed for the house.

Sol and Emilio were standing over the unconscious men in the bedroom. Nick injected them. "That'll keep them out for a few hours." The young girl was cowering in the corner sobbing and clutching the rags of her clothes for protection. Sol had released her after the chief was down. "We're here to save you," he told her in Spanish. She was in shock. With care he wrapped her in a blanket and helped her to stand. Her legs wobbled and he signaled Emilio take her out to the van.

The girls in the cage were trying to all fit into the corner farthest from the door. "We're here to save you," Nick repeated. Sol appeared at his side with clothes he handed out. In a daze they dressed. As he and Sol led them out, they glanced at the bodies on the ground. More than one shivered before looking away. They huddled together in the van, clinging to each other for support.

Sol shook his head at the scene. "Do we need to sedate them?"

"Not yet," Nick remarked. "We'll see how the trip back goes."

When they returned to the house, Zyra was standing over the unconscious Juan Soto. "We need him?" Sol stared at her. "Trash we must get rid of later," she said as her hand withdrew her knife from its sheath.

Nick turned away. Sol put his hand on Nick's shoulder. "Let's go. I'll help you with the chief." Neither glanced back.

Chapter 5

At the Hacienda, Nick began setting up the interrogation room. It was a small room with no windows and a single door. Abutting the courtyard wall, it was insulated from outside sound. The first item seen upon entering was a large casket-like box. The exterior was matte black and seemed to suck the light and life from the room. Tubes and wires from the box connected to a tank and monitors on the wall similar to a hospital room. A lounge chair faced the box with a computer mounted on a swiveling arm next to it. A smaller chair was off to one side.

Nick flipped on switches and started pumps. He lifted the lid of the Isolation Chamber and put his hand into the circulating brine inside. It was cool. The heating system would bring it up to body temperature in an hour.

He sat in the chair, swung the computer around and booted it up. The monitors on the wall lit, displaying flat lines. On his computer he ran through a series of diagnostic tests. He checked the recording equipment to ensure it would preserve every word uttered. After thirty minutes, he left, closing the door behind him.

Police Chief Jesus Borova was unconscious and nude on a gurney. Borova was not a small man. Parts of him hung over the sides of the gurney which Nick rolled onto a portable scale. *Shit, 110 kilos.* He would need help getting him into the chamber. After taking his pulse, blood pressure and temperature, he gave the man an injection. All information was entered into the laptop. Nick didn't want him waking up until he was in the chamber and prepped.

He walked to the communications room where his thumbprint opened the door. "Hey, I need some help getting Borova into the chamber."

Sol looked up. "Emilio is at police station. Our bugs he planted give us update about chief's disappearance, apparently not an unusual event. His assistant is trying to locate him for a meeting. He wasn't at home. He's calling the whorehouses now. The suggestions about his whereabouts are fascinating."

Ilia stared at the monitor. "They're sending a car to the ranch house we hit. This should be interesting." Another monitor from the overhead drone tracked a cruiser leaving the police station. "To cover their discovery, I'm launching another drone. It should arrive on station about the same time as the car. We can use it as a repeater for the bug Sol left behind."

Sol turned to Nick. "I help you with chief."

Together, they grunted and struggled to move the chief into the chamber. "Thanks, Sol. I can take it from here."

Though Sol didn't know much about the Isolation Chamber, an expression of relief crossed his face. "I help move him out when you ready." He closed the door firmly as he left.

Nick knew he didn't want to be in the room during the interrogation. Though Sol didn't understand what was going to happen, he'd spoken of interrogations in Israel. His voice broke during the descriptions of what went on.

Nick stuck the monitor pads on the chief, inserted IVs, placed a bone mic next to his ears. On the computer he entered the sedative used to knock him out. On the screen were the traces showing bodily status and brain activity. Brine temperature was body temperature. With one last look at the floating body, he shuddered. *Closing the lid is Borova's exit from this world.*

Nick sat in the lounge chair, pulled the laptop over and began keying in instructions. The computer would give him suggested drug dosages for different effects. These interrogations took hours. The baseline was the unconscious state.

Nick added adrenaline and amphetamine drips as he watched the breathing and heart rate rise. He added curarine to paralyze the body. The trick was to add enough to keep him from moving but not suffocate. Next he added some LSD, then tetrahydrocannabinol to take the edge from the LSD. He turned on the sound suppression system. As he watched, the chief began to wake up. He could see him trying to move, see his brain activity increase.

His panicked voice came through the speaker.

"What is wrong with me? Where am I? Why I see or hear nothing? I can't move?" He screamed. "I can't feel...." He screamed again. "There is nothing!"

Nick let him struggle for a while. The shouts increased, the pitch rising to a scream. Nick added some sedative, watched the heart rate and breathing calm. He spoke into the microphone attached to the laptop.

"Jesus, you are no longer in your world." The bone microphone would transmit the sounds directly into his head. With the sound suppression system, his ears would pick up nothing, not even his own screaming. *"You are with me now."*

"Who are you?"

"I am your God."

"Am I dead?"

"You have entered my world, the one after your death."

"No! I cannot be dead."

"Do you remember what happened to you?"

"I was at the house fucking that little puta. Men burst in. They shot me. The pain was horrible. My whole body jerked. I could not control it. I fell, then everything went black."

"And now you are with me."

"You are God?" He moaned. "Dios mio. I didn't go to confession yesterday. What will happen to me?"

"You are Catholic. You know. For you to enter heaven, you must confess your sins, all of your sins. You must repent. If you do not, you will burn in Hell for eternity."

"I confessed to Father Diego last week. I cannot remember my sins."

"You are with me now, not Father Diego. When you confessed to Father Diego, you were supposed to be confessing to me, but you did not do that. You did not repent. You continued to commit sins."

"Father Diego said I was absolved."

"He hasn't that power. Only I do. I am sure you will remember. Start with what you did last."

"I fucked that chica."

"You raped that girl, didn't you?"

"She wanted me to."

"Hell is looming, Jesus. Lies are sins and you continue to commit them. Soon you will feel the heat as your soul burns."

"No! No! Yes, I raped her. I'm sorry."

"I don't hear repentance in your voice." Nick

increased the LSD. *"I am going to put you inside her head. You will feel her terror, her pain."*

"How can you do that?"

"Remember the room you were in, the wooden wall, the lantern, the bed. Do you see them?"

"Sí. I am in there."

"Only now you are on the bed, your mind is numb from the drugs. You try to move, but your arms won't work. You struggle but your body is like lead. Screams echo in the room. They are your screams. There's a noise, the door is opening. Someone's coming! Your eyes are squeezed shut, but you must look. What do you see?"

"A man comes in. He wears a uniform of police."

"What does he do?"

"He slaps me, takes off his belt and hits me more with it. I try to flee. I try to protect myself from the blows, but I can't move. He rips my clothes off." The chief screams, "No No. Help me! It hurts. It hurts. Help meeeeee!" He sobs.

Nick let him cry for a few minutes. *"Are you sorry?"*

"Dios mio. I am sorry," he wailed. "I am so sorry."

Nick didn't know how much of this he could take.

"Who recruited you to do this?"

"Alfredo Bautista. He paid me, but I had to pay my officers."

"Who were the officers you paid and who helped you?"

Names spilled out of the man like a fire hose. At last he began to wind down.

"In the end I didn't get that much money."

"You sold your soul for a little money and a chance to rape those girls, didn't you? Picture them in your head. See their faces. You are them!"

The chief screamed again.

"How many of them died?"

"Only a few. We couldn't sell the dead ones."

"Who killed the girls?"

"Juan Alfredo Bautista, I swear. I never wanted to see them die."

"Where are their bodies?"

"Behind the rancho. There is a field. We buried them there."

"Did others in the government know or participate?"

"Sí. The mayor, the council, they all know."

Nick was ill. He needed a break. He turned off the psychedelics, the stimulants and increased the sedatives. He was tempted to increase the curarine, but stopped. *The hell this man will face is a more just punishment. And it will last a lifetime, however long that is.*

For the first time, he looked forward to interrogating someone–Juan Alfredo Bautista. *It's more than information I want.*

Chapter 6

Rapha Sanchez watched Katherine Russell's car from a different room in the apartment. He'd told the family living there he was a photographer and wanted to take pictures of the plaza from their upstairs apartment. *It's been an hour. Somehow she had made me, won't come out this way.* He glanced at the plaza one more time. *She has to return sometime for her car.* He waited an additional hour hoping for another chance to shoot her.

At last he dressed in his mariachi clothes, put his rifle in the guitar case and left, leaving fifty dollars on the kitchen counter. As he walked past Katherine's car, he dropped his keys. Bending down, he attached a tracker beneath the rear bumper. *I can watch her travels from my hotel room. I need rest.*

Once in his hotel room, he splashed water on his face, looked longingly at the bed, but went to the desk and opened his laptop. He brought up a map of the city with her car showing as a red dot. *If it moves, I'll know.*

After months of following her trail of bodies, he'd caught a break when he saw her entering a gated community. He'd staked it out all night and followed her today. In the plaza he never had a clear shot, he told himself. Now he could track her.

He sat on the bed, yawned. He could use a short nap. *I need to call headquarters first.* He got out the satellite phone.

"Nesbit here, Sanchez," came the answer.

"I found her. She's in Nogales, Mexico, sir."

"Did you take her out?"

"Didn't get the chance," he lied. "She may have made me, but I have a tracker on her car. I'll find her."

"Get it done. We have other work to do."

The line went dead without a goodbye.

Rapha checked his computer. *The car hasn't moved. I'll set up an alarm. I need sleep.* After the news of the two latest attacks, one a couple days ago, the other yesterday, he'd driven for twelve hours straight to get here. Both attacks had her signature–sniper covering for a ground assault. It was right out of the military training manual. She left no signs she was there, only bodies.

He undressed and headed for the bathroom. After washing his face and brushing his teeth, he stared at himself in the mirror. *Not a pretty sight–*eyes swollen from lack of sleep, hair long, in need of a haircut, grizzled and needing a shave. There hadn't been time. He shook his head. *This woman Katherine Russell.*

Sometimes her assassinations were solo hits, but lately there were attacks on cartel operations in Mexico. These attacks were a team effort. She had friends in on this. Why the cartels? Was another cartel paying her and her team for that? Whatever her agenda, it was always deadly.

He lay on the bed and stared at the ceiling. After his brother's murder, he'd started an online search for information on Katherine Russell. There was a lot of redacted information. The only photo he'd found was from her days in the army. It was years old, and she was in her cammies with a Model 700 sniper rifle. Her army records were exemplary, a reputation he envied. She'd received several awards before she was wounded.

After receiving the message that her family had been murdered in Arizona, she'd suddenly resigned and returned to the US. That's when she dropped from sight for several years. The information about her actions during the Bio-Cyber War was heavily redacted.

Several years later, her name came up as a possible suspect in the downing of a helicopter carrying high level representatives of the Military Industrial Complex. There was no proof against her, but the circumstantial evidence was strong. It was her signature mode that pointed to her.

After the death of a prominent senator and strong supporter of the military a couple of years ago, Nighthawk Securities was contracted to kill her. It had not gone well. After murdering Miguel, she'd killed Jackson Jenkins, the head of Nighthawk. Again, no evidence, but witnesses said that a blond woman had been with him in the parking lot. *A trail of bodies.*

He lay on the bed, staring at the ceiling. His brother Miguel had been assigned–his little brother. Miguel was good but hasty at times, missing clues. He was always eager to prove himself. The two of them had been typical brothers, competing with each other. A vision of Miguel in uniform rose in his head. They'd been in the Marines together, served in Afghanistan. Afterward, they'd joined Nighthawk Securities. Usually they worked as a team, but not this time.

When the contract came up for Katherine Russell and her husband, Rapha had been on another assignment. Miguel had insisted he could handle the assassination alone though it should have been a two man job. It cost him his life. Rapha had to exact revenge on this woman. *Why didn't I pull the trigger when she was in the plaza? I won't hesitate again.*

Chapter 7

Nick and Sol removed the unconscious Police Chief Borova from the chamber and strapped him to a gurney. Sol helped Nick roll the chief into an adjacent room where he began cleaning him up, when he awakened and began mumbling. Sol leaned close to inspect the inert body for signs of trauma. It was unmarked.

Borova's eyes flew open. His neck twisted violently as he whipped from side to side looking like a trapped animal sizing up its cage. He squeezed his eyes tightly shut. Sol jumped back in surprise.

"No no no! I confessed everything," Borova wailed. "This is wrong! I should be in Heaven," his voice rose in panic. Then he screamed, "No, I did what you asked. You cannot send me to Hell." His shrieks echoed from the walls as he violently thrashed within the restraints. In a falsetto voice he shrieked, "No No. Help me! It hurts. It hurts. Help meeeeee!" The screams from his flashback came from his soul. The chief was making a hard landing from the psychedelics. Nick rushed to his side and gave him a sedative.

"Not that I care but he will be easier to handle unconscious," Nick stated, glancing at Sol.

Sol stared, face pale, mouth agape, eyes wide in horror. "What you do?" his voice a whisper.

Nick's eyes were cold as he looked up. "Gave him less than he deserved." He nodded to the now still figure on the gurney. "He said it. I sent him to Hell."

"What do we do with him now?"

"Killing him would be a mercy. His mind won't come back." Nick stared at Sol. "You dispose of him, but listen to the recording of the interrogation first." *It might influence what you do to him and how you feel about it.*

Nick turned back to the interrogation room. "I have to get Bautista ready." He felt Sol's glare boring into his back as he closed the door.

There was little cleanup to do. *It's not like these guys will suffer from a disease if the brine is contaminated.* He chuckled at his joke, but it was humorless. He refilled the drug reservoirs, checked the brine temperature, reset the computer for a new interrogation.

When he left the room, the gurney with the chief was gone. In the next room another unconscious figure was strapped to another gurney. Nick looked at him. Bautista was small. He could get him in the chamber without help. That was good. He wanted Sol to listen to what type of man was on the other gurney.

The prep ritual was the same. Bautista weighed sixty-five kilos. He had a crucifix on a chain. Nick entered that into the computer along with the amount of sedative and the time he'd given it to him. He lifted the small man into the chamber, attached the sensor pads and the IVs. He dimmed the lights.

In the lounge chair, he pulled the laptop in front and checked the screen. Everything was normal for a sleeping man. Did Bautista really sleep like this? Did memories of the girls and boys he'd sold into slavery haunt him or was his soul as black as Borova's? Though exhausted, Nick wanted this to be over. With a deep breath he started the amphetamine and adrenalin drips. He added the curarine slowly, watching the respiration. He turned on the sound suppression system inside the chamber.

The crucifix told him Bautista was Catholic which provided an opening avenue into the man's head. He'd interrogated all types, including atheists. Once they were convinced they were dead, the questioning was pretty routine. That first hurdle that was hard.

On the monitor, he watched Bautista's respiration, heart rate and brain activity increase. Now to make him believe he was waking up dead. The door opened behind him. It was Zyra.

"Nick, I watch, yes?" He nodded as she took the other chair. "I learn to do this better someday. The times I do it before not so good."

Nick cringed at that thought. *What was "Not so good?"*

A yell came from the speaker. Bautista was awake. On the monitors they watched him struggle to move, his pulse rate and breathing increasing. He yelled again. "Where am I? What's going on? Why can't I move? Why can't I hear my voice?" Nick said nothing, allowing him time to understand he had no sensation of his own body.

Nick turned to Zyra. "Let's get something to drink."

Zyra's brows knitted together. "You leave him?"

"He won't go anywhere. He needs some alone time. You're welcome to stay, but say nothing. If anything happens, come get me."

Towering over Nick as she stood, she said, "I go with you."

Nick set some alarms and they left the room.

In the communications room, Dawn and Kiki watched the screen showing her car. Sol stared at Nick and Zyra. "I call the boss when you have information from Bautista. He wants report—wants to know what we found."

"We need a break," mumbled Nick by way of an explanation. He looked at Kiki who nodded. She knew what these interrogations took out of him. "Where are we with Kiki's car?

Dawn pointed at the red dot on her monitor. "Nothing's happened. We reviewed the time span. The only thing that caught our attention is this mariachi. He drops something beside your car. There's enough time to plant a tracker."

Zyra chuckled. "Perhaps we track the tracker."

"We get car tonight," said Sol. "Take it to your house, then stake out. Ilia, put bird drone there. We see who comes and goes." Ilia nodded agreement.

"I can go with Ilia," said Dawn.

Kiki laughed. "We need somebody who will blend in, not attract attention. Dawn, with your super-model's body, golden skin and blond hair you could blend in Southern California or Sweden, but not Mexico. Sasha's not a good choice either. I'll go."

"I'll wear a disguise," Dawn countered. "You'll see. It'll be fine." She laughed as she left the room.

Kiki shook her head. "I'm not sure what kind of disguise will work for her."

A few minutes later, Dawn reappeared with a dark brown wig, darkened skin and a pregnant suit. She held her arms out and turned for inspection. "Yes?"

They all laughed at the transformation. "Okay," said Sol.

"You'll have to practice your waddle," said Kiki. More laughter.

Nick turned. "I have to get back."

"I go too," declared Zyra. "See what we learn."

Chapter 8

Bautista's voice was hoarse from screaming. Nick sat in the lounge chair, pulled the laptop in front and rested his hands on it, fingers poised like a gamer ready to start. Zyra took the small chair to his left. "

Are you done yet?" said Nick.

"Who's that?" *"You were raised Catholic. Who do you think this is?"*

"You are God? My mother believed in you. My sister still does. I do not."

"Okay, I am whoever you want me to be."

"You're my imagination. You're not real."

"If that's what you choose to believe, but I'm here with you."

"Where am I?"

"You have left your world and you are in mine

now."

"What happened to me?"

"What do you remember?"

"If you're God, you know what happened to me."

*"I do, but do you? Tell me the story.""*I was at the ranch to pick up the new batch of girls."

"Who were you picking them up for?"

"If you're God you know."

"I'm not the one with the scrambled mind. Can you even remember?"

"Am I dead?"

"Do you feel dead?"

"I don't feel anything."

"But you can remember things?"

"I was getting them for Eduardo Robledo, my boss. I bring the money to pay the chief, but…. That's when the attack happened." He inhaled deeply. "Cuate, my guard, was shot in the head. He was dead, I saw his brains splatter the ground. I was shot and fell. The pain was terrible. I watched a black devil-woman kill my guard with a knife. A man injected me with something. Everything turned black. Did he kill me? Am I dead?"

"The world you lived in is gone from you. Do

you believe I am God now?"

"Sí. I am going to Hell."

"If you confess your sins and repent you may not. Confess."

"I have not confessed since I was a niño."

"Then you have a lot to talk about. Start with your latest memory and we will go back through your life together."

It took hours of talking and coaxing to get the whole story out. It was typical, an impoverished boy growing up in the streets, struggling to stay alive and finding a family with the cartel. Alfredo Bautista was smart, a quick study learning who to give his loyalty to, earning trust. He moved up in the kidnapping arm of the Sonora Cartel, becoming the payoff man and the inspector. If those who were kidnapped had no value, he disposed of them. Once the ransom was paid, he decided whether to return the person. Mostly, he did not.

Bautista was the liaison between the cartel and the local authorities, making the payments and placing orders for product. He knew the names of those involved. In the end, the corruption rose through the local police, federal police, the army, and politicians up to the Minister of Defense.

Bautista didn't know personally many of those high up in government or law enforcement who were involved. He knew them by reputation. The situation was worse than Nick imagined. And he knew these men were immune to justice.

Exhausted, Nick shut him down, putting him back to sleep. *It's probably the best sleep he'd had since childhood. This man's soul is black.* Rising from the chair, Nick blinked and stretched. Sometime during the interrogation Zyra had left. Nick hadn't noticed.

Sol shook his head as he entered the communications room. "I listened. Unbelievable. The whole government corrupt. I don't think can be fixed. Must call boss. What he will do with info, I know not."

"Before you do that, tell me where are we with getting Kiki's car?"

"Emilio and Dawn will pick it up and drive it to your house. They swept it and found a tracker."

"Where's Kiki?"

"She and Zyra take care of chief. He will be found. Another message to bad guys. Finished with Alfredo Bautista?"

"Yeah. He's wrung out. Nothing else to get out

of him."

"Kiki and Zyra will take him. They create scene with bodies to incriminate chief. Cartel be not happy their section head dead." Sol picked up his phone. "I need to call boss."

"You want me to leave?""Usually am told not to involve anybody else in talk with boss. This time, no. You might know something to add."

Wearily, Nick sat down. *Even after the interrogations are over, they're not over.*

Chapter 9

"You have news for me?" Julio asked as a greeting. *Only one person would call me on this number.* His office and residence was in the Presidente InterContinental in Mexico City and overlooked the city with a spectacular view. Though he owned other houses throughout Mexico, here was where he felt the pulse of Mexico.

"Yeah," said Sol, "not good. We raid kidnapping operation, free five girls, and capture two people."

"Well, that's good. Find out anything interesting?" *What was not good?*

"The police chief was there. We interrogate him. He named the officers in department part of operation." Julio said nothing, awaiting more information. "We interrogate Alfredo Bautista, leader of kidnapping section of Sonora Cartel. He tell names throughout local, state and federal law enforcement, and the army.""You have a recording of this?"

"You want copy?"

"No. Keep it well hidden and protected." *We will use it at the right time.*

"Bautista didn't know all names of government officials involved. We must question higher up for that. Those he named have support of those above them."

"This is good news. So we can prosecute these men you spoke with?" *This could go far in taming the cartels, bringing them into a coalition.*

"No sir. They did not survive interrogation." Sol looked at Nick who nodded.

"I see. So we cannot bring these individuals to justice. Is there corroborating information that would allow us to go after those they named?"

"From the information we have," Nick interjected, "I don't believe justice could be served at any trial. The corruption rises too high."

"Who is that?"

"It is Nick Sabino, the interrogator. He is with me to add information if needed."

There was silence. Julio remembered Nick. *Would Nick remember me if he met me? Of course he would.* "Then we will have to take care of it through other means." *It will be bloody bringing the cartels into a National Collective, but big changes were seldom made without bloodshed.*

Sol stared at Nick. "We under your direction, sir."

"Thank you. I have another call coming in. I will call you back." He hung up. *Did Sabino recognize his voice? Would he be a complication?*

* * *

Sol looked at Nick. "Well, we see what happens. I have hope this mess in Mexico can be straightened out."

"Sol, do you know who that is we spoke to?"

"No. He uses great pains to keep identity secret. Phones scrambled. Coded email. Payments directly into our accounts."

"I think I recognize his voice.""What! Who?""I'm not sure. Kiki would have to hear his voice to confirm."

Sol shook his head. "Nobody supposed to hear conversations but me. Don't know what he will do since you were here."

"You did record this, right?"

"Told not to, but am not stupid. Yes, recorded.

* * *

Julio looked at his phone. He recognized the number, *Eduardo Robledo, head of the Sonora Cartel.* "What can I do for you, Eduardo?"

"One of my operations has been hit. My man has disappeared along with the chief of police who was also my man. A lot of money and my product are gone too. How did this happen? You promised protection."

"I am aware of the incident. Our agreement was that we would not interfere with your drug or immigrant smuggling. We would protect those operations from attacks by others. You were not to continue the kidnapping or slave trade. This was the operation that was hit, correct?"

"Sí. How did you know?"

"Little escapes my attention. You did not abide by our agreement. These are the consequences. There is room for you to make a lot of money with the other operations. Divest yourself, and we will protect you."

"I cannot give up those parts. My cousin runs it, and they are too profitable."

Julio hung up. *Either Robledo would learn or he would be replaced.*

He dialed another number. "Señor Presidente, our operation *Fantasmas* is moving ahead. We are having the expected opposition, but it's being taken care of. We will need a replacement for the chief of police in Nogales, someone we can trust. A number of officers there may also need to be replaced. The new chief will tell us if they understand the rules."

"Do you have anyone in mind for chief?"

"Not at this time, but the new chief should bring in his own crew."

"Gracias, Julio. I'll consider any recommendation for people ready to step into those positions." The line went dead.

Julio dialed another number. He had to move fast while things were in disarray. "Pablo, gather your closest people together and take a trip to Hermosillo for five days. When you return, you will be the new head of the Sonora Cartel. Let me know of any resistance."

"Sí, patron."

Julio called Sol back. "Eduardo Robledo, the head of the Sonora Cartel is our enemy."

"We take care of him. You have replacement?"

"It's handled. Get me the list of those officials your source named. I will decide what to do."
"Yes, sir."
Time to start cleaning house.

Chapter 10

From the communications room at the Hacienda, Ilia and Kiki watched the couple approach her car. Dawn had the pregnant waddle down pat, looking to be about seven months along. As they approached her car, Emilio pulled out what looked to be a cell phone. It was a bug sensor.

"I'm picking up a tracker on the car. What do you want me to do?"

Sol and Kiki glanced at each other. "Leave alone," said Sol. "Drive car to house and park in driveway. We watch to see what happens from here."

Emilio held the car door for Dawn as she struggled to sit down. "I don't know how women can do this," she said pushing the bulge to one side, "and this one is foam rubber, weighs nothing.

Every woman considering children should be forced to wear one of these before doing the deed."

The sticker on the windshield of the car opened the gates at the community where Nick and Kiki lived. Once inside the house, Emilio linked into the surveillance system and the drones Ilia had watching. After thirty minutes, they watched a Jeep Cherokee park outside the wall surrounding the community. The driver got out and jumped the wall into the neighborhood.

"It's all clear," Ilia said over the com system.

Emilio, who had slipped out the back of the house and jumped the wall, circled the block and put a tracker on the Cherokee. "Now we follow him."

"It looks like he's putting a remote cam outside your house," Ilia remarked to Kiki, watching the overhead drone view.

"Yeah, he's got the cam up in a tree and is walking down the street like a resident out for a stroll. We're getting pics to run facial ID."

"Emilio, he's on the way back," Dawn cautioned.

"It's okay. I'll circle around and come in the back."

"Our tracker is higher tech than his," noted Ilia. "With rotating frequency, he won't find it with a simple signal detector."

"You two stay there tonight. We track him from here," Sol instructed.

"Roger that," Dawn said. "Now I can get out of this damn suit."

* * *

On the drone monitor, Kiki and Ilia watched the man get back into his car and drive away. With the tracker, it showed up as a red dot moving through the streets until it stopped at a hotel. "Okay, we know where he's staying," she announced.

"I need to go over there with some equipment so we can tap into the hotel security system," Ilia replied. "We'll find his room and bug it."

"How will you get him out of the room?" Kiki asked.

"I'm working on that," Ilia responded.

Chapter 11

In his hotel room, adequate by Mexican standards, not quite by American, Raphael Sanchez booted up his laptop to access the app tracking Katherine Russell's car. The red dot showed it at the house he'd visited. In another window, he brought up the camera he'd planted across the street, aimed at the parked car. He set up an alarm system that would alert him of movement of the car or someone in the view of the camera.

Time to report in. He unpacked his satellite phone and called Nighthawk Securities. Colonel Michael Nesbit answered after the first ring. "Nesbit here."

"Colonel, I've got a tracker on Russell's car and a camera watching her house."

"I thought you'd tell me she was a done deal."

He detected irritation in the colonel's voice. "I didn't have a clear shot, but I can find her. If she moves, I'll know." *And then my brother will have his revenge.*

"One of our main contracting firms is interested in your mission. One of their partners in Mexico got hit, took out some men, stole some property and money. A couple of their key figures have disappeared. I told them we have a man in Nogales, which got their attention. The contract to find these people and remove them is ours if we can handle it."

If we can handle it. "What information do they have for us?"

"The partner is the Sonora Cartel. The hit was on one of their kidnapping operations. Alfredo Bautista, the cousin of Eduardo Robledo, head of the cartel, ran it. He's missing and Robledo is pissed. The chief of police is also missing. The cartel is offering a huge reward for the cousin's return and the heads of those responsible." Colonel Nesbit chuckles. "Nothing for the police chief."

Yeah, that figures. "No clues who's responsible?" *I believe Katherine Russell was involved, but I need confirmation before saying anything.*

"Kidnapping is Los Xecas' business, but they haven't moved this far west. The Sonora Cartel's main business is drugs and smuggling. It does only a little kidnapping and human trafficking. There's been no ransom demand, so it doesn't appear that Bautista was taken for that reason. Besides, it was more of a rescue mission. The girls were returned to their families."

"Los Xecas would have sold them," noted Rapha.

"Exactly," Nesbit agreed. "Incidentally, there was a hit a couple of days ago against a startup cartel trying to move into Sonora's territory. Fourteen dead. Sonora says they didn't do it."

"Usually these cartels have eyes and ears everywhere," Rapha mused. "They knew nothing?"

Nesbit sighed. "Strange. They're calling whoever did this the *Fantasmas,* Ghosts. Nobody knows who they are. They appear and disappear leaving bodies and very few witnesses. Any chance they're tied to your target?"

He thought a moment. "I'm not sure why Russell's down here, so it's possible. *But what would she be doing hitting cartel businesses?* So far, the only person I've seen with her is her husband, Nick Sabino, though she could be part of a team. I've been able to follow her by tracking the bodies she's dropped, but in the past they weren't cartel bodies. That's a recent development. Before this happened, her targets were military leaders and political figures."

"What? Where's the profit in that?" Nesbit sounded incredulous.

"I've wondered the same thing. These hits were on some nasty people, and if I were a goody-goody, I'd target 'em too. But no money tied up in those hits. Go figure."

"Unless there's a long-term political angle," the colonel murmured. "Stay on her. Meantime, I'll start looking into money. Somebody's financing the *Fantasmas* and somebody's financing Russell."

"Yeah, follow the money."

"Sanchez, if we end up with a contract, I'll get you some help. We could use this contract."

"Yeah, Thanks, sir. I'll keep you informed of anything down here." *Help, huh. Usually they just muddied the waters. I need to be the one who kills this bitch.*

"Call me tomorrow with any updates."

"Roger, sir."

He glanced back at the screen with the red dot. It hadn't moved. The camera of the front showed nobody moving. *Tucked in for the night, huh. I'm gonna put you to sleep–permanently.*

Chapter 12

Kiki rolled over and nestled against Nick. He sighed in his sleep. Without disturbing him, she rose and headed for the shower. The hot water caused her to cringe. After scrubbing and shampooing, she turned the water to cold, then gasped at the shock. *Now for coffee and information.*

Entering the security office with the steaming mug in her hand, she nodded to Ilia. *Did he ever sleep?*

"Your *Friend* hasn't moved his car. Last night, I tied into the Hotel Colonial de Nogales security. It's been quiet. I also installed a radio monitor on the roof. We picked up a satellite call last night. It was encrypted, so I suspect it was your *Friend.* I'd like to put more eyes and ears on this guy."

"He's not my fucking *Friend*!"

Ilia held up a hand. "Okay, no need to get hostile. We have to call him something. What do you want to call him?"

"How about asshole," she snapped.

"Too many of those around." Ilia frowned. "Did you get up on the wrong side of the bed?"

"Sorry. I'm a little on edge. Killer any better?"

"Too many of those too. Come up with something else."

"Bogey. How's that?"

"That will work until we get a name. I've got facial recognition running now."

Sol walked in with his coffee. He slurped and turned to Ilia. Anything on Kiki's *Friend*?"

"Bogey!" said Kiki and Ilia together. Sol jerked at the shouts, spilling his coffee.

"Don't ask," Ilia laughed. "His car hasn't moved, and he hasn't made any calls since the one last night."

"Let's see if we can force the action," said Kiki. "If we move the car, what will he do?"

Sol nodded. "Good idea. We get Emilio to go for groceries. If our Bogey follows, Ilia can put some bugs in his room." He looked at Ilia.

"That will work. I can do that."

Ninety minutes later, Kiki and Sol watched the red dot of their Bogey's car move. "Emilio, the fox is after you," said Sol. "Get him to hang onto you for hour." He turned to Ilia. "Go!"

Sol stood, pushing the chair back. "Now we watch F…the Bogey. You want coffee?"

Kiki shook her head. "Got some. As soon as Ilia gets back, we should talk about Eduardo Robledo. It was his cousin we took."

"Yeah. Robledo's refusal to stop kidnapping operation put him in crosshairs. Boss want him taken. We conference with boss."

An hour later, Ilia returned. "You have any trouble?" asked Kiki.

"No. We have the room next door. The camera is looking through a pinhole, and there's a holographic mic from our room. They're passive so he won't find them in a sweep."

Sol nodded. "Yeah, good job. Emilio heading back to house. We see what happens." They all glanced at the monitor to assure that the red dot was moving.

Sol faced Ilia. "Boss send me address of Eduardo's house? Get plans. We conference later to plan raid."

"How about a drone over the site?" Kiki ventured. "An overhead view would give us the layout and surroundings."

"The DEA's drone spends a lot of time over it," Ilia noted, "but we don't control that. Nick and I can get one up in thirty minutes. Can we bring Dawn back to help me with the monitoring? We can leave your car at your house, turn the lights off and on to make it look like someone's there."

Sol picked up his phone. "Dawn, you and Emilio go out back to road outside community. Don't be seen. Set up house to look like people there. Nick or I pick you up on road in thirty minutes."

"What about our *Friend*?" Dawn asked.

"Ugh, that name is Bogey now. If looks like someone in house, Bogey not suspect. We need to do planning. Best if you here."

"Just when I was getting settled in," Dawn said, a whine in her voice. "Okay, we'll be ready," her tone brighter. "Do I need to wear my pregnant suit? That thing's hot."

"Welcome to world of undercover." Sol snickered.

* * *

Sol addressed his team as they sat in the semi-darkness of the communications office. "We go after Eduardo Robledo. Head of Sonora Cartel heavily guarded. We have house plans, or maybe we hit him someplace else, if better."

"Is dead or alive mission?" asked Zyra. "Dead easier."

"True that, but need his information." Sol looked at Nick, who grimaced. "Ilia, we want his communications monitored and him tracked."

"I'll set up an AI to filter for what we need." Ilia said. "Dawn, put our vulture drone over his house. Tonight we'll bring in a low level raven to get more information. We need to pay special attention to his security staff housing. When Robledo's there, so are his men."

Sol pointed at the large monitor on the wall with the overhead view of Robledo's mansion. It was off of Highway 43 south of the city, once a huge rancho located in a valley. The countryside on the surrounding hills was grassland and scrub oak. It was only ten miles from their Hacienda, "Kiki, when attack begins, you must keep guards in those barracks." He pointed to the long building about fifty yards from the main house. "If they get out, we seriously outgunned."

Kiki walked to the big screen. "Typically, snipers like longer range, but our guns have to be silent, and the 300 Blackout is quite effective under two hundred yards." She pointed to a brushy spot two hundred-fifty yards from the barracks.

"I'll be here. I can cover the front of the house and the front of the barracks. At the house, there are guards stationed at the front door and the back and one on the roof. We'll need someone else here," she pointed to another spot behind the barracks, "to cover the back door. This barracks has no windows, so the only ways out are these two doors. Covering the back door also gives line-of-sight to the back of the house. When I take out the roof guard, that's the signal for someone," she looked at Dawn and Nick, then Sasha and Zyra, "to take out the guards at the back of the house. Once the roof guard is down, I'll go after the ones at the front door. I'll then cover the front exit from the barracks. Questions?" Nobody spoke.

"When the first shots are heard, people will try to get out. We'll use suppressors on all our guns to delay alerting them as long as possible, but if they shoot, it'll be noisy. That's when things will get busy."

Sol looked at the faces around him. "Emilio and I go in front," he circled the mansion. "We take out guards that Kiki not get to. Nick, you and Dawn cover back of barracks and back of house. I know you are not sniper like Kiki, so need to be closer. Sasha and Zyra in back as soon as guards down. We need guards gone without noise."

Zyra grinned. "You mean like with knife? Sasha and I do that."

"Ilia, you stay on monitors and drones. We need constant updates."

Zyra smiled. "When fun kick off?"

"For now, we must learn. Ilia, Dawn you keep drone over house, tap into cell phones, watch guard patterns. Use infrared to learn how many guards inside and outside. Track shifts, mine the data and tell us when is best, but needs to be soon."

"What about our Bogey? Who's going to keep track of him?" Dawn asked.

"Unless he alerted, no problem." He looked at Ilia. "You can use alarms if he does anything?"

"I'll alarm if his car moves or if he makes any calls."

"Boss say that Eduardo capture is priority. We go after him."

Chapter 13

On her heads-up display visor showing the overhead view from the drone, Kiki watched her team move toward the large well-lit villa in the wide valley. It had a magnificent view of the moonlit rolling hills surrounding it. Music drifted across the open space. It was a peaceful and idyllic scene except for the armed men patrolling the house. Highway 43 was not a busy route, so it was quiet this time of night. The Sonora Cartel was *old-school*, depending on guards, not using electronic sensors.

One-by-one she highlighted the sentries with her infrared laser. Acknowledgement came from each of the team. She switched to night-vision and infrared to check the perimeter for additional guards. There were none. The drone overhead marked each target into a site screen. Using heat signature, it also marked the three at the back of the mansion. It was a real-time projection. If they moved, it followed them. On the heads-up display, eight red dots glowed outside the building. She was responsible for the one on the roof and three or four in the front. The IR sensor on the drone marked four more inside the house. One of those was Eduardo Robledo. Four green numbered dots were stationary around the grounds. One was her, two were Nick and Dawn, and the other was Ilia in the van. Four more green dots advanced toward the front and back of the house.

The IR sensor showed twenty more red dots in the guard barracks. It was critical they stay there. A silhouetted figure appeared in the doorway of the house. "Hold," she said. She marked him with the laser. On her visor, his red dot approached each of the others in turn. Obviously, he was the security supervisor for this shift.

Within twenty minutes he disappeared back into the manor. "Clear. Take 'em." She watched, alert to any problems in taking out the guards. Her silenced 300 Blackout was equipped with subsonic 220 grain bullets. There would be little sound as her deadly shots backed up the team. She would start with the guard on the roof, then the one nearest to her and work across the front. Dawn and Nick had the same guns focused on the rear of the barracks and the house. The shots had to be kill shots. Wounded men screamed and raised alarms. It was up to Zyra and Sasha whether the sentries at the back could be taken by knife or shot.

Each of the advancing team members carried a nine millimeter UZI with an integral suppressor capable of almost silent death. Her friend, Zyra, also carried a knife honed to razor sharpness. She liked to dole out death in close quarters. Zyra and Sasha were the best close-quarters killers on the team. Kiki couldn't cover the back of the house, so they got the hard job. Nick and Dawn would back them up if necessary.

Her first shot would signal the start of the assault. A last check of everybody, and she lined up on the roof lookout. He peered over the edge and stepped back to light a cigarette. The glow from the lighter highlighted his face. Her bullet struck him between the eyes.

Quickly, she aimed at the nearest sentry on the ground. He had his back to her looking up at the roof. The splat of the bullet and body falling up there had made a noise. Her crosshairs focused on the man, an easy shot from two-hundred yards. After the soft pop from her rifle, his head too snapped forward, his rifle clattering to the ground. The next guard, nearer the door raised his rifle and ran toward his fallen companion. Her slug hit him center of mass taking out his heart. The guards on the far side of the house from her both went down. Sol and Emilio, she knew. All of the red dots in the front had changed from red to yellow on her display, and the supervisor hadn't appeared in the doorway. The green dots of Sol and Emilio advanced toward the front door, stationing themselves on either side. No alarm had been sounded, death had been silent.

Kiki checked the display of the rear of the house. The green dots of Zyra and Sasha were next to the yellow of the guards. All of the outside guards were down.

"We're ready," said Zyra. "How's the front?"

Kiki glanced at the heads-up. All the red dots were yellow. "Ready in the front. How about the back?

"We're clear here," said Dawn, excitement in

her voice.

"Focus on the rear door," Kiki instructed.

"It's a go," said Ilia. The green dots entered front and rear of the house. Her scope swung around to cover the exit from the guard barracks. She had a clear view but inside was darkness. There was sure to be shooting from the house as the team encountered the sicarios inside. It was up to her and Dawn and Nick to keep reinforcements from joining the fray.

Their recon with the drone had shown thirty-five guards. That meant that there were twenty-four in the barracks. If they made a rush out, she'd have to be quick. She replaced the magazine in her rifle and moved the three thirty-round magazines close for ready access. It was several minutes before the rattle of automatic gunfire echoed across the hillside. In the green glow of the night vision scope, the first man emerged from the barracks. She fired. He collapsed in a heap in the doorway. A head peeked out. She fired again. The doorsill behind him spattered with gore and brains. There was another rattle of gunfire as someone inside the barracks sprayed through the gaping doorway. She waited for the next victim.

"We've got people trying to get out through the rear door," cried Dawn.

"Stop 'em," answered Kiki. This was Dawn's first hot-action duty. That's why Nick was with her. The rattle of automatic fire from the rear sounded. "If these guys are trained, they'll rush the door. Move and set up on automatic fire. Empty a magazine into the doorway, then move so they can't locate you while Nick covers the door. It'll make them think there's more of you."

A fusillade of shots came from the front door, none near her. Figures leaped over the bodies in the doorway and ran out. Two rapid shots and they both were down. Silence filled the air. "Status?" she called.

"Quiet at the back door," said Nick.

"We have the package," said Sol. "Clear the road."

"Suppressing fire," Kiki called as she began to put rounds through the door to move everybody back. As the team exited the manor, Zyra and Sasha broke off, running to each side of the barracks. Sol and Emilio passed her dragging an unconscious figure as she watched Zyra toss a grenade through the door. The echoing explosion was followed by another. Sasha had done the same in the back. Those booms were the sniper teams signal to withdraw.

Kiki watched the green dots that were Nick and Dawn move away. She dropped back a hundred yards and sighted on the doorway again. Nothing moved in the dust cloud. She put more shots through it. As Zyra passed her, she pulled Kiki to her feet. "We go."

Kiki shouldered her rifle and backpack. They ran for the two vans. Scrambling inside, she glanced at the bound and blindfolded figure. "Eduardo Robledo?"

Sol nodded. "I'm sure Nick pry useful information from him before he disappears."

Kiki frowned at that. Shit! Nick hated these interrogations. And what would they do with the information? What would their boss do with it? This hit was sure to catch the attention of the Bogey? Was he someone from the cartels who was onto them?

Chapter 14

Sol glanced at Nick and Kiki as he dialed their employer. On the big screen monitor in the communications room, the drone view showed chaos at Robledo's house. Black SUVs and police cars jammed the driveway. Bodies on stretchers were carried to a van, placed inside. The stretchers were carried back to the buildings for more. Teams of men combed the area for clues as to who did this. The phone was picked after the third ring.

"Hola, Sol."

"We hit Sonora cartel headquarters."

"I know. I received a call. You have Eduardo Robledo alive?"

"Yes."

"My man to replace him is on his way to Nogales. He was the number two man, so he shouldn't have trouble taking over. There may be some holdouts or contenders, but he'll handle them."

"Will he need help?" Sol asked.

"If so, I'll call you. What about Robledo?"

"We interrogate him tomorrow." Sol glanced at Nick, who nodded.

"I want to be there."

Nick shook his head. Kiki stood with her mouth in a tight line after hearing the boss's voice.

"We cannot do that. We cannot guarantee your safety, and questioning procedure has no room for anybody else."

"I'm afraid I must insist. I may have questions that need to be asked. I'm also curious about your interrogation methods."

Nick mouthed the word *audio*, and pointed at his ears. Sol nodded. "We set up link. Audio-only. Protection for both of us. It will be real-time so you can ask questions and hear answers. Everything recorded so you refer back if needed."

The man used to getting his way sighed. "That will be acceptable. Call me when you are ready."

* * *

Eduardo Robledo was short, with beer keg abs

and black hair. His moustache obscured his upper lip and a good part of his mouth. Nick guessed his age at thirty, not too young in a business where the life expectancy was measured in years, sometime months, certainly not decades. Kiki poked her head in the room.

"You need help?"

"I could use the company." When the door was shut behind her, he asked, "Did you recognize the voice?"

She nodded. "It was Julio Cardenas, a voice I won't forget. You knew."

"I wasn't sure until today. He is the last person I want to know about our interrogations. That is why this will be an audio-only link. You tried to kill him. What do you think he'll do when he finds out you and I are here?"

"I didn't try to kill him," Kiki snorted. "I let him go. We've saved his life twice, but we did force him back into Mexico and thwart his plans to take over Southern California as a new state in Mexico."

"Let's get Robledo in the tank and go talk to Sol before we link up."

* * *

Thirty minutes later, they closed the

interrogation room door leaving Eduardo in the Isolation Chamber, the first stage of his voyage out of this world.

In Sol's office with the door shut, Nick put his hands on the desk and leaned forward. "Sol, we may have a problem. Kiki agrees with me that we know who our employer is." He glanced at her then back at Sol. "His name is Julio Cardenas. During the rise of cartels, he was the biggest boss in Mexico. In a joint operation of FBI, CIA and an Israeli contract team, he was captured. Kiki and I were an unwilling part of this group."

"What kind of operation was this?"

"At first, Kiki and I were interrogating terrorists for the FBI and Homeland security. Then the CIA got involved and it branched out to other areas. We disagreed and were held prisoner on a boat when Julio Cardenas was brought onboard. The Israeli team had captured him. He was to be interrogated about drug operations, something we didn't want to be a part of. When we objected, we faced prosecution for bullshit charges. We escaped, taking him with us. After we turned him loose, he grew a lot stronger."

Nick paced. "During the Bio-Cyber war, he

teamed up with the gangs taking over California. In return for his help, they were going to give him Southern California. We were part of a team that stopped him, forcing him back to Mexico. He knows us." Nick stopped and turned toward Sol. "The short version is that we don't know what he'll do when he finds out we're on your team. We didn't leave things on a friendly basis after our last encounter."

Sol frowned. "I know only the name Julio, but his past not a surprise. Only strong could take and hold position he has."

Kiki shook her head. "Whatever that is."

"I had to submit a list to Julio for approval. He knows who is on my team. He knows you are here and does nothing. I think he is fine with it. Certainly, he recognizes talent."

Kiki and Nick glanced at each other. Kiki sighed loudly. "I will be watching him. Do you know more about what his position is, what organization he is with?"

Sol shrugged. "I know little for fact. I make assumptions he is trying to be biggest boss. But our directions regarding drugs and immigrant smuggling I understand. Kidnapping and human trafficking is puzzling. Why he against those?"

"Is he the top of the pyramid or is there somebody else?" Kiki stared hard at Sol.

Sol chuckled. "I've wondered myself. This *need-to-know* basis. I have suspicions, but not ready to share yet." He looked from Nick to Kiki. "Are you ready to start interrogation?"

Nick blew out a breath. "I have to wake him up and get him in the mood to talk. We'll let you know when to make the link."

Chapter 15

Once back in the interrogation room, Nick plopped into the chair, sighed and checked the chamber and monitors reading Eduardo's vitals. Without looking up he said, "What do you think, K? Should we pull up stakes and flee? The trimaran is calling."

A half smile crossed her face. "We could do that for a few years again. Then what? I kinda like splashing bad guys. We do that for The Prophet, but his jobs are only occasional."

"Yeah, but I wish we knew who we were doing these hits for. We know the prophet." He smiled. "With him, we are sure they're truly evil people."

She glanced at the chamber. Her brown eyes glinted as she pushed her dark hair away. "Let's see how this plays out for awhile longer." Her voice hardened. "So far, you can't deny the hits are on evil people." She shrugged. "We can always run. The trimaran is berthed at Puerto Peñasco, and that's only a few hours away."

Nick stared at her, turning this over in his mind. He nodded and pulled his computer in front and began typing in commands that would awaken Robledo. Kiki sat in the other chair and booted her computer up. She brought up a bio of him, looking for things to use.

"He has no religious tats or jewelry, so religion probably isn't the best way into his mind," she noted. She began reading: "He was raised by his grandmother who took him to church every Sunday. He was even an altar boy, but then he left his home suddenly, living on the streets. Something really bad must have happened. His priest was murdered soon after. Coincidence? I think not."

Nick blew out a breath. "Okay, another avenue. What else?"

"He went to prison for robbery. His cellmate was murdered, his throat slashed."

"Did he do it?"

"Probably, but there was never a trial. He escaped."

Nick hit the com button. "Sol, make the linkup for Julio. Robledo is almost ready."

Eduardo's scream interrupted him, filling the room. "Where am I?"

On the monitor, he and Kiki watched his heart rate and blood pressure surge as he struggled to move. The EEG trace became a series of jagged spikes. Panic was setting in. Nick tweaked the sedative and increased the psychedelics.

Robledo's voice rose to a shrill cry. "Why can't I feel anything? Am I blind? What's happened to me?" He shouted, on the edge of hysteria. "I can't even hear myself. I don't understand."

"Eduardo, you are with me now."

"Who are you?"

"You don't recognize my voice? Perhaps it has changed since you altered my throat."

"Who are you?" he whispered.

"It's your cell partner, remember?"

"Sache? I killed you."

"Yes, you did. Cut my throat with that shiv. What did I do to deserve that?"

"I had to get out. A new trial was my chance, so when I was scheduled to go to court for murdering you, I had my escape ready."

"So I was just another pawn in your game."

"Wait! If you're dead, then I'm…"

"And we had such great plans to take over the drug and people smuggling business in Mexico. We talked for hours."

"I did everything we talked about. My Sonora Cartel has the transportation routes into the United States from California to Texas. We control the border. Everybody has to come to us to move their product."

"I knew you could do that. Yet you are here in this place with me now. All your work and plans for nothing. What happened?"

"It was Los Xecas. They have the kidnapping, extortion, and protection in most of Mexico, but not in Sonora. We have that."

"Then they attacked you?"

"It had to be those God dam Xecas."

"Didn't you have protection?"

"I did. I was betrayed."

"By who?"

"All of those bastards. The governor, the Minister of Security, the police, the army. I pay them all, but they let Los Xecas come in."

"The Xecas offered more?"

"The governor and the Minister of Security each got $50,000 every month. The local police got $5000 per month. General Fimbres got $10,000 a month. And at first I paid individuals to look the other way and for information. Everybody got paid."

"You were paying out a lot of money."

"I was making a lot of money. Then this man, Julio, says he will take care of the payments and guarantee security. But only if I give up the kidnapping, extortion and human trafficking. I think the Xecas were paying him to get those operations. It's what they do. I couldn't allow that. Sonora is my territory. This Julio let the Xecas come in. They killed me." Robledo emitted a sob. "What happens now?" he whimpered.

"Didn't you have agreements with the Americans for protection?"

"I did. The Americans gave me information to protect myself. In return I moved their fentanyl, heroin and crystal speed for them. By ship they would bring in chemicals to make them. They set up labs in my towns to make their drugs, and my Sonoran sicarios would move it across the border."

"Which Americans?"

"They called themselves The Company. They had technology and money. When we began to have trouble with El Presidente and his enforcement policies, they spoke of a plot to remove him."

Julio's voice spoke in his ear bud. "Ask for names."

"A coup to remove El Presidente? Were there others to help do this?"

"I know that the Secretariat of the Interior is ready to step in when the presidente is removed. He is friends with this group, maybe the American CIA, I think. They are also going to replace the Minister of Cartels."

Nick was surprised at this title. He'd never heard of such a position in the government. *"What is this position?"*

"It is some secret thing only shared between the cartels. He is like the don of dons. Neither the public nor the American government can know of him."

"What about those CIA people?"

"They are the ones who recommended that position. They wanted to organize the cartels. That requires a boss."

"What's his name?"

"We were never told. His identity is kept secret. We only know him as Julio."

Nick sucked in a breath. There were many Julios in Mexico. It was a common name, but a coincidence? He wanted to ask Julio about it, but kept quiet.

Nick asked more questions, but it was clear they had the important info. He increased the sedative and decreased the psychedelics and the stimulants. He watched Eduardo become unconscious.

The voice in his ear bud spoke. "You will never mention this to anyone. Destroy this part of the recording."

Chapter 16

The interrogation had run late. Sol asked for a debrief in the morning, and they were only too glad to put it off. Kiki and Nick had retired to their bedroom. Kiki paced the bare room containing only the bed and a small desk. The walls showing only cracks and patches matched her dark mood.

"Nick, we're fucked. If we tell Sol about this Minister of Cartels and the coup and Julio finds out, we'll be in trouble. If we don't tell him, Sol will feel betrayed when he learns that we knew."

"He won't find out."

She spun to face him, her brown eyes blazing. "Of course he will! He's not dumb. He will hear the recording tomorrow, and any gap will be a glaring omission. I don't want to lie to him."

Nick shook his head. "K, I'm more concerned about an American agency behind the overthrow of a legitimate government. They got away with it in Central America for a while, and they might be able to get away with that in some third world African nation. Mexico is our neighbor, right on our doorstep. Millions of Mexicans are living in the U.S."

"This is worse than the attempt a few years ago by the DEA to create a war between the cartels. The bloodshed was horrendous. The promise to stop that violence is what got El Presidente elected."

Their minds prickled. It was The Director, a spirit or an alien without a physical form that existed to eat human emotions. Nick had encountered it while interrogating a terrorist years ago. At first he doubted his sanity, but Kiki heard the voice in her head too. Only one other person had been able to hear it, and he was dead.

They both clamped down on their emotions so as not to feed it.

"Good evening, Nicholas and Katherine. It has been a while since I spoke with you."

Usually Nick and Kiki abhorred this being they'd named The Director. Other aspects of it existed, all part of one, but with different tastes.

This was the only one that communicated with them, preferring the emotions of hate and fear, likening those to flavors. The entity claimed to not be able to read minds, but it could create thoughts that led to the emotions it preferred. War was a banquet.

"It has been a while," Kiki sneered, "and I had almost forgotten about you. I hoped you had died."

"Ha ha. I do not die. I simply am. I have missed our conversations, but I have followed you. This is a bit of a situation, is it not?"

"It's a mess," declared Nick. "We are sure Julio Cardenas is this Minister of Cartels, and our group is working for him."

"That is true. I must say that under his direction the levels of violence and fear have diminished. My best caterers, Los Xecas, are even realizing that there is more to be gained with organization. My tasty meals from them have diminished."

Kiki's laugh was harsh. "Pardon me if I'm not sympathetic."

"These Xecas instill a unique level of terror in their enemies because they are particularly vicious. You must be careful of them for it is their

special areas of kidnapping and human trafficking that you attack."

"Los Xecas are mostly in the eastern section of Mexico, we are not," Kiki pointed out.

"That may not always be so."

Nick sat on the bed with a big sigh. "We are worried that Julio Cardenas has reason to attack us. The knowledge of the existence of this Minister of Cartels position and that we know who he is makes us a target."

"It does, but he still has use for you. In addition to your past relationship with him, your knowledge of him is another reason he has to fear you, and the flavor of that is tinged with admiration. He does care for you both for twice saving his life. He believed that you, Katherine as **La Diabla** *were killed by the gang attack. After the assassination of Sean Gallen, he believed you were a ghost, a true devil."*

Kiki began laughing. "Scared the shit out of him."

"That was a particularly tasty treat. Your name on Sol's team list shocked him. It was you and your young commandos who forced him back into Mexico, dashing his plans for California. He

fears. It is in his nature to strike against fear. Be very careful of him."

Nick and Kiki locked eyes. "What of the cartels we've struck?" she asked.

"Los Xecas believes your group is part of another cartel. They are combing sources for information, and their methods of requesting information are brutal. They are hunting you, and they are good. Following them is a smorgasbord of flavors. Ta ta for now. You may have another enemy. I will talk to you soon."

"Nick, I'm worried. We're amassing enemies."

"I know, and some of them are American."

She crossed her arms. "We've opposed Americans before."

"K, I'm beginning to feel surrounded." He walked over to her and hugged her tightly. "Odds are not in our favor. At some point we'll run out of second chances."

She nuzzled into his embrace. "Let's get to bed."

Their lovemaking had a tinge of desperation. Afterward, she stared at the blackness. *What would I do without him? I'll do anything to protect him.* Tomorrow they would tell Sol. He had to know.

Sleep did not come easily.

Chapter 17

Kiki strode up to Sol's desk with Nick behind her. He furrowed his brow as he watched Nick close his door. His office, once a small bedroom, had nothing on the walls. The only furniture was a cot, Sol's desk, clear of anything personal and three metal folding chairs. She leaned forward; her hands flat on the desk's scarred surface. "We need to talk."

Nick joined her as they sat in the two folding chairs facing the desk. Kiki glanced at Nick. "The interrogation was very informative, more so than we anticipated."

"I have not listened to the tapes," Sol offered.

"Julio wanted us to edit them before anyone listened," Nick noted.

Sol's mouth fell open. "What? Me too?" Kiki

nodded. Sol straightened in his chair. "Why would he want that?"

"Eduardo revealed information that threatens Julio. The Sonora Cartel and others have an arrangement with Americans, he thought the CIA. These Americans have hi-tech and money. They feed him information, and he moves their drugs to the border. Those drugs come in by ship at Guaymas."

"Ship!" exclaimed Sol. "Not by air or truck?"

"He said ship," confirmed Nick, "and he was specific about opium, white opium and the raw chemicals for manufacturing fentanyl. That makes me think the source is overseas, probably Asia."

"And that reminded me of Air America from the Viet Nam war," offered Kiki. "Eduardo also said something about trouble with the present Mexican administration and a possible coup."

"A coup against Mexican government with American involvement! If this information got out, it could be diplomatic disaster," exclaimed Sol. He rose and began to pace.

"Which U.S. agency has orchestrated government overthrows in foreign nations?" She watched Sol's eyes widen as he thought about it.

He turned and faced Kiki. "This is what he wanted edited out?"

They both nodded. "Have you heard about the government position Minister of Cartels?" Kiki asked.

Sol's puzzled look told her he had not.

Nick sighed. "Eduardo named people within the Mexican government dealing with the cartels and the amounts of money they were paid. The corruption goes to the highest levels."

Sol sat again. "The presidente?"

Nick shook his head. "He didn't say that specifically, but he spoke about this unknown position in the federal government. Julio may be the one holding that position. Julio's reaction to Eduardo's information was that we were to say nothing to anybody, including you."

"If he is this Minister of Cartels, he may be trying to organize the cartels at a national level and using us to enforce it. We are the sacrificial goats," Kiki exclaimed. "If we're caught or killed, the government can deny any knowledge." She glanced at Nick, who nodded. "We can think of no other reason he'd want this to be kept quiet."

"A position of Minister of Cartels would cause

an international uproar and scrutiny," stated Nick.

"Not to mention how the cartels would react to being forced to obey another boss. Their independence would make Julio an enemy to all of them. Know anything about this?" Kiki watched for any sign of deception in Sol's answer.

Sol looked down at this desk and paused. "I have suspicions. I think the presidente is trying build a strong government, a thing lost these last years. He made a campaign pledge to reduce the violence and murder rate." He looked up, frowning. "The path to that means not battling cartels, but organizing and incorporating them as part of government, making them a legitimate business."

"That would make Mexico an international outlaw if it became known," stated Nick.

"Perhaps not," offered Sol." Netherlands and Uruguay legalized drugs. Have not collapsed. Many countries not enforce drug laws, particularly producer nations."

"Yeah, and others use drugs as a weapon against the United States," Kiki asserted. Nick stared at her. "China is the greatest source of fentanyl and amphetamine that ends up in the U.S.," Kiki continued. "Think of the resources spent fighting drugs and what that sucks up, not to mention the losses addiction causes. If we look at drugs as a weapon, the damage to the nation is huge."

"And they get paid to do it," Nick muttered, shaking his head.

"I not blame Mexican government for wanting to profit," Sol said. "Risky narrow path they travel."

"The corruption is so deeply ingrained throughout government and law enforcement, the presidente has to do it outside of normal channels," Kiki said. "So enforcement of this new policy falls on us."

"You believe the presidente is behind this, and you're all right with it?" Nick asked.

Sol shrugged. "So far it's bad guys we're attacking."

"They all look like bad guys," snorted Kiki.

"This is history in the United States repeated," Nick observed. "The attempt to legislate morality was tried in the Prohibition Era and found unacceptable for a number of reasons. It led to the rise of gangs, which we're still fighting today. When Congress repealed Prohibition, gang activity fell tremendously. Their main source of revenue, illicit alcohol, went to the government. They had to find new ones because prostitution and gambling wasn't enough–illegal drugs became the logical move."

"You think Mexico will legalize drugs as a way of fighting the cartels?" Kiki sneered.

"The battle against the cartels is an America war exported to Mexico. If you consider the cartels a business supplying a product, there is no battle. The war is the U.S. laws. During Prohibition, much of the rest of the world, including Canada and Mexico supplied the alcohol. Refusing to make the U.S. problem Mexico's will certainly reduce the violence," stated Nick.

"So we are transition team," Sol declared.

"One of several in the future. We're the experiment. As this Minister of Cartels, you don't think Julio's in it for the money?" Kiki snorted again.

"I think the government is in it for the money," Nick offered. "It's a win-win-win. They reduce the violence, reduce the cartel influence and receive billions in U.S. funding without Congress. They become THE cartel. Our government has threatened to impose sanctions if Mexico legalizes drugs. This is a way of doing it covertly." He smiled, looking from Kiki to Sol.

"Julio Cardenas is still a problem." said Kiki. "Sure, he wanted southern California back as a part of Mexico, which sounded patriotic, but profit and power have always been his goals. Even if the presidente is on the level, how can he trust Cardenas?"

Sol's jaw tightened. "When you have job to do, you don't always hire ones you trust. Hire ones who get job done."

"Keep your friends close and your enemies closer, huh?" smirked Kiki. "I just hope the presidente is playing it straight and knows how to get off the tiger he's riding."

Nick stared at her. "At some point we might be that exit ticket."

Kiki watched understanding dawn on Sol's face.

"Cartels not give up power easily. Government targets," observed Sol, "Julio and presidente. CIA not want to see change. They lose out. Who has more experience deposing governments?"

Kiki shook her head in disgust. "Now Cardenas has another reason to get rid of us. But what worries me more is getting on the wrong side of the

CIA, the biggest international gangsters in the world." *I'm not sure David Kennedy would agree with that.*

"Unfortunately, finding out truth may cost us our lives," Sol remarked.

Chapter 18

The *Fantasmas* were again gathered in the communications room. Ilia looked from his computer monitor to Kiki. "Facial recognition finally came back on our Bogey. He's Raphael Sanchez: ex Special Forces, vet of Middle East conflicts, presently working for Nighthawk Securities. It took a while to find information around the *Access Denied* on normal channels. I had to hack in. Even with that, there are still some gaps in the bio so I'm continuing to try to get to the un-redacted reports."

"Nighthawk Securities, huh." Kiki's tone was hard. "Nick and I had a run-in with them a couple of years ago. They were doing some black ops contract work that included making Nick and me disappear. I had to take out two of their operatives."

Could this be a grudge match?

Sol looked from Nick to Kiki. "They work for who at time?"

"It was a dark government operation, rogue group." She held up her hand. "I can only say we were working with the good guys."

Nick glanced at Kiki before turning to Sol. "We have a friend who might have some info about this. Years ago, we worked with David Kennedy, the ex-director of the CIA. He may be able help us. We can give him a call."

"You trust him?" Sol raised his eyebrows.

"Yeah, with our lives. We, along with Ilia, Sasha and Zyra all worked with him." The three team members nodded approval.

"That level of trust we need. Go ahead."

Kiki gave Ilia the number. After several minutes, they heard the phone ring.

"Kennedy here."

"David, it's Kiki. Can you talk? Are you on a secure phone?"

"I'll call you back in ten minutes."

Ten minutes to the second the phone rang. Kiki looked at her phone, *Unknown Number*. "David, thanks for getting back to me."

"I was in a meeting that I didn't want to attend anyway, needed a break. What's up? This is a social call, right?"

"Sorry, we'll have to save the pleasantries for a little later. David, Nick and I are working on a contract and hit a snag. We need some information on an individual named Raphael Sanchez. He may be with Nighthawk Securities. Can you check on him?"

"Can you tell me anything about what you're doing?" Sol was shaking his head.

"All I can say for now is that it's not domestic."

"I too, am doing some contract work–for the Company. Let me take a look at this guy. I'll get back to you as soon as I have anything. We can catch up then. Gotta get back to my meeting."

"Is this wise?" asked Sol. "He's working for our potential enemies."

"We've been through some harrowing times together," stated Nick. "If it comes to a choice, he'll go with us."

"Hope you are right."

Two hours later the phone rang. *Unknown number.* Ilia answered.

"Kiki Russell, please."

"I'm right here, David. You're on speaker phone with Nick and some other old friends."

"Kiki, you always keep things interesting. I don't know what's up with Sanchez, but the search triggered some alarms."

"Did that cause a problem?" she asked.

"Let me tell you some of what I'm involved with here. The Company asked me to help them with some operations in Mexico."

Looking at the other faces in the room, Kiki said, "I knew you did work there years ago." *Shit, this could put him in a bad situation.*

"I did, and still have some contacts, though the landscape has changed dramatically with the rise of the cartels. If you're there, be very careful. That's dangerous territory."

Yeah, as in more dangerous than the Sandbox was when I was there. "Thanks for the warning. Sanchez appears to be tracking me. What can you tell me about him?"

"We're in discussions with Nighthawk about doing work for us. If Sanchez is in Mexico tracking you, it's not on our dime...yet. One of our partners has been hurt by a new group they're calling the *Fantasmas.*" Nick's mouth fell open, Sasha and

Zyra both raised their eyebrows. "Nighthawk may be contracted to erase them." There was a pregnant silence. "By the way, I have to congratulate you on the security you're using. Our NSA boys haven't been able to track you, but they're working on it. Don't get complacent. They're good."

"You're scaring me, David. We talked to someone who may have been with your partners. He spoke of help from the Company. He also spoke of a plan to create a government change. Know anything about that?"

This time the silence came from David. "Did this come from one of Nick's interrogations? Wait, don't answer that. Kiki, whatever you're involved in, it is deep doo doo. Let me just say I'm trying to steer the Company back from operations against our neighbors. I'm fighting some strong opposition because of the black ops revenue involved. Money without oversight is very attractive, and anything that threatens that is a target."

"David, is this another Air America or Iran Contra operation?"

"I can't answer that. Get out as soon as you can."

"Thanks for the warning. Talk to you again,

socially next time," laughed Kiki. *That's as strong a warning as I've ever gotten.*

"I hope so. Give my best to Nick." He cut the call.

"Why wouldn't the CIA want to work with the Mexican government?" asked Nick.

Sol chuckled. "CIA have been playing one cartel against the others to get the best deal they can. The Mexican government would be a monopoly. They could cut the CIA out."

"The warning from David was clear," Nick stated.

Chapter 19

Sol glanced around the faces in the communications room. The monitors displayed views from the drones. The one overhead showed clear roads. The movement of a car would set off an alarm. Another circled Sanchez's hotel. If his car moved, they'd know. "Tell me more of David Kennedy. I need confidence in him."

Kiki gave a lopsided grin. "Nick and I were teamed up with Ron Carson and David Kennedy during the Bio-Cyber war."

"Ex-president Ron Carson?" Sol's eyes widened in surprise.

"Yeah," said Nick, "but he wasn't president at that time. My interrogation techniques had proven to be quick and accurate, so we were enlisted to track down the source of the smallpox attack. When that led to Russia, Zyra, Ilia and Sasha were brought on board." He glanced at them. "We found the source and retrieved vaccine for America. Ron Carson and David Kennedy did the logistics of that mission and others."

Sol pursed his lips. "Rumors at Mossad about mission into Russia with our agents. Also about disabling president there." He glanced at Ilia, Sasha and Zyra. They were frozen. Only Nick and Kiki moved, shaking their heads that no further information would be forthcoming. "Okay, I get secrecy."

"Kennedy's proven to be a good friend," Kiki smiled. "After Carson became president, Nick and I worked with him on Carson's dream of moving ahead with the Orbiting Power System. David was instrumental in bringing that to reality. He had his leg blown off in a bomb attack by those opposing the OPS."

Sol grunted. "I remember when that happened." He chuckled. "In Israel, we watched Carson maneuver politics to get funding. How lucky to uncover plots to bring about war. Those responsible disappeared or died, no trials." He studied Nick and

Kiki. Their faces remained impassive. "And the Prophet. You knew of him?" Sol's eyebrows rose.

"We have met him." She added nothing more, glancing at Ilia, Sasha and Zyra. Surprise was written on their faces.

"Amazing man by all accounts," Sol said. "Made changes in world. Your story fills in some holes in your history. Interesting. Perhaps someday you share more."

"Perhaps someday," Kiki offered.

Silence filled the room.

Dawn broke the stillness. "What do you want to do about Sanchez? He's a threat."

"If we take him out, things escalate," stated Sol. "More agents come to investigate, probably finding our bugs and taps. They learn more than we want. More danger than now."

Kiki chuckled. "Let's feed him what we want him to know, minor trips, little exposure."

Nick frowned. "Kiki, you could be in danger."

"We'll be careful. Thus far he doesn't know we're onto him," said Kiki.

"We all will protect her." Ilia coolly explained. "So far he only has a tracker and a camera. No bugs. Meantime, we'll monitor his room and calls.

Learn more about him and Nighthawk's mission. He will have to report back at some time. We'll be ready."

* * *

Sol nodded as he watched everybody file out of the room. *There is a lot more to Nick and Kiki than I have been able to find out, and my sources are good,* he mused, walking back to his office.

He sat behind his desk and stared at the blank wall. Her reputation as a sniper had been easy to uncover, but after their involvement in anti-terror operations, they had disappeared, presumed dead. He'd found some information about their role in the Bio-Cyber war through reports redacted from the Mossad agents who'd participated.

Information about their role in retaking California from the gangs was spotty. But again, there was a gap of more than a year where they'd disappeared. Reports of Kiki's death were corroborated by several sources. *But here she is. Obviously having a president, now ex-president, and ex-director of the CIA on your side creates layers of protection. The question now is where are Kennedy's loyalties?* The *Fantasmas* had a contract. To leave would do damage to his and

Mossad's reputation and future work. *But the admonishment by David Kennedy to get out rings of true peril. We have a decision ahead.*

Chapter 20

Rapha's cell phone signaled he had a text. Only one person would send him texts on that phone. He sat on the edge of the bed and read the brief message. *Call me. MN.* He moved to the desk and got out the satellite phone. It was more secure. The call was picked up immediately. "Colonel Nesbit."

"This is Sanchez."

"We have a contract. Someone hit the Sonora Cartel and kidnapped the leader. They are our client's partner, and they want the leader returned, or maybe just his head—their words. Proof of death will do. They're afraid he will reveal information they want kept secret. They also want to end these attacks. Eliminate whoever did this. Is your target is involved?"

"She may be, but I have no concrete

information. I tried to follow her but lost the trail at the edge of town. A day later bodies, cartel bodies, turned up. It's not conclusive, but the circumstantial case is strong."

"Yeah, it is. Your mission has been modified. Primary: find the captured cartel head, bring him in or eliminate him. Second: information gathering and recon. Take your target out but not before you find out why she's in Mexico. We need intel. Use whatever methods work. If she's not involved, start looking for who is. These attacks are organized, using military tactics. The Xecas are ex-Special Forces and tech savvy. Watch them or find one to question."

Rapha grimaced. "How will I find them?"

"I'll get info from our client. They can give us names and locations of Xecas operations."

"Yes, sir."

"Call me with good news next time."

The connection was broken before Rapha could say more. He stared out the window at Nogales. *Shit! I was recon, a sniper, not an intelligence man. The last thing I want to do is start hunting Xecas. That could be fatal.*

Chapter 21

Sol gazed at his assembled team. They had new marching orders. "I got call from boss this morning. He has information Mochis Cartel is planning to take parts of Sonora Cartel territory. They want corridors to U.S. border. Sonora charges very large fees to use their corridors. War to be bloody. Attempts to negotiate not accepted. We are to set up operation in Los Mochis and observe."

"Just observe?" asked Kiki.

"Depends on what we find. After our raid on Sonora Cartel headquarters, new head moving in next week. Attack right after he takes over could be bad. Before that is to happen, we will stop it or weaken for sure."

Emilio smiled. He was from Los Mochis and his knowledge would be valuable. "Who's going to

Mochis?"

"At first, you and Ilia. Establish surveillance and monitoring. Our boss gives us contact in Los Mochis named Rosalinda Villa. She help set up."

Kiki looked at Nick. She flicked her dark hair away from her brown eyes. "We worked with a Rosalinda Villa in the battle to get California back from the gangs. She was pretty ruthless when it came to the Mexican cartel there. Any chance she's the same person?"

"I ask her background." He looked at Ilia and Emilio. "Do complete real-time tie-in to systems here. We want to see what you see, hear what you hear. Dawn handle this end, Ilia in Mochis. I let you know of the schedule, but it happens soon."

"I have a little more information about our Bogey," revealed Ilia. "He made an encrypted satellite call last night. I'm still trying to break the code. The call lasted only a few minutes, but if I had to guess, I would say it was to Nighthawk. My program is grinding on it now, and I should have something in a few hours. I can say that most of the talking came from whoever he called. Our Bogey said very little."Sol's brows knitted together. "Getting orders?"

Ilia grinned. "If he was giving a report, it was short."

"We kill him before he report," Zyra sneered.

Sol held up his hand. "No. Better devil we know than a new one. When Ilia breaks code, we learn more."

"If he has new orders," offered Nick, "he may act without Kiki's car moving. That would be something to know."

"Good observation, Nick. Ilia, work harder on code."

"I think Nick and I should talk to our contact in the U.S. We need to know more about the landscape down here. Face-to-face would be best."

"Will reveal anything confidential?" Sol asked. "You know him."

Kiki pulled out her phone. "We can ask."

Sol nodded. She dialed.

"I don't know who this is, but if my suspicion is correct, you want something from me."

"Hello, David. Suspicion confirmed. Would you be able to meet with us tomorrow or the day after?"

"Us being you and Nick. It's the weekend, so sure. Be good to see you. Call me with the details when you can." He hung up.

Dawn looked up flights. "There's a direct out of Sky Harbor into Dulles leaving in six hours. You can make that."

Kiki called David back. "We'll arrive at Dulles at ten tonight."

"Out of Sky Harbor?"

"Yeah."

"I know the flight. I'll meet you at the surface transportation pickup. Call me with the station number. Looking forward to seeing you."

"And us you."

"That was easy," commented Sol. "What you tell him about us?"

"As little as possible. David will stop us if we get into sensitive areas."

"All sensitive, Kiki. Remember who he works for. Don't test loyalties. More than your lives at stake." *I'm not comfortable with this, but I hope they can keep us out of CIA eyes.*

Chapter 22

Kiki watched the shadows lengthen on the Virginia countryside. They would arrive at David's summer house in Lake of the Woods after dark. Her reverie was interrupted when David asked about their trip.

"We drove to Phoenix." She stopped.

"Yeah, and?"

"Sanchez has been following me, put a tracker on the car and a camera outside my house."

"You drove your car to Phoenix? He followed you into the U.S.?"

"We drove another vehicle. The car's in my driveway in Nogales."

"And the camera? Did he see you leave?"

"We hacked the signal and looped it. We'll have to show some movement at the house or he may investigate."

David nodded. "Very good. Okay, short trip. No Washington D. C. sightseeing."

"It was good to be back in Arizona even for a short time," Kiki noted. "The flight was uneventful, the best kind."

"So you and Nick are close to the border?" David probed.

"That's not a very subtle interrogation," Nick chuckled from the back seat.

"I'm out of practice," laughed David. "Let's skip the toing and froing. Why are you here?"

Kiki gazed at their friend. "Your warning about the CIA has us worried. How much can we tell you?"

"I'm a contractor to the Company. They have the loyalty they buy. You are my friends. I will not betray you."

"We knew that David," Nick sighed. "I think we just needed to hear it."

"David, four months ago Sol Ayub asked us to join a team in Mexico to stem the cartel violence. We weren't sure, but when he told us that Ilia, Sasha and Zyra had already joined, we went ahead. Living in Tucson, we're more exposed to reports of cartel violence. It's gotten out of control lately."

David looked at Nick in the rearview mirror. "They wanted you for your interrogation technology."

"And me for my talents," laughed Kiki.

"That's a value not to be underestimated," commented David. "Who's paying?"

"We're not sure. Our instructions come by phone call." She glanced back at Nick. "The voice sounds like Julio Cardenas. We're ninety percent sure."

"Now that's interesting." He paused. "Cardenas dropped off the radar after you chased him back to Mexico."

Kiki laughed. "Tammy A did that, but he thought it was me, or at least my ghost."

"Does he know you're alive and on the team?"

"Yeah, Sol gave him a team list. He approved everybody."

"Forgiving you seems out of character." Again, there was a pause. "Okay, so you're doing what in Mexico?"

"We've been instructed to hit kidnapping and human trafficking operations. Drugs and immigrants are left alone."

"You hit one last week, didn't you?"

"Yeah. They were kidnapping children and selling them."

"Your boss seems noble, but what you hit was part of a CIA operation."

That was a jolt. "The CIA is involved in human trafficking and kidnapping?" cried Kiki.

"Not directly, but that cartel is a partner. You hit them, you hit a company operation."

"Our government is partnered with a drug cartel?" asked Nick.

"Ugly as it is, the cartels set up the manufacturing operations for fentanyl and amphetamines. The Company brings in the raw materials from Asia. The cartels move the finished product and heroin across Mexico and into the U.S. Black ops require black money. The Company offers information and protection in return. They also facilitate the movement of Mexican product at times."

"And they needed your help with this?" remarked Nick.

Kiki said nothing. *If this ever came out the shit would really fly. Heads would roll.*

"Look, operations like this have been going on

since the Viet Nam war. It's nothing new."

"Old doesn't make it right," snapped Kiki. "Even if we're on the side of morally right in these attacks, we'll be crosswise with the Company."

"Afraid so. They're talking to Nighthawk Securities about sending a team to eliminate the threat. That team will have the backing of the CIA and the NSA. They bring all the toys and all the money."

Oh shit.

"What about this plot to depose the president? Are they behind that?" Nick demanded.

"Where did you get that information?" Kennedy's voice was sharp.

Clearly he's surprised we know about that. Another nuclear news bomb if it ever gets out.

"I interrogated the head of the Sonora Cartel."

"Ah yes, your interrogations. I'm recommending that you both quit this job and leave Mexico."

"You're onboard with this!" Kiki spat. "What's happened to you?"

"I'm not onboard. But if I want these actions to go away, I have to work on it from the inside. Sniping from the outside only drives it farther into the dark."

"Does that mean you're going to let the ouster of the Mexican president go ahead? Or are they going to assassinate him?"

David shook his head. "I just found out about it last week. I'm not sure there's time before it happens."

She gave him a dirty look. "Does the CIA have a team in place?"

"We're supplying information only. The president will be removed by his own people." David waved to the guard at the entrance into the Lake of the Woods community. "It might be best if we talk only pleasantries in the house. It's probably clear, but I haven't swept it in a week."

The house was on the lakeshore. Through the floor-to-ceiling windows, Kiki looked at the wavy glittering lines reflected by the water from lights of the houses across the lake. The living room had oak floors with Persian rugs and leather upholstered chairs. Behind the bar was a mirror with expensive bottles on glass shelves.

"Drinks?" offered David. "I have twelve-year-old McCallum, or perhaps you'd prefer some six-year-old Bundaberg rum or Don Julio tequila?"

"I'll try the Bundy," said Kiki.

Nick held up his hand. "Scotch."

With three fingers of the requested liquor in each glass, they walked onto the porch, slid the Adirondack chairs across the wood deck until they could rest their feet on the railing. "This is just the place to spend the summer," sighed David. "When you're not battling in Mexico, what else have you and Nick been up to?"

Kiki laughed. "I'm still teaching Force Recon part time. Nick's got a clinic, but we've been on vacation for the last few weeks. How's Ron doing?"

"Ron Carson is CEO of the Orbiting Power Company. He's amassing political chits for a run at president of the World Government, when it forms. It's an amazing thing with Ron. While we all age, he seems to get younger. He laughs it off as good genes, but I'm not sure."

Kiki snickered. "Cosmetic surgery, perhaps? I never pictured him as the type."

"Whatever his secret, he's doing very well. He's at his ranch in Idaho at the moment. I'll be sure to tell him I saw you. I know he'll be disappointed at missing you."

"How's the leg?" Nick glanced down.

"I've grown used to the prosthetic. My toes still ache every once in a while, but I'm getting along fine."

"What are you doing with yourself?" Kiki said for the sake of anybody listening.

"I'm retired. I fish," he nodded toward the lake, "I play golf, but I have to use a cart these days." A smile crossed his face. "I've been thinking of writing my memoirs."

"Be careful with that," snickered Kiki. "Some people wouldn't want all your exploits made public."

"I know how to keep secrets. How long can you stay?"

Nick smiled. "We leave in the morning. Going back home. I have a practice to get back to."

"We really do need to get together, sort of a reunion. Ron and the Prophet would like to see you."

"We hear things about the Prophet occasionally," Kiki said. "He hasn't contacted me for a job in a while."

"After the bloodbath with the Military Industrial Complex, things have quieted," David murmured.

You both must be tired. I'll show you to the guestroom."

Yeah, only a rogue target once in a while.

As the bedroom door closed Kiki looked a question at Nick. On a small piece of paper he wrote: *We save the presidente, of course.* He chewed and swallowed the paper.

Chapter 23

Arizona was already into summer with temperatures near one-hundred. Nick drove up the curved driveway to his mother's house. It had been his house since his mother died, but he still thought of it as his mother's. The house, built by his dad, sat on a hill south of the city of Casa Grande. From the patio it was possible to see almost one-hundred miles on a clear day. As the van stopped before the carport, the front door flew open and a slender woman with sandy blond hair ran out.

"Nick, how great to see you!" her arms wrapped around him.

Over her shoulder Nick watched Kathy's husband embrace Kiki. When Kathy released him, he turned and shook hands with Bob. "Good to see you. Looks like you're doing well."

"Kath and I really wanted to get out of the city, and your offer to stay here was perfect. And thanks for the work we're getting from you. I get to be creative with things I love. I've got some new toys to show you. They're almost ready for Mexico. Ilia did request replacement batteries for you to take back."

Kiki headed for the front door. "Let's head out to the pool. I could use a beverage."

Cold IPAs in hand, they watched the sun sink behind the mountains to the west.

Kathy held up her bottle in a mock toast. "Nice to have you back."

Nick glanced around the patio and back of the house. "You've kept the house up nicely. Thanks. It's always better to have someone living here."

Nick and Bob had gone to school together. Nick leaned toward medicine, like his dad. Bob, with an amazing aptitude in aeronautics and electronics, had gotten certified in aircraft maintenance and worked for a high-end company until the downturn in costly private aircraft. Upon retirement, he'd dabbled in drone design.

Kathy had worked for the government in Customs and Import inspections, but she liked micro electronic design. When Sol contacted Nick about work in Mexico, he asked if Nick knew anybody who could do hi-tech design. Sol wanted top end drones and surveillance equipment, and he didn't want any tracks from vendors. Bob and Kathy were eager to join this "Adventure."

Bob laughed. "What the hell happened here? When we moved in, I had to patch up the bullet holes in the wall. You're welcome, and thanks for the place and the job. It's one of the most interesting I've ever had, getting to play with hi-tech and having the money to build it."

"Someday we'll tell you the whole saga," Nick answered.

"What new toys are you developing for us?" Kiki asked.

"I built a couple of drones that are solar powered. They can stay aloft indefinitely, even at night."

"They look like vultures?" Nick's eyebrows rose.

"Of course one does. I also have a few smaller versions–ravens. These are new and improved– better electronics and energy storage. I've also refined the cell phone monitor software. Coupled with the drones, we can pinpoint any phone, tap into any conversation." He pointed up. Overhead a vulture circled in the last golden rays of the sun. "Check your phone. Here's a site to tie into." He gave them the address.

On his phone screen, Nick looked down at the four of them on the patio as seen from 1000 feet above. He glanced at the vulture again. It was hard to pick out, as the sun had set. On the screen he saw his pale face staring up. "Wow, the resolution is great."

"Watch." Bob pressed some buttons on his phone. The scene changed to an infrared view. "It can also do a night vision view." He pressed more keys. Data scrolled across the screen. "That's the status screen; altitude, power charge and amount of time aloft depending on the mode it's operating in. With a Doppler beam from here, it can read air currents to minimize the need for power." He pulled out a device that looked like a cop's radar gun. He swept it around, and the display on the screen translated to colored shades representing updrafts and downdrafts. "I can program it to seek whatever currents will keep it at the desired altitude in this area."

With the drone switched to night vision, the four of them sat by the pool in a green halo. "It can also be used in a sentry mode, sending an alert if there's movement."

Kiki's mouth dropped open. "This is stunning. Who has anything like this?"

Bob wore a sly grin. "Just us at this point. I had to hack into military research programs for some of the techniques, but nobody has been able to miniaturize everything and fit it into this airborne package. The battery was a big problem, but I went to a flywheel setup that's lighter, stores more energy and helps stabilize the drone. It also has no heat signature, so IR can't see it. Everything's carbon fiber and Mylar so radar has a hard time finding it."

"How long does the energy charge last?" asked Nick.

"That depends on how much it's using. If we're continuously broadcasting back, a couple of hours. On intermittent broadcast, it'll go for four or five hours."

"That's better than what we've got now," Nick commented.

"For the charging system, the top of the wings

and body are micro-thin solar cells. The undersides are also cells tuned to absorb infrared radiation. I can direct an IR laser at it and charge the power back up. But I have to be in visual range." He pointed to a box at the edge of the patio. "That's the charging station. The computer keeps it aimed at the drone. It's charging right now." There was no light or sound coming from the box. "Let me bring it down so you can see it." He tapped the command on his phone.

Nick looked at Kiki. "This technology is amazing!" They held up their beers in salute.

"Yeah, I've had fun putting it together. Kath is a whiz at working with robots under a microscope."

The beers came up again in a salute.

From the darkness came a rustling. Air woofed past them and a large black shape landed to one side. The wings folded like a bird. "Come on. Take a look," the pride easily apparent in Bob's voice. The body was five feet long. Up close it was not birdlike. The head was almost rectangular, the body thick. Bob entered another command and the wings opened out. "Nine-foot wingspan," he said as they stepped back to allow full spread.

"It didn't look that big from the ground,"

commented Kiki.

"That's because it was higher than a normal bird flies. Gives a wider view and makes it more difficult if someone chooses to shoot at it."

"You've got the smaller version too?" Nick asked.

"The raven drones don't have the same capabilities, but yeah, cameras and some solar charging. They can link together for wider surveillance and shared functions."

"I'm wowed," declared Kiki.

"I'm doing the final tests now. I should be ready to bring them down to Ilia in a week or so."

"How are you going to get something this big across the border?"

Bob laughed. "They'll fly, of course. How long can you stay?"

"Short trip. We need to be back tomorrow." Nick read the question on Bob's face. "There was some business in D.C." He considered Bob for a moment, pausing, not sure he wanted to open this discussion. "Speaking of D.C., What can you do with encryption?"

"Everything is double encrypted with rotating frequency broadcast. Ilia set that up. It's very tough to break, tough to find."

"We may have to get better," muttered Kiki. "It's possible that we'll have the CIA looking for us."

Kathy's mouth fell open in astonishment. "CIA as in our own government?"

"Long story," Kiki stated.

"And you need to know it," Nick confirmed. "Here's the short version. You know of our basic contract to help stifle the violence in Mexico." Kathy and Bob nodded. "We captured some of the bad guys and I interrogated them." The expressions on Bob and Kathy's faces conveyed that images of waterboarding or bamboo shoots under the fingernails and worse were arising in their minds. "Not that kind of interrogation," he continued. "There's no physical harm. It's worse," he muttered.

Bob and Kathy stared at him, trying to discern what that meant.

"The information we got implicated the CIA in some of their operations including one we hit. It's where we captured those Nick questioned. In addition, our bugs overheard conversations about a team possibly coming to Mexico to attack us."

"A CIA contract team?" questioned Bob.

"We had to go to D.C. to confirm," answered Nick. "They'll bring in hi-tech."

Bob scowled. "We have to be cautious. Along with NSA, they are the best. Electronic cat and mouse." He started to rub his hands together then stopped. "This could get deadly serious."

"How about dinner at Cocina de Sabino? I'd like to see my brother and his family before we have to leave." He looked at Kiki. Only she had noticed the change of subject.

Chapter 24

Kiki faced the team at the Hacienda. After a brief meeting with Sol, he wanted her to deliver a report to the group. They were in the communications room, monitors showing views from the drones. The one showing the taps on the Bogey phone was flat line–no activity.

"On Sunday, we met with David Kennedy near Washington D.C. to find out more about the CIA involvement in operations here in Mexico. He is presently contracting with them. Some of you know David as someone we can trust." Ilia, Sasha and Zyra nodded. He confirmed that the CIA has partnered with some Mexican cartels. The cartels smuggle drugs for them, they supply information and influence. It's a source of money for operations where they don't want any congressional involvement."

Zyra smirked. "Ya. Mossad has secret operations, but they get approval first."

Sol guffawed at that.

Kiki continued, "David was aware of the program to oust the president, but didn't agree with it. He's trying to dissuade them. Our attack hurt their partner, though Nick and I didn't confirm our involvement. So far, none of us have come up by name. They are moving ahead with a contractor to stop us. Nighthawk Securities is used for black operations and wet work and is the prime candidate for the contract. The contractor will have the support and use of the resources of the CIA. Kennedy warned us to be very careful. He strongly suggested we get out."

"CIA very powerful," Zyra said, "like GRU, eyes and ears everywhere."

Sol stepped to the front of the room. "The danger factor up. We have choice. We are mercenaries, don't do suicide missions. We can get out of contract and leave now or not. I think nothing less of anyone who wants to leave." He paused, then sighed "If we stay, we will be proactive against CIA to survive. Must be an endgame."

"I feel what we're doing is for more than the money. I'm staying," Kiki's hand was up. *Especially after the rescue of those girls.* "On its present course, Mexico will self-destruct. I want Mexico to survive."

Nick's hand followed hers in approval. One-by-one the others raised their hands to stay.

Sol studied them each for a moment. "Okay, I glad to see it. Ready for plans."

"We attack," declared Zyra. "But not direct way. Divert attention to others. They take blame."

Kiki's eyes sparkled as an idea grew. "Los Xecas. We make them the fall guys."

"How?" asked Nick.

Kiki laughed. "If we attack Los Xecas and leave evidence that it was a CIA-backed assault, they will go after the CIA operatives and partners."

"Sol's hand was on his chin. "Hmm. Los Xecas partnered with CIA once, but not so much now. They know who operatives are. They know who partners of CIA are. I call Julio."

Kiki glanced at Nick then back at Sol. "How much are you going to tell him?"

"Only what necessary. Any leaks and we all

dead. Kiki, your idea. We hit their headquarters in Nuevo Laredo. You and Ilia pull up satellite maps. Put plan together."

* * *

Back in his office, Sol dialed Julio's number.

"Sí, Señor Ayub. What can I do for you?"

"We got problem with CIA. If we continue, they deploy team to hunt us."

"You want to quit?"

"We took vote. Everybody staying, but need a plan. Need address of Los Xecas headquarters in Nuevo Laredo."

"What are you going to do with that?"

"We watch them."

"And then?"

"We watch them."

"Okay, when dealing with Los Xecas it is perhaps best if few people know." He gave Sol several addresses. "I'm not sure which is their headquarters. Be cautious, my friend. Action against them is like kicking the dragon."

Chapter 25

Kiki eyed the computer monitor over Ilia's shoulder. On the screen was the Google maps image of Nuevo Laredo, Mexico across the Rio Grande from Laredo, Texas. Sol handed them the suspected addresses of Los Xecas operations. As they entered them, teardrops appeared on the screen showing places around the city. When they zoomed in, one was a large manor to the south of town. Another was a house in a residential neighborhood. The third address was in the middle of town, near a shopping plaza. The fourth was an isolated building in a fenced area less than 600 yards from the river and the international border. A flag indicated it was a radio tower. *I like that one: open country around it, not too far from the border.*

"Ilia, do you think that radio tower is the

communications center for Los Xecas?"

"Los Xecas are techies, so it would be logical. With a facility there they could stay in contact with operations over all of northeastern Mexico."

"I like it because it's isolated. Less chance of civilian casualties. In fact," she pointed to a park-like area across the river in the U.S. "that looks like a place we could stop and picnic, control the drones, and have line of sight to the property."

"Yes. A good location," Ilia murmured.

Kiki stepped back and faced Sol. "I wish we had the new drones from Bob. The one we saw was amazing. We could watch continuously."

Ilia smiled. "He has told me about them. Probably more important is that we could tap into the phone calls."

"Make do with what we have," Sol said. "Who is going?"

Kiki looked thoughtful for a moment. "Ilia for drone control and communications, Nick, if we need a doctor."

"Hopefully not needed. What is plan?"

"I'm going to take my car. Ilia and Nick can follow in a van. Moving my car will attract our Bogey. Hopefully, he'll follow. After that, we'll have to assess what to do. I'm still formulating the plan."

"How soon you ready?"

Kiki rose and headed for the door. "We'll start packing now."

Sol glanced back at the monitor. "Tie everything to our system. We watch from here too."

"Roger that." Standing in the doorway, Kiki turned to face him. "Sol, keep us informed about our Bogey."

"Dawn, drop off Kiki and Nick behind house so Bogey not see them enter. Nick, go for groceries in Kiki's car. Keep Bogey believing tracker working and both of you at house." Sol gave her a half smile. "We watch and listen. After Nick return, start trip. See if he follow."

* * *

Sol called as she crossed the border. "Bogey moving, heading for border. Think he will follow. Be careful. Not get isolated, Give him chance to take you."

"Nick and Ilia are a couple of miles back in the van. We'll stop in Deming to eat, someplace with lots of people."

"Dawn says Bogey tracker relayed through

153

satellite. He not need to be close. After delay to get through border, he will be ten minutes back. Danger area after El Paso. Night and long stretches of nothing–ideal place to force you off road. Trip sixteen hours. You break up, stop somewhere?"

"Too much risk. We're driving straight through, stops for bathroom, gas and food only. We'll be careful. Keep us informed of anything."

* * *

Seven hours later they were through El Paso, Texas. The traffic had been bad during evening rush hour, but as soon as they cleared the city they had the road to themselves. Kiki had an audio book on to help keep her alert. West Texas was so boring. The sound of her phone jarred her. "Yeah, Nick."

"Ilia's decryption program finished with the satellite call from our Bogey yesterday. In addition to interrogating and killing you, Sanchez is to gather information about Los Xecas. That includes talking to them. Blackhawk's not sure who's responsible for the latest hit. He's sure it was the *Fantasmas* and that includes you. They want to make sure it wasn't Los Xecas."

"He's going to talk to Los Xecas?"

"Their client wants that info."

"He's trying for a twofer? This trip east takes him closer to Los Xecas for a parlay…and I'm vulnerable."

Chapter 26

Rapha was awakened by the shrieking alarm. Katherine Russell's car was moving. His computer screen showed the red dot traveling toward the Diconcini Port of entry into the United States. *Shit! By the time I get there, she'll be way ahead of me in line, and those lines move very slowly. After crossing, she'll be miles away before I'm even to the inspection station, putting her out of range of my tracker. Shit! Shit! Shit!*

He grabbed his *go bag*, laptop and satellite phone and ran downstairs. Everything else he'd need was in the car. As he pulled out of the parking lot, he called Blackhawk.

The colonel picked up on the second ring. "Nesbit."

"Russell is on the move and heading toward the

border. I may lose her because the wait time to cross is forty minutes. That'll give her time to get out of range of the tracker by the time I cross. Do we have anything in the air that can help?"

"Let me check status," Colonel Nesbit growled. "How'd she get so far ahead? Wait, doesn't matter. Our client might have something to use, but I don't want to go to them yet. I'm going to send you Global Entry permission. Get in that lane. You'll beat her across."

Rapha heard his cell phone signal he'd gotten a message. "Okay, got the permission. I'll keep you up to date."

The Global Entry line was only three cars long. He breezed through in ten minutes. His laptop showed Russell was still in line in Mexico. He parked at the Burger King and waited, setting up the tracker reception on his dash display. Twenty minutes later he watched the red dot get on I-19 and head north. He called Nesbit back as he followed.

"She's heading toward Tucson. I got up on her tail, and she's alone in the car. I'm about two miles back. If I get a chance, I'll take her, see what we can learn. Then it's lights out."

"I'm sending you info on Los Xecas. After the

Russell affair is over, contact them."

"Roger that." *I-19 meant that she was heading for Tucson, then...? She could be shopping in Tucson, or go to Phoenix, or head east toward El Paso.*

In Tucson, the red dot merged onto I-10 heading east. He called Nesbit again.

"She's on Interstate 10 heading toward El Paso. Do you want me to bump her off the road?"

"Let's see where she's going. If she exits where you get a chance to take her, do it. What's traffic like?"

"Moderate, as you'd expect for a weekday morning. I'll stay back."

"I'm going to link your tracker through a satellite cell system. You won't have to be close." The line went dead. He settled in for a long drive. This Arizona-New Mexico stretch of Interstate-10 was straight roads and open vistas. At Deming, she exited at a busy tourist stop. Filled up with gas and got food. He pulled in one island over and did the same. He was itching to take her. He glanced at the other people. *Too crowded.*

Late-afternoon traffic in El Paso was bad. Again, she stopped for food and gas before getting back on the Interstate. Rapha looked at the Google Maps display of what was ahead–hundreds of miles of nothing. *I might get a chance in a few hours. After dark would be best.* Traffic dwindled to occasional cars. The sun went down as they passed the exit to Ft. Stockton. *Christ, she only used the restroom once at the second stop. She must be wearing astronaut diapers.* He looked longingly at the empty soda bottle on the seat. It was only twelve ounces. *I gotta piss more than twelve-ounces.*

Darkness and lonely roads lay ahead. Rapha glanced at the map display looking for an exit. Fifteen miles past the Bakersfield exit was a connection to Highway 305. *Nothing but the road there, no stores or gas station. Perfect.*

Rapha looked in the rearview mirror. The only headlights were a mile back. He began to close the distance between the cars. He could force her onto the exit ramp then off the road. The exit sign flashed past, one mile to go. He eased up beside her. A glare from his mirror hit him in the eyes. A car behind him blinked its lights signaling to pass. *Where did that come from?* He slowed and pulled in behind Katherine's car as the exit flashed by.

Shit! He pounded on the steering wheel as a white van roared past him, and pulled ahead of Katherine Russell's car. It was going faster. The distance widened and she sped up to keep the same spacing with the van. He dropped back.

The van was still within view as they passed the town of Sonora. He glanced at the map, looking for another chance. *If only that van was farther ahead.* An hour later, traffic began to pick up as they approached San Antonio. They'd been driving for thirteen hours. *This woman is a trooper. Surely she'll stop there.*

He closed the gap again hoping for another chance to take her. She exited the loop onto Interstate 35 South and stopped again for gas. Rapha did the same, staying as far from her as he could at the busy truck stop. This time, she went into the restaurant for a sit-down breakfast. He followed, taking a booth near the door but with a clear view of her sitting alone at a table near the window. The waitress took her order before walking over to Rapha's table and setting a glass of water in front of him. Glancing at the menu, he said, "I'll take the Southwestern omelet and coffee."

When he looked up, she was gone! A flash of panic hit him. Where? His head swiveled, taking in the restaurant. She'd left a jacket on the back of the chair at her table. *Restroom. Of course. I could use that too.* As she emerged, he went to the men's. *Sweet relief!* When he returned, she was tapping on her phone. Their meals arrived.

Rapha texted Nesbit on his phone: At truck stop south of San Antonio. She's on I-35.

Within a minute, Nesbit texted back, advising that she may be heading to Laredo, known center for Los Xecas. Either business with them or her usual style of greeting. Stay with her.

After four cups of coffee and with an empty plate in front of him, he watched her head for the restroom again. When she came out, she headed for the cashier. Rapha took one last bathroom break. With the tracker, he could find her. He'd take her in Laredo.

Chapter 27

Laredo was a Texas border town, and that in itself an apt description. As the sun neared its peak, Kiki looked across the Rio Grande at Mexico. The countryside looked much the same, but not the building construction.

Ilia called. "We need to eat before we get a room and rest. Let's stop at Denny's. After we're checked into the hotels, we'll put a couple of drones up and start reconnoitering."

With her com set on, Kiki slid into a booth. Comfort food and a seat that wasn't moving refreshed her. She was just another business person on a call–a Zoom conference call with Ilia, Nick and Sol. "What's first?"

"You have reservations at the Laredo Executive Inn in town. Sanchez must believe you're alone, so

Nick and I will be a block away at the Hotel Ava. It puts us close enough to Nuevo Laredo to control the drones," said Ilia. "I'll put a couple of drones up from the hotel roof. Nobody will see us."

"How long can they stay aloft?" Kiki remembered the new version Bob was finalizing.

"If we use the updrafts to conserve energy and intermittent broadcast, they'll be on mission for four or five hours. Once we see what the surroundings are like, we can put a raven drone near the best site to keep an eye on it. It will monitor cell frequencies so we can intercept calls."

Kiki looked through the window at the dusty town. "How long do you think we'll be here?"

"We should have enough information to formulate a plan within a couple of days."

"And then?"

"We'll go back to the Hacienda. Along with Sol, we'll come up with a plan to set Los Xecas and the CIA against each other. That'll keep them off our backs at least for a while."

"We're in conference now. We could strike while we're here," Kiki remarked.

"Not what we are supposed to do," growled Sol. "Not your decision. You only geared for observation. Plan may require more equipment."

Ilia smiled at her. "We need to set the van up as our command center. Let's eat and go check in."

After returning to the Hacienda, they would have spent thirty-two hours driving. Kiki felt a little irritation that this was only a recon mission.

The receptionist who greeted Kiki was a pretty Latina with a ready smile and eager to help. "I'd like to get two adjoining rooms above the second floor and with a view of the river." The girl bent over her terminal.

"Your reservation was for one room, but I have two on the fourth floor. Is that all right?"

"Perfect," answered Kiki. She handed over her credit card naming her as Alicia Williams. "My husband and I will have one room. The kids get the other. We need time alone," she chuckled. "What's room service like here?"

"We have full restaurant service. The menu is in your room."

"You have pizza?"

The girl laughed. "No but we do have hamburgers."

"My kids like pizza. Can I get one delivered?"

"The Pizza Palace is a couple of blocks away.

They deliver, and I'll direct them to your room. Do you need help with your luggage?"

"That's what the kids are for. Thanks."

Kiki was in contact as she entered her room.

"How is it?" asked Nick.

"Adequate, not luxurious but nice." I've got a view of the river and Mexico."

"Connecting room?"

She opened the door. "It's a mirror image room. What's happening with Sanchez?"

"Out tracker shows his Jeep parked in front of your hotel. He's probably checking in now. I'll hack into the hotel security system in a few minutes so we can follow him. We all need rest. That drive was grueling, especially for you. Nick and I switched off on the driving, so we're not as knackered as you probably are."

"Yeah, I'm beat. You can come over whenever you want." She gave them the room numbers.

"We'll be over. I want to set up on the hotel security system, then I'm coming back here. I'm hitting the bed."

Ten minutes later there was a knock on the door. Kiki peered out. It was Nick and Ilia with two rolling suitcases in tow. In the second room, Ilia began setting up the electronics. Nick and Kiki hugged, holding each other up as exhaustion tugged them down. Finally, she pushed back. "Ilia, I'm going to order a pizza. What do you want on it?"

"Pepperoni, sausage and mushrooms."

Nick frowned. "Let's get half ham, pineapple, bell pepper and spinach and half meat."

"Sounds good to me," Kiki said. She looked up the number for Pizza Palace and placed the order for delivery to Laredo Executive Inn and her room.

"Let me show you what I have," Ilia called from the other room.

The TV in the room had a wide view across the river, the default screen from the hotel. His laptop had a view from the drone circling overhead. Kiki's laptop showed a squiggly line. "Our drone is picking up a satellite call. That's the Sanchez's signal," he pointed at her computer. "They're still using the same coding as in Nogales," Ilia explained. "I'll get a camera in his room when he leaves."

At the push of a button, Sanchez's voice came over the speaker. "I just checked in, sir—same hotel as Russell. I'll find out what room she's in today. We drove straight through, sixteen hours. I need some sleep."

"Yeah, I'm sure it was exhausting. Set up your tracker alarm and get some shut eye. If anything comes up, I'll call you."

Kiki's phone rang; the front desk. "Ms. Williams, your pizza is here.

"Please have it sent up. Thank you."

"How hard will it be to put a camera in Sanchez's room?" asked Kiki.

"While poking through the hotel security system, I discovered there are cams in each room. I guess theft is a problem. Unless there is a need, they are turned off for privacy. We have a need."

Kiki looked around trying to see where the camera was. *Where would I put one?* She started inspecting the lamps and the phone. Five minutes later there was a knock at the door. As she went for the pie, she asked, "You can disable these rooms, lock them out?"

"Already done."

The aroma of hot pizza filled the room. Whether it was because she was so tired and hungry, it was one of the best she'd ever tasted.

"I'm going back to our hotel," Ilia announced. "I need sleep. I'll bring a drone back at midnight for a battery recharge but put another up so we'll have continuous coverage of the radio tower. That's the most promising site. I've set the monitor in Sanchez's room to alarm if he gets up. Before dawn tomorrow, I'll put a couple of drones up from the Laredo Water Museum. At that hour nobody will see me. We'll check out the addresses we have to see what's going on."

"Tomorrow we'll discuss what's next." He stumbled from the room. "First one up calls the rest to meet. Enjoy your evening together."

"You're staying?" Kiki smiled at Nick.

He took two extendable braces from his bag and placed them under the knobs of each door. "Double security," he explained. "For privacy. No surprises."

Chapter 28

Breakfast was room service, the works—pancakes, scrambled eggs, bacon and sausage, all the things teens would order. And coffee, lots of coffee. Ilia's knock had awakened them thirty minutes ago. After finishing their hearty breakfast, they began the vigil of Los Xecas, concentrating on the building near the radio tower. A review of the tapes from last night showed activity in the early morning hours. From the connecting room, they conferenced in with the Hacienda. Sol and Dawn were on the line.

"From our assessment of last night's tapes, much of their business takes place late at night and in the early hours." Ilia fast forwarded, stopping to show the vehicles. "As you can see, the parade ranges from the large SUVs to police cars to army

Humvees. Our cell monitors picked up conversations and orders going to phones across the country, all the numbers recorded. We can go through it later. They take advantage of the radio tower. Being there is certainly no accident."

Nick had been online gathering information. "Los Xecas is powerful and widespread. As with all cartels, divisions have occurred and groups split off. Some go to war with the Xecas, but not for long, others pick businesses that don't compete. Some think Los Xecas are the most powerful, others disagree. Opinions are fluid. Of no doubt is that they are the most vicious."

Ilia had plugged into the in-room TV, and he and Kiki stood in front assessing the view of Nuevo Laredo. Everything was shared with the Hacienda. "These are the three operating centers for Los Xecas," Ilia pointed at each. "We'd have to be on station for weeks to learn what each does, so let's concentrate on the communications center." He pointed to the one near the radio tower. "This one is not their headquarters, but it is the central point for control over their operations."

Kiki stepped forward. "From across the river here at the Laredo Water Museum," she pointed, "there is a clear view of the buildings and the radio tower. On the maps it's listed as a communications center for the city and the police. It is, but not only for the city of Nuevo Laredo."

"Los Xecas have communications across Mexico from here," Ilia added.

Kiki moved her fingers from the Laredo Water Museum to the radio tower. "The range is 800 yards. We can set up our observation post in the van, never leaving the U.S. If we want to wreak mayhem, I can do it from there."

"What will be targets?" Sol asked.

Ilia brought up video footage of the site. "People are moving in and out continuously. This black SUV belongs to their leader. He showed up at four this morning. We'll watch tomorrow to see if there's a pattern."

"You could hit target?" Sol asked.

"Yeah. Not easy, but yeah," her voice confident.

"Strike would hurt them," Sol said, "but not our objective."

"How do we tie this to the CIA?" Nick asked, glancing around the room. Kiki and Ilia let Sol's statement pass. The room was silent.

Dawn spoke, "We still have our Bogey. Perhaps

we could lure him to Nuevo Laredo. Use him in a setup."

Kiki laughed. "Good thinking. The old *two birds with one stone.* So how do we do it?"

Nick regarded Kiki. "Maybe we do a double *kill two birds with one stone.* We know that Sanchez has orders to meet with Los Xecas and to kill Kiki. If they're both in the same place, he might try to take her and meet with the Xecas."

Ilia snapped his fingers. "We move Kiki's tracker to the Los Xecas headquarters. Sanchez will follow. But he's Nighthawk, not CIA."

Kiki laughed. "I'm sure under proper questioning he'll talk about the CIA. Los Xecas can be very persuasive."

Nick grimaced at the thought. "How do we set this up? How do we make the tie-in, get them to associate Sanchez with the CIA?"

Kiki's eyes twinkled. "Leave that to me."

Chapter 29

"Ilia, can you activate a camera in the hallway in front of Sanchez's room? If he makes any move to leave the hotel, I want to know."

Ilia glanced at her.

"His movements are critical," Kiki explained.

"Sure. I'll put a raven in the trees opposite too. My guess is he is probably trying to find you. He might consider this an opportunity. He's seen nobody with you, so I'm sure he thinks you're alone."

They glanced at the monitor of Sanchez's room. He was in the bathroom. "Guess he's up," Kiki remarked.

They watched him walk out of the bathroom with only a towel around his waist, and pick up the satellite phone to make a call. Nesbit answered immediately.

"Talk to me, Sanchez."

"Sir, her car hasn't moved. She must be in her room. I tried to call her, but she's registered under another name. I'll find out her room number. Do you want me to get her?"

"Not just yet, I want to know what she's up to. Stay on her car. I'll see if we can get into the hotel phone system. As soon as you know what name she's under, we'll find out who she's talking to."

"Roger that, sir."

"Meanwhile, I'll get info re Los Xecas. I want you to talk to them. First get assurance that they were not responsible for the attack in Nogales. See it they would consider an alliance with us and our client." The call ended abruptly.

* * *

"I'll launch another raven." Ilia went out to the van parked a block away. In fifteen minutes, he was back. "It is done." He tied into the visual from the drone and displayed the view on this laptop. With a simple joystick he guided it to a tree branch with a good view of the hotel where Sanchez and Kiki were staying. The gray Jeep was in the same place it had been parked last night. Ilia tightened the focus on her floor and opened a movement alarm program. In addition to the hall cam, anyone moving through that field would trigger an alarm.

Nick turned to Kiki, with a perplexed look on his face. "What are we doing here?"

"I know this was to be a recon assignment, but I consider it a mission of opportunity. We're already here. Why stop?" Kiki brought up a Google Maps scene of Laredo. "I've thought about it, and we have the opportunity to accomplish what needs to be done." She paused and glanced at Nick. He looked doubtful.

"Before dawn," Kiki said, "You move the van to the Laredo Water Museum. I'll drop off the tracker to be picked up by the vulture drone." She pointed to the spot. "It's across from the Los Xecas operation in Mexico."

She moved her finger to the U.S. side of the border. "I'll set up my hide in the van on the U.S. side. Ilia will launch the vulture drone with the tracker. It'll fly low and follow the streets at road speed to the border crossing." Her finger traced the path. "Once it flies over the border, the drone will follow the road toward Highway 2." She glanced at Nick, who was staring at her, not the map.

"Before that intersection, it will move along this dirt road, lay the tracker in this copse of trees, then rise up to give us an aerial view. We'll need to monitor the cell and radio traffic too." She watched Ilia. "Doable?" He nodded.

Nick frowned. "You're depending on Sanchez to follow."

She smiled. "I'm counting on it. If he doesn't, nothing lost but a little time." Turning back to the screen she pointed. "This spot where the tracker will be is visible from the parking lot of the Laredo Water Museum." Her finger traced the line of sight from the trees to the parking lot. "The museum is closed, so no one will be around."

Kiki smiled, looking from Nick to Ilia. "The range is six-hundred yards. Two-hundred yards farther is the Los Xecas headquarters compound, also visible." As her finger traced the path from the parking lot to the Los Xecas compound, it was highlighted on the monitor.

"Nick grinned. "While Ilia is guiding the vulture, you and I use the van to raise mischief from within the U.S. I like it."

"Are you going to kill Sanchez?" Ilia asked.

"Not here, not now. We need him. I'll take care

of him later. Other questions?"

"How are you going to do that?" Nick asked.

"Not sure yet. It depends on what he does and how Los Xecas responds to their boss getting shot."

Ilia's mouth curved into a smile. "Nice plan. Nobody exposed."

The alarm sounded. Ilia pressed some keys. Their heads swiveled toward the monitor showing the hall outside of Kiki's room. A figure stood outside her door. He leaned close, listening.

"Shit! Now what?" Kiki whispered.

"Pretend you're on the phone to Nick in Nogales." He signaled for Kiki to talk.

"Hey, Nick. How are things in Nogales?"

Ilia glanced at Nick. He spoke through cupped hands to simulate a speakerphone. "It's quiet here. Nothing going on. How was the trip?"

"It was long and boring. The audio books helped. You should listen to *Nimitz Class,* by Patrick Robinson. That book had me mesmerized. The miles just rolled by."

"How are things in Laredo?"

"This is not my idea of a vacation town. I'm just getting ready for tomorrow."

"Be careful. I wish you'd taken somebody with

you. Los Xecas are really dangerous."

"Nick, this is recon only. I just want to get an idea of what they're doing."

"What about the hotel room? Is it secure?"

"Nobody's going to get in here before I can blow them away. I'll be back in a few days. Don't worry." *That should make him think twice about busting in.*

On the screen they saw Sanchez plant a bug high up above the door. He walked away. On the monitor of his room, they watched as he returned. With his own laptop, he linked into the bug he'd just planted.

Ilia signaled for Kiki to keep talking. "Nick, it's getting late and I'm still pooped from the drive. I'm going to take a nap. I'll talk to you tomorrow. Bye, Hon."

Ilia made more keystrokes and the sound of a local television program came on. "His first move," he whispered. "We must be careful to ensure he thinks you're here alone. Given the opportunity, he'll try to take you."

Chapter 30

The alarm woke Rapha. Katherine Russell was on the move, going somewhere in her car. Even though he'd slept in his clothes, it was several minutes before he ran out to his Jeep. Being pre-dawn, it was early, still dark outside. Wiping sleep from his eyes, he checked the dash monitor to make sure it showed her car. There was little traffic on the streets. *Where the hell could she be going at this hour?*

He waited a few minutes before following so she wouldn't spot him. Two blocks down the red dot turned right. He followed. She stopped, then started again, turned right again and headed north. At Jefferson, she turned east, passing under the I-35. Rapha closed the gap. If she got on the interstate, and he was held up for any reason, she could move away quickly. He thought about the conversation last night. The international border crossing was a few miles ahead. *Could that be where she's heading?* But she surprised him by taking San Dario north. He dropped back. *Where is she going?*

On his screen, her red dot took Miles Rd. before getting on I-69W. *She is going to the border.* At the entry, the red dot slowed as she joined the line to cross into Mexico. She was a mile in front of him. This time of the morning, the line into Mexico wasn't long and moved quickly.

He crossed and followed. His map showed her taking another road south. These were good roads to accommodate the growth of Nuevo Laredo and the cross-border traffic. On each side of the road were newer houses, the neighborhoods well lit, streets newly paved. She veered off onto another road.

I better close the gap, get nearer. Again, she turned off, but this time it was onto a dirt track. He followed, turning off his headlights as he eased down the road. *I should be able to see her taillights, but there's nothing ahead. She must have turned off her lights too.* The red dot stopped.

As the sky lightened in the east, he could see a thicket of trees and brush ahead. *She has to be in there.* Rapha pulled off to one side and got out of his car. *I'll either capture her for interrogation or kill her.* Part of him relished the idea of questioning her–with prejudice. A vision of her bound under a bright light, fear in her eyes, rose. He'd questioned prisoners in Afghanistan, but others were better at getting answers. He did like watching the fear grow as they understood he was in total control. *Either way this is going to end.* He crept toward the trees.

Ahead and to the right was a well-lit area, surrounded by a six-foot high chain-link fence, razor wire on top. Armed men patrolled the fence line. They didn't wear uniforms. He pulled out his phone to check the last text. Colonel Nesbit had sent him the addresses of Los Xecas locations in Nuevo Laredo. *Shit! We're at the communication headquarters! What is she up to?*

He eased closer to where his tracker indicated she was. It brought him nearer to the fence. The ground was exposed, but with his black clothes he should be invisible. Something was happening inside the compound. He froze, watching a black Escalade drive in. Two men moved toward it. The driver got out and held the door for a man in the back seat. He wore a suit and held a briefcase.

The air around Rapha cracked, a sharp blow that stung his ears. He hit the ground, recognizing it as a supersonic bullet passing by him. The gun had been suppressed, but the bullet couldn't be quieted as it traveled faster than sound. *Is Russell shooting at me? Did she get behind me?* Cautiously he took a quick peek at the copse of trees. Nothing. There was shouting from beyond the fence in the compound. The man in the suit lay on the ground.

Guards ran toward the still figure while others looked through the fence for the source of the shot. A bang sounded as a flash glared in his eyes a mere ten feet away. The sound of the shot boomed from behind him. *This shot was meant for me. Or was it?* His mind processed. *If the shooter could hit the man two hundred yards farther out than I am, how could she miss me? Of course! It had to be Katherine Russell. She wasn't in the trees!*

There was another bang and flash as another marker round struck the ground five feet away. Yelling from the fence area snapped him back to reality. They'd seen the marker round and were coming for him as the shooter. *I have to get out!*

Bullets snapped around him as he ran for the Jeep. He jumped in, started it and in a cloud of dust spun around and headed for the road. *Los Xecas won't believe I am innocent in the death of the man on the ground. I have to get away!*

Once on the road he pushed the gas pedal to the floor. If he could make the border, he'd be safe. On his console, he speed-dialed Nighthawk.

"It's early, Sanchez. What's going on?"

"I was set up. I'm in Nuevo Laredo, Mexico and Los Xecas are chasing me. They think I killed one of their men. It was Russell! I know it."

"Can you make the border?"

"Maybe, but there was a line to get across into the U.S. a mile long. If I stop, I'm dead, or worse. I need extraction."

"How far behind you are Los Xecas?"

"I guess more than a mile, about a minute at the speed I'm driving."

"Hold on, I'll pull up a map. When you get on Highway 2, head west, pedal to the metal. I'll see what I can do."

Rapha glanced in the mirror. The headlights weren't gaining on him, but he wasn't losing them either. Traffic was picking up as he neared the turn to the border. *I have to focus.* Semi-trucks were lined up to make that turn. He took the curve where Highway 2 went west on two wheels, forcing oncoming cars off the road. He flashed his lights in a rapid staccato trying to clear a path. *Los Xecas will set up a roadblock ahead.*

"Sanchez, you hear me? I made an emergency call to our client. They've called up favors. I've got you up on a drone pic. DEA had one in the air. They're scrambling a chopper from the Laredo airport headquarters. It's going to get in front of you and touch down. Get on it. The chase cars may get there before you're in the air, but this is the best we can do. This is a hot LZ. Leave everything and get on that chopper."

"Thanks, boss."

"We're going to owe DEA and CIA big time on this. Shit rolls downhill. You're going to owe me."

If I make it.

Chapter 31

By the time the vulture drone arrived in a position to see what was happening on the road, Sanchez had abandoned his car, and the chopper was lifting off. Ilia called Kiki and Nick. "You heading back to your hotel?"

"Yeah. How'd it go?"

"I'm there watching the excitement now. Did you leave anything behind in your room?"

"I didn't figure on going back to it, but we need to pick up the gear from the room next door. I'm bunking with you guys tonight."

"We'll get our own room," Nick called from behind the wheel.

"I'm recording everything, video, audio and cell calls. Lot of excitement going on where Sanchez made his exit. We have tons of stuff to sift through.

I'm forwarding it all to the Hacienda."

"What happened to Sanchez?" Kiki asked.

"He was extracted. Classic, right out of the Viet Nam history book. How soon until you are here?"

"Five minutes," Nick answered. "What about our vulture?"

"It is circling the extraction site now. I will leave it on station until there is nothing more to record. We will recover it when things cool down."

"We're here," Kiki announced. A few minutes later, she entered the room carrying a long athletic bag. Nick followed with another. "I want to see the footage."

"I want coffee, Irish coffee," Nick asserted.

"You want popcorn to go with the show?" laughed Ilia. He tilted the screen back on his laptop so they all could see it. "From the start. This is where the bird put the tracker on the ground." The camera rose as the bird gained altitude. They could see the well-lit compound with the guards and the dirt road coming in. "Sanchez turned off his lights here. I'll speed up the action." The guards trotted around the fence. The darkened Jeep crept down the road. They watched Sanchez get out and look at the trees searching for Kiki. In the lights from the compound, a guard held the gate open as the Escalade drove in.

After the suited man with the briefcase got out of the car, he straightened his jacket. Suddenly, he flew back, smashing into the car door and collapsing on the ground like a puppet with the strings cut. The guards froze, some for less than a second. Two quickly recovered and ran toward the downed man, the rest turned, searching for the shooter. "Good military discipline," commented Kiki. The flash of the spotter round near Rapha drew their attention. Some began firing immediately, trying to pin him down. Others ran to vehicles and raced from the yard. There was only one road out. They knew where he had to go.

They watched Rapha run to his Jeep as bullets peppered the ground around him like a hail storm. In a smooth motion, he jumped into the jeep, cranked it over and raced away in a huge cloud of dust. They watched him speed down the dirt track. As soon as he was on the paved road, he shot forward. Two cars appeared to join the race as they sped out of the view. "The vulture couldn't move fast enough, so there is nothing to see until it catches up." Ilia fastforwarded the view. He slowed to real speed as Sanchez' Jeep came into the picture. Armed men surrounded it, some pointing rifles at the rising helicopter. Nobody fired. "Sanchez was in the chopper already," Ilia explained.

"Why didn't they fire?" asked Nick.

"Good discipline," answered Kiki. "That's a U.S. helicopter, probably DEA. Killing DEA personnel in Mexico has consequences that go on for years. They learned that lesson about fifteen years ago. There's also a machinegun mounted in the doorway of that chopper pointed at them."

The men turned to the car and began methodically taking it apart all the way to the frame. Anything of interest was stuffed in bags. "I speed up again here." The figures raced around, until one man directed them back to their cars. He shot the fuel tank while another man tossed a road flare under it. Within seconds the Jeep was engulfed in flames.

"Well, that was satisfying," exclaimed Kiki. She chuckled.

"How's this going to tie into the CIA?" asked Nick.

"The extraction by a Blackhawk helicopter will

tie it to the U.S.," Kiki declared. "From there, we'll see what happens."

"We need to get some rest and be out of here before nightfall," Nick announced. "The sixteen hour drive back to the Hacienda will be exhausting."

Ilia finished packing their gear into the rollaway suitcases. "Let's go to our hotel." Pulling both pieces of luggage through the door, he turned to Kiki. "You and Nick have the connecting room at our hotel. I will have the vulture fly north. We will pick it up on the trip back. I think I will leave the raven that is watching your door in place until we leave."

In their connecting room, weariness hit Kiki like a wall. "I'm exhausted." She took her boots off and crawled into the bed fully clothed. Nick lay beside her. Her mind tingled. She looked at Nick. He rolled his eyes. He'd felt it too. It was the Director.

"Nice job with Raphael Sanchez. The hatred and fear is spewing out of him. He knows you set him up. Los Xecas are giving me tasty hatred too. Their anger is a spicy flavor, something to relish. Katherine, you still provide me with delicious meals."

She answered in her head. "Your wellbeing is not a concern of ours. We did what was necessary to get him and the CIA off our backs."

"Sanchez will be debriefed very soon. They will realize what the intention of your actions was. Your respite will be short-lived. They will come after you with more intensity than before, but this time they will not underestimate you. You must be very cautious. If you choose to stay with this plan, I do not see a good outcome. I must go. Thank you again for a nice meal."

She studied Nick. "Should we drop out?"

"Yes, but not immediately. There are still things I'd like to see accomplished."

Chapter 32

In the early morning light, Rapha watched the helipad grow larger as they approached the hangar where the DEA had a special operations center. A man in a white shirt and striped tie stood with his hands on his hips watching them land. The blast from the rotors whipped his black hair and raised dust. He covered his eyes. His tie flapped like a flag in a hurricane. As they touched down, Rapha stepped out. The man motioned for him to approach.

"We have a debrief set up inside. On me now," he snapped.

The man spun and marched into the hangar. *This guy is pissed, hot enough to fry an egg on his forehead.* Rapha followed him into an office. The door slammed behind him, rattling the glass. The man closed the blinds. "Before I get your boss on the line, I want to know what the fuck is going on!" His voice rose in both tone and volume. "You work in my patch without telling me? Who authorized this?" His face got redder as spit flew from his lips.

"Sir, my name is Raphael Sanchez. I cannot tell you anything else. My boss will fill you in."

"Sit your ass down," the man thundered, pointing at a folding chair. He loomed over Rapha, his face like overheated steel, red hot. "Your shit operation trampled all over my own ops. You endangered my agents. There will be an international incident complaint filed by Mexico. All for your worthless ass."

He stomped over to his desk and the phone. Rapha felt a shiver run down his back as he watched the man jab number buttons so hard he was sure the phone would break. He pushed the speaker button as the phone rang.

"David Kennedy," came the answer.

"This is Assistant Director Brian Olson, Texas Sector of the DEA. Who are you?"

"I'm David Kennedy with the CIA. I have Michael Nesbit, commander of Nighthawk Securities, a CIA contractor on the line with me."

"I need an explanation why your director had me jeopardize my operations here, endanger my agents, and violate the international border," Olson shouted.

"Were your men fired on?" Nesbit asked.

"No, sir. The men chasing your agent were U.S.-trained Los Xecas sicarios. Looking down the barrel of an M-249 machinegun gives one pause. It was good discipline. Now tell me what's going on."

David cleared his throat. "Agent Sanchez was on an information gathering mission, nothing else."

"Across the border without notifying the agencies operating in the area. What kind of shit operation do you have going?"

"Assistant Director Olson, I..." David tried to interject.

Olson glanced at his phone. He had a text. "I'm getting reports that a high-level member of Los Xecas was assassinated this morning. Sanchez was there. That doesn't sound like information gathering," sneered Olson.

"Sanchez, did you fire a weapon?" Nesbit asked.

"No, sir."

"Why did they think it was you?" Nesbit continued.

"Someone behind me fired. I heard the bullet pass me. They then fired marker rounds to reveal my position."

"A very convenient explanation. And just who do you suspect fired these rounds?" snapped Olson.

"Assistant Director Olson, we cannot tell you anything more about this mission," announced Kennedy. "Thank you for your help. This is a confidential matter. You are to speak to nobody about it."

"Jesus H Christ! You will not be able to keep this quiet. Just as I have plants within Los Xecas, they have spies in my organization, and they're very good at breaking encryption. They know we are aware of their agents. We're both careful about knocking off each other's citizens. We're also very cautious about violating sovereignty. Unlike you spooks." Acid seemed to drip from those words. "Within hours, their headquarters and the Mexican government will know about this. Los Xecas are not forgiving. I do not want a war between DEA and them."

"You want them to know it wasn't DEA, is that right?" observed Kennedy.

There was a pregnant silence.

"My director will certainly be in touch with yours," fumed Olson.

"Hashing this out is above our pay grades. I apologize for any inconvenience," David said.

"The next time one of your spooks gets in trouble in Mexico on an illegal mission, my phone may not work," Olson huffed. "Get your man off my base before I turn him over to Los Xecas."

Chapter 33

Kiki's phone buzzed against her hip, jarring her out of the half-sleep. Not many people had this number. Exhausted, this interruption to her rest period was more than irritating. They were breaking the sixteen-hour drive into three-hour shifts. West Texas could kill you with boredom. She stared at the caller ID trying to get her eyes to focus. *Unknown.* Unknown wasn't anyone she knew so she declined, giving Ilia a quick look. He glanced at her and returned his focus to the road.

They had pulled off the road fifteen miles outside of Laredo and retrieved the vulture drone. After San Antonio they called a break and ate dinner at a truck stop. Nearly midnight and they were two hours from El Paso.

Kiki's phone rang again, *Caller Unknown.* This

time she accepted the call.

"Well you sure made a fucking mess in Nuevo Laredo, but that was your plan, wasn't it?"

"Hello, David. I'm fine, thank you. How are you?" She didn't bother asking how he got this number.

"I'm pissed. Can you tell? You've made a lot of trouble for the Company."

"You scared me the last time we talked. I'm just trying to buy some time before I get out." From the corner of her eye, she saw Ilia glance at her.

"We're going to be busy putting out fires for a while. But people are already starting an investigation into who was behind this. The squabble between cartels won't play for long. Then the search begins and you better be far away."

"I'm sorry for any trouble you're facing."

"No, you're not," his voice was icy, "but I understand. When you get back tomorrow, and after I've had a chance to cool down, we'll talk again. Drive carefully." The call was ended.

Shit! He just showed her they would be able to find them way too easily. She called Nick who was driving her car and put the call on speaker. "David just called. The good news is we caused enough of a stir to keep them busy, maybe too busy to think about us. The bad news is when the investigation does start, they will probably find us. We pissed off some powerful people.""They gonna kill us?"

"That or offer us jobs. My bet is on the former."

"How long before we really have to worry?"

"He didn't say, but my take is not more than a couple of weeks."

"I guess we'll have a lot to talk about tomorrow."

* * *

Sol greeted them as they drove into the Hacienda. "Get a few hours rest. Debrief this afternoon. Dawn intercepted calls about serious hit on Los Xecas. We get your story after you sleep."

In the darkened bedroom, neither Kiki nor Nick could relax enough to sleep. She turned to face him. "Do you think Sol understood what this mission might cost?"

"He's a smart guy. He knows this contract is over." Nick chuckled. "I have a hard time picturing us in the unemployment line explaining why we aren't looking for work."

She laughed. I'm glad you can joke about our situation." Kiki knew Nick used humor to shield any fear he might be feeling. "We all made enough money. Time off won't hurt."

"Sol's a professional. You don't get old in his job without knowing when it's time to quit."

They lay together in bed, neither asleep, neither wanting to talk more.

* * *

The late lunch meeting was a team affair. Nick, Kiki, and Ilia took turns explaining how the mission went.

"So to summarize," Sol said, "you did not use this trip for reconnaissance."

"I saw an opportunity," Kiki acknowledged, "and I took it. The CIA is busy with Los Xecas and our Bogey, Sanchez."

"Won't last," Sol snorted. "CIA involved, will talk to Los Xecas. Realize this was setup." Kiki grimly nodded. Sol continued the summary of their situation. "Most of cartels have limited tech, except for Los Xecas. If we are targeted by pros, danger level goes up. If Los Xecas team up with Nighthawk Securities using CIA assets, we have to be gone. Their tech too good. Ilia cannot cover tracks enough in time. I call our boss. Tell him things too hot."

"There won't be a problem with him, will there?" Dawn asked.

Nobody answered.

Chapter 34

Rapha Sanchez poured himself a tall glass of Don Julio tequila and sat on the bed in his new Nogales hotel. He shook his head. The debriefing had been brutal. After his harrowing experience in Nuevo Laredo, he'd been put on a plane. Nobody told him where he was going. In fact, no one spoke to him at all.

At Langley he was escorted to a small office where Colonel Nesbit met him. CIA Assistant Director Dick Forester and ex-director David Kennedy were introduced and sat across the table in the small interrogation room. Forester started the questioning which he knew would mercilessly continue for hours, asking the same question with different words.

"Why didn't you go through the DEA channels

to contact Los Xecas?"

Nesbit answered, "We didn't want to involve DEA. Our understanding was that they were not on friendly terms with your operations. Isn't that the case?" Both agents ignored the question.

Forester stared at Nesbit, ignoring Sanchez. "Why was your man alone?"

"Raphael Sanchez was to meet with them informally to be assured that Los Xecas weren't the ones attacking your partners."

David Kennedy clasped his hands together on the table, then gazed at Sanchez. "You were in Nuevo Laredo solely to meet with Los Xecas?"

Nesbit nodded at Rapha, indicating he should answer. "I have been tracking Katherine Russell. I believe she has assassinated numerous people including two Nighthawk Securities employees. She may also have taken part in the attacks on your partners."

"Did you follow her or was she there at the same time by chance?" A smile played across Kennedy's face. "What was she doing in Laredo?"

That stopped Sanchez cold. *Why was she there? Her usual style was a high-profile target or several bodies.* "Sir, I truly don't know. From what I saw, she appeared to be alone. I thought I would have an opportunity to pick her up for questioning. She's our best lead as to who is attacking your partners."

"Instead you are now a target of Los Xecas and your actions revealed DEA involvement," Kennedy rebuked. "For your information, the DEA and Los Xecas have a tacit truce, which is now in jeopardy. With the leaks from that bureau, the CIA has entered the picture. Until we can smooth this over, we are at war with them." He placed his hands flat on the table and pushed himself upright. "I have to question Nighthawk's competency and our contract." He glanced at Forester.

"Sir," protested Nesbit, "Raphael Sanchez was obviously set up. If anything, this strengthens the case of Katherine Russell's involvement in the attacks. I suggest we put a team together to eliminate her and anybody else she's with."

"It looks like her mission was to do exactly what happened in Nuevo Laredo," sneered Kennedy. "Perhaps we should be looking at contracting with her." He again glanced at Forester.

"Sir, Nighthawk will put its own team together. We will take care of her," pleaded Nesbit.

"On your dime," stated Forester. "We will

supply you with tech support, but that's all."

When they were finished with Sanchez, he was admonished about the need for secrecy. *As if they needed to remind me.* On the flight from Langley, he was the only passenger on the jet. The only crew was the pilot and co. Upon landing, the jet taxied into a hangar. The crew spoke not a word to him as they handed him keys and pointed to a new SUV.

The drive from Ft. Huachuca seemed endless, but gave him time to think. *Whatever the reason Katherine Russell was in Nuevo Laredo, I was caught in her trap. Her group knew I had a tracker on her car and probably put one on mine. They had undoubtedly bugged my hotel.* He glanced at the reservation card for a different hotel sitting on the passenger seat. Whatever room he had been given, he knew had been swept for bugs.

He pounded on the steering wheel. *They set me up to create a mess with the CIA. She lured me to a point where she could easily have killed me. She didn't. She used me. Was she counting on Los Xecas to do that for her?*

His new hotel was the Francisco Grande, only a block from the border. From his eighth-floor room, he looked out over Nogales as he took a big sip of tequila. The glow from it traveled from his throat into his stomach. They had received new marching orders. He was now the advance scout and recon man for a Nighthawk Securities team that would arrive as soon as he located Katherine Russell.

Another sip of tequila. *Somehow I have to pick up her track again. Her trail of victims led me to her before. Do I have time to wait for the next ones to fall?*

He sectioned the view of the city as if he could pick her up by just watching. High in the sky, a buzzard flew lazy eights.

He took another gulp of tequila. NSA was going to help by monitoring cell phone calls, but that wouldn't be up and running for a couple of days. At his computer, he fast forwarded through the three days of surveillance footage from his camera at Russell's house. *Nothing. Nobody entered or left. She wouldn't go back there, would she?*

Another big sip and his head spun, fuzzy from two cross-country trips and no sleep. The tequila helped, he felt better. Sighing, he realized what a close call he'd had with Los Xecas, minutes behind him, intent on revenge and murder. *Probably beheading too, either before they'd killed me or not. That was their style.* Fully clothed, he lay back. His eyes were closed before his head hit the pillow. That's when the dreams started.

Chapter 35

Nesbit and Sanchez had left the office with their tails tucked between their legs. Dick Forester glanced at his notes and faced David Kennedy. "Find out what you can about Katherine Russell."

Kennedy stared at Forester for a few seconds. *If he knew who she is and what she's done for this country he won't be so eager to get rid of her. But telling him of my association with her will put me at risk of losing my job, maybe my freedom. He has been known to fly off the handle, but I have to try.*

"Sir, I worked with a Katherine Russell during the Bio-Cyber War. She was a top sniper in Afghanistan, and the chance that there are two of them with the same name is slim. Here's what I know. Several years ago, she and her husband worked with Homeland Security to stop the terrorist attacks against the families of servicemen serving in the Middle East. That murderous campaign started with the slaughter of her family."

Forester's gaze was glued to Kennedy. "I remember that episode. Our inability to protect those families was a devastating blow to morale of those serving."

"Yes, it was. Local law enforcement had been unable to make any progress on Russell's case. She and Nick Sabino returned from Afghanistan and hunted them alone, killing several members of a drug gang contracted to the terrorists. When she was captured trying to nail the Arab head of that operation in America, Sabino contacted law enforcement for help. Due to the nature of the killings, a team had already been formed including FBI, Homeland Security and the locals."

"I thought that being on that team was a plum assignment, put me in a good position to advance." Forester frowned. "It didn't turn out that way. Glad I didn't make the cut. Continue."

"In exchange for their help in reacquiring Russell, Sabino agreed to lend his interrogation expertise. He was a whiz. He could get accurate information in hours that would take weeks or months normally, if at all. Unfortunately, one CIA agent decided to force them into extended work they didn't want to do. They disappeared for two years, location unknown."

"Who was this agent?"

"Dianna Coleman. She's presently at an asylum, diagnosed insane, though she is lucid at times."

"I remember her file." Forester shook his head. "A sad story because she was on the up-and-up, a real goer. Freddy Foster, the FBI agent on the team, got blamed for the damage to Coleman and the loss of a helicopter. She spent a couple of years in some career hell."

"Yes, sir. Two years later just after the bio-cyber attack, Russell and Sabino surfaced, contacting Foster and offering to help. It was Sabino's interrogations that put us on the path to getting the smallpox vaccine and nailing those responsible for the attack. That's when Ron Carson and I worked with her and Sabino."

Surprise showed on Forester's face. "Ex-President Ron Carson?"

"Yes, sir. He was Secretary of Interior at the time. It was later when he became president."

"He got a lot of mileage about getting the U.S. out of that mess," Forester remarked. "Catapulted him into the White House."

"He was one of our best presidents, sir." Forester nodded agreement. "Russell and Sabino fought the gangs in California as guerrillas until the U.S. was able to retake the state. That put her on a kill list with the gangs. She and Sabino faked her death and disappeared for two years again.

"Later, Russell and Sabino helped President Carson uncover and stop the plot the Military Industrial Complex hatched to start a war in the Pacific and a bio attack in the Middle East."

"I thought that stopped with the deaths of several of the principals."

David stared at Forester.

"Jesus H Christ!" He threw his pen on the table. "That's who we're dealing with?"

"I believe so, sir."

"What the hell are they doing in Mexico, besides fucking up our operations?"

"That I don't know, sir."

"Can you contact her and get them out?"

"Leaving has been my advice. I believe they are trying to extract now."

"So you've already been in contact with them." Forester's face grew red. "Well, they better get the fuck out. Heroes or not, I'm not letting them fuck with my black budget. Too much is at stake."

David moved his pen across his own tablet with one finger. "Their deaths would bring some powerful people into the picture. It could expose operations we really want hidden."

Forester blew out a noisy breath. "If you can't get them out and get these attacks on our partners stopped, they may have to just disappear again, permanently this time."

"Yes, sir. I'll try to convince them." *Threats hadn't worked out too well for Kiki's enemies in the past. I wouldn't want to be in Forester's shoes if this doesn't work and she finds out.*

Chapter 36

Sol didn't look forward to calling Julio, but it had to be done. He'd soldiered enough to know when discretion is the better part of valor. Their small force would be no match for the CIA and their contractors. He sighed, glanced around his bare office and dialed Julio's number.

"Sol, I was about to call you. We have a problem. The Los Mochis Cartel is planning to take over part of the Sonora territory. It will be a bloody war. Many will be killed."

"We have another problem," Sol interrupted. "A security contractor hired by the CIA will be hunting us. We're going to have to pull out, at least for a while." *There, I've said it.*

"We have a contract, work to do, lives to save."

"Julio, I will not sacrifice my people in a situation we cannot win. The contractor will have CIA tech support. We won't be able to hide." A silence grew.

"How long before this hunt begins?"

"We created a diversion in Nuevo Laredo that will give us at a week, but no more than two. I don't want to wait until then."

"I heard about an attack on a Los Xecas communications center by a gringo. Los Xecas are looking for DEA or CIA agents to take revenge. That was you?"

"Yeah. We had an agent tracking us. His company is a contractor the CIA uses, so we needed to get rid of him without exposing ourselves. It will buy us time until Los Xecas figures out the agent wasn't the shooter. The Americans probably already know. Then we'll have three groups after us: Los Xecas, Nighthawk Securities and the CIA. We have to leave now."

"I see your problem. Sol, we can still take care of the Mochis trouble. Besides, you won't be in Sonora. I'll double the payment for this job. After that you can leave with my blessing."

"Send me all the information you have. I'll discuss it with my team. One more thing you should know. Nick Sabino recognized your voice during the interrogation. Don't worry. Nobody will find out. I realize the problem security is for you." He heard a sigh.

"I had hoped to stay more invisible."

* * *

Sol called a meeting in the communications center. He reviewed the mission to Nuevo Laredo and finished with the involvement of the CIA and DEA in searching for the *Fantasmas*. "If caught, there will be no trial. Public can't know activities of American government agencies. Would come out in trial. Kiki, how much time before hunting season opens on us?"

She stood and surveyed the team. "First off, when the hunt begins, the techies will come in with their latest and greatest. If the *Fantasmas* are still in business, we will be caught. My guess is more than a week, but less than three. It depends on when the agents can focus on more than covering their butts. Nick and I have run up against Nighthawk Securities before. They're not slouches; ex-military, Special Forces and Navy Seals. We do not want to engage them in any type of open fight. They'll have helicopter gunships, armored Hummers and plenty of firepower supplied by Uncle Sam. When we disappear, it will have to be to the four winds."

Her phone rang. She glanced at the caller ID. *Unknown. Maybe David Kennedy.* "Hello?"

"Kiki, you need to make vacation plans."

She recognized David's voice. "David, we're having a meeting about this right now. Can I put you on speakerphone?"

"I'm not happy about more people knowing of my involvement." He paused, before adding, "It's too late for that, isn't it? Ah shit. Go ahead."

Kiki hit the button. "You're on."

"Okay, we debriefed Sanchez. No one in the company believes this was anything less than an attempt to put us in conflict with Los Xecas. We will have to devote effort to calming that conviction down so we're not targets. Right now Los Xecas are shooting first and not talking. Within a week we'll get them to sit down with us."

"I'd hoped to buy more time," remarked Kiki.

"Nighthawk's agent is back in Nogales,"

continued David, "trying to locate you while a team is being assembled to join him. Since they fucked up, this is on them, so they'll want it over quickly. As soon as we straighten things out with Los Xecas, we'll put efforts into helping them. It's going to get very dangerous there. Best pull a Houdini."

"David, thanks for this. I know if you become compromised it could be bad."

"Bad! We're talking fed prison at best for me. For you guys, you'll just disappear. They may hand you over to Los Xecas to mend fences. I needn't tell you what will happen then. I had to tell my boss about you and Nick. Despite your record of helping the United States, the attacks have to stop. Even that may not be enough to save you. Get out."

"Thanks, David." The call was ended.

"That's good asset and good friend you have," remarked Sol. "Nothing about him will leave room." Heads nodded agreement. "Employer agrees we need to disband and disappear. He has one more job before that takes place." Kiki scrunched up her face. "It is short job in Los Moches. The Mochis Cartel sending men to Sonora to take over territory and operations. War would be bloody. He wants us to stop that drive. We set up surveillance post. Info determine what we do."

"Is doing nothing an option, considering our situation?" posed Kiki. "I do see how disappearing from Nogales could buy us a little more time, but hitting the Mochis Cartel will bring in the troops. We'd have to have our escape completely set up."

"If smells bad, we leave," asserted Sol. "Boss offered double payments for job."

"Or we could vote to not do it at all," snapped Kiki. "I take David's advice to heart. This is a risk for all of us."

"Double payments I like," asserted Zyra. "Sasha and I not have to work for long time." She smiled at the stunning blonde beside her.

"Zyra, you like the work too much to quit," Kiki joked. "I can't picture you retired."

"Okay, long vacation."

Nick looked at Kiki. "I have another reason to do this job. Since we began, violence against civilians has dropped. This last mission would send a message."

"Who vote no?" Sol looked around the room. No hands went up. "So all okay with it?" his gaze fixed on Kiki. She forced a smile and nodded. "I tell him we go. Get all information for us. Ilia, Emilio, pack whatever you need in van, leave in morning." *Hope I am doing the right thing.*

"We need to find Sanchez." He stared at Kiki.

Chapter 37

Ilia and Emilio loaded the van with everything they could think of. As the sun was coming up, they were on Highway 15 heading south. The rolling grassland turned to desert. Three hours later they were bumper-to-bumper in traffic in Hermosillo. After an hour, they'd cleared the outskirts and continued on toward Guaymas. The desert became greener as they entered Los Mochis—a six hour trip. Sol had sent them the address of Don Zacaros, the head of the Mochis Cartel. He'd also sent them contact information for a local asset, Rosalinda Villa, who would assist them.

Ilia called the number Sol had sent. "Hola, this is Rosalinda."

"I am Ilia from Nogales. Can we meet?"

"Sí. I will be at the OXXO on Highway 15 in thirty minutes."

Parked at the convenience store, Ilia and Emilio watched cars come and go. When the tall beautiful woman dressed in a black skirt, white silk blouse and spike heels got out of the black Lexus, their gazes were glued on her. She walked directly to their van and leaned in the open window giving them a breathtaking view of her cleavage.

"You are Ilia." It was a statement, not a question.

"You are Rosalinda?" She smiled. He gestured toward the passenger seat. "This is Emilio. Our employer sent us here to meet with you."

"Call me Rosa. He asked me to find you a house to rent. I have several. Follow me."

Ilia and Emilio watched her walk back to her car. It was a Cadillac walk.

The early afternoon traffic was light as they drove into town. The first house was near the city center. In the Mexican style, it was surrounded by a high wall with an iron bar gate which was opened by a guard as they approached. The white plastered walls of the two-story house gleamed in the sunlight. Red brick lined the courtyard with potted plants scattered along the wall. Wrought iron chairs and a table were under a bright yellow umbrella. A stairway gave access to the roof.

Rosa opened the heavy oak double doors. The furniture inside was heavy wood construction with bright colored cushions. Spanish tile was plentiful, on the floors, and kitchen cabinets. There were two bedrooms with baths downstairs with two more upstairs. The windows upstairs had views of the city.

"This is a beautiful home," commented Ilia.

"I can get this for one month or two–longer if you want a lease."

Ilia glanced around the house. *The upkeep of this house will require a maid and a gardener. Being in the city center, there could be no hasty exit. The address given to us of Don Zacaros is not far. Maybe not far enough.* "It is more than we need. What do you have that is simpler and nearer the outskirts of the city?"

A momentary frown crossed Rosa's face. She shrugged. "Let's go look at another."

The trip following the Lexus took twenty minutes, traffic had increased. They curved onto a residential street lined with trees. Rosa turned into a driveway, stopping at a large wooden gate set into a tall wall, the plaster a desert sand color. When Rosa got out of her car to open the gate, Emilio jumped out and opened it for her.

They drove into a concrete floored courtyard. The house was single story with a metal studded oak door. A stairway led to the roof. Inside, the floors were saltillo tile, the walls white plaster. The furniture was utilitarian, the kitchen had adequate counter space. The stove was gas, the refrigerator old. There were three bedrooms. The master had a bathroom. The other bedrooms shared a large bathroom. The views through the bars on the rear and side windows were of similar homes in the neighborhood, some shielded by trees.

Ilia glanced at Emilio. "Let me talk to my partner for a few minutes." Rosa went into the courtyard. "What do you think?"

"This is an older neighborhood. It was one of the nicest when I lived in Mochis. The people living here were longtime residents, moderate incomes. It's minutes from the highway, yet not that far from Don Zacaros' house."

"Yeah, no taller structures around so our antennas and satellite dish won't be spotted." Ilia pulled out his phone. "Good strong cell signal." He walked to the door. "This will be fine," he called to Rosa.

She came in with a clip board. "This house has been vacant for awhile. You can get it month-to-month or sign a lease."

"We'd like a two-month lease. Can we move in immediately?"

"As soon as I file the papers this afternoon, it's yours. Maybe one hour. I will call you."

* * *

They set up the third bedroom as their communications center. In addition to the queen-size bed, it had a desk and dresser. On the walls were paintings of the Sea of Cortez. Their satellite dish and antennas were installed in the patio, not visible outside the wall. Ilia called Dawn.

"We're all good here. Rosa got us just what we needed. We launched a vulture drone and have it circling our target address now. I'm triangulating so that calls from that area are running through the telecommunications program for word recognition. We can filter down to those phones tied to Don Zacaros. Hopefully we'll be able to isolate his phone. Everything is mirrored into your system so you see what we see, hear what we hear."

"Didn't take you guys long to set up. I'll let Sol know. Between you and us, we should be able to monitor 24/7."

"What's going on there?"

"Sol's a little nervous about David Kennedy working for the CIA."

"Don't worry about him. Sasha, Zyra and I worked with him before. He's solid."

"We're packing up to move out of Nogales at a moment's notice," a tone of sadness in Dawn's voice. "The Hacienda will maintain the communications center, but we'll be able to jump ship within two hours if needed. Other than that, things are quiet here."

"Any luck finding Sanchez?"

"We're monitoring the frequencies he used with the satellite phone before, but nothing. He's not in the same room at the hotel so we pulled the bugs. His camera is still active at Nick and Kiki's house. We're thinking of using that to lure him out. Kiki and Nick will return to clean the place out. They'll be seen going in. If the Bogey shows up, we'll follow him."

"As soon as you find out where he's staying,

bug him. He'll report back that he's located her. Nighthawk will send a team."

"Roger that. I've mirrored things up here to you too, so you and Emilio can watch from your end."

"Good. You keep watch on our security here for awhile. Anybody good can set up an observation post without setting off the alarms. Emilio is going to give me a tour of the city. Let us know if anything goes on. We need to scope out the neighborhood and get something to eat. Grocery store after that."

"Unless something occurs, I'll talk to you tomorrow, let you know if anything happens with Sanchez."

"I like it, but be cautious. He could shoot first and interrogate after. He is probably that pissed."

"Not a very attractive image there. Yeah, we go with backup."

Chapter 38

The tone on Rapha's computer woke him. The motion sensor on his camera at Katherine Russell's house had triggered the alarm. He had the curtains drawn so he could catch up on much needed sleep. At the desk, he watched as she and some guy unloaded bags from the trunk and took them into the house. This was the first time his camera had picked up movement since the disastrous trip to Laredo. Had they been on another trip? Where? *No more bodies have dropped in Nogales since I've returned from Langley.* He shuddered at the memory. *It doesn't matter where you've been. I have you again.* He called Colonel Nesbit. "I've found her."

"Where is she?"

"She and a guy are at her house. It looks like

they returned from a trip."

"Watch her. Our files say she's married to Nick Sabino. Might be him. Don't lose her again."

"I'll stake it out, don't want to try a tracker again."

"Just don't get spotted. Call me when you're in position."

"Roger, sir."

* * *

"Sol, our vulture spotted an SUV parked behind Kiki's house outside the gated community." Dawn turned to face Sol in the communications room. "Someone's sitting inside. The car's been there two hours."

He came over to look at the overhead view from the vulture. "Hmm. Has view of back of house. Probably accessing feed from camera in front. Neither Kiki nor Nick can leave unseen. Find frequency of camera in front."

Dawn started a scan. On one monitor screens of static flipped through. A view of Kiki's house flashed. "Got him!"

Sol leaned forward. "Scan satellite frequencies from hotel bugs planted before."

"Nothing. He has to become active before we'll

find what he's using."

Sol called to Zyra in the next room. "Can you come to the communications room? I've got a mission."

Three minutes later she strode through the door in her usual black skin-tight, Sasha close behind. Sol pointed to the view of the SUV. "That's our Bogey, Sanchez. He's staked out Kiki's house, and we need to plant a tracker on the car without him knowing. Can do?"

"Da. Dark in one hour. We go then. If he sees us we kill him?"

"No. We need him. He is info ticket to when bad guys come."

"I hope he doesn't leave before we get there," remarked Dawn.

"Let's do something to keep his interest." Sol called Kiki. "Go out, put something in trunk of car."

"What?"

"Bogey watching front and rear. Must keep him there. With suitcase he think you leave. He must stay."

Watching through Sanchez's camera, they saw Kiki walk out of the house carrying a suitcase. She looked up and down the street before walking to her car and placing it in the trunk. A last glance at the street and she returned to the house.

"Check your frequencies in case he makes a call."

"Got it." cried Dawn. "They're using the same encryption as before." She hit a key on the keyboard. Voices came through.

"Sir, the tango put a suitcase in her car, then went back inside."

"Stay on her. You lose her and you can explain it to Los Xecas," Nesbit growled. "Got it?"

"Yes, sir."

* * *

Sol called Kiki again. "When I call, go into back yard with Nick. Dig hole. Bury something."

"What do you want me to bury?"

"Doesn't matter. You are holding Sanchez's attention while we bug his car. You are being watched by sniper who wants to question you. Still might kill Nick and wound you."

"Thanks," she snickered. "Make yourself a target but don't get shot. Easy."

"Take phone. Drone on infrared view. I forward to you. If he pulls out weapon, you'll know."

They waited until the sky darkened. On the infrared view, Dawn and Sol saw Zyra approach the car. In her black skintight, she would have been invisible with any normal view. "Zyra, hold." Sol commanded. He called Kiki. "In position. Go."

At the Hacienda, they watched Kiki and Nick enter the back yard. Nick carried a shovel. Dawn focused the drone view on Sanchez's car. He was looking through binoculars, both hands holding them. "Go Zyra." With the IR view, they watched her hunched figure approach the rear of the car and place something under the bumper. On the map view screen a red dot appeared. "Up and running, Zyra." She moved away. Sanchez remained glued to the binoculars. "Okay, Kiki. You and Nick can go back inside."

As the back door closed, Sanchez dialed Nighthawk on his satellite phone. Dawn keyed to the frequency.

"I'm at dinner, Sanchez. What's happening?"

"Russell and Sabino buried something in the back yard. I couldn't see what it was."

"Keep watching. We'll get it when the coast is clear."

"Boss, I've been here more than a day. I'm

going to need some help."

"I've got somebody on the way. She's booked into your hotel. Go there when Russell and Sabino are tucked in for the night."

"Roger, Colonel. Thanks"

"Shit," Dawn exclaimed. "They'll be more of them."

Sol nodded. "Was going to happen. He didn't say it was his hit team." He called Kiki. "Tracker planted. We'll turn it off and on remotely to keep him from finding it"

"How did you keep Zyra from killing Sanchez?"

"Told her he was important. Sanchez called Nighthawk to report. Company soon for him."

"The hit team?"

"Not yet. Just relief. Meeting at hotel tonight. We learn more, patch you in."

"Thanks, Sol. Maybe we need to think of a way to delay the hit team."

"All ears."

"Nick and I will talk about it. Let you know if we come up with any ideas."

"Nothing to get us killed, okay?" Sol said.

Chapter 39

After watching Russell's house go dark, Rapha waited another hour before driving back to his hotel, The Francisco Grande. Judy Brown was waiting for him in the lobby. He'd been introduced to Brown before but hadn't worked with her. She was about five-foot-eight with sandy-blonde shoulder length hair and a pretty face that belied her occupation. The baggy jeans and loose shirt hid her slim figure. In D.C. she'd done mostly tech work, but he knew this wasn't her first field trip.

"You checked in?" he asked.

"Yeah, but I drove straight from the Tucson airport. Didn't get much to eat but peanuts and crackers."

"La Roca is walking distance and stays open

late. It's a nice place."

"Let's go."

She was quiet during the two-block walk. Most of the shops were shuttered, but people were out on the street. Music blared from the nightclubs. One block after crossing over the railroad tracks, they walked along a narrow street and entered a courtyard. La Roca was a four-star restaurant carved back into the cliff. The bottom floor around the courtyard was shops. The upstairs was the restaurant with window tables that overlooked the courtyard and the street. They climbed a flight of stairs where a formally dressed maitre d welcomed them.

A boisterous party was underway with mariachis circling the mass of tables pushed together in the center of the main dining room. The maitre d showed them to a window table overlooking the courtyard and street. Within seconds, a tuxedoed waiter appeared with an easel holding the menu. Another server behind him set bowls of salsa and tortilla chips on the table.

Judy favored Rapha with a smile. "You seem familiar with this place. Go ahead and order."

Rapha ordered margaritas and mochomos to

start. After the waiter returned with their drinks, he asked what they would like to order. For Judy he ordered coconut shrimp and for himself green chili enchiladas. When they were alone, he pulled out his phone.

"This is Russell's house." He showed her the screen. "My camera will detect movement and give me an alarm if they come out of the house or the car moves."

Judy nodded. "You have a tracker on the car?"

He shook his head. "No. I did that before. They detected it and used it to mislead me. I was in a mess. That's one reason you're here. We need twenty-four hour surveillance."

"I heard something about a fuckup in Nuevo Laredo. That was you?"

Rapha grimaced and nodded. "Nearly got killed. My balls are on the line here."

Her mouth twitched. "Aren't we taking a risk right now leaving the house unwatched?" She glanced around the restaurant.

He frowned. "Yeah, but I'm pretty sure she's tucked in for the night. My camera on the front will let me know if there's movement. When we get back to the hotel, I'll take the rest of the night. You can relieve me in the morning."

"Colonel Nesbit briefed me a little. This Katherine Russell is supposed to be some kind of super sniper, right?" She raised a brow.

"I was in Afghanistan while she was there. She was good, so good the rag-heads put a bounty on her, a large one. When their attempt failed, they sent a team to the U.S. and slaughtered her family. She resigned from the military and returned home to hunt them down."

"It's what I'd do," exclaimed Judy.

"Yeah, me too. I have a lot of admiration for her. It's strange, but if you look at her bio, she went pretty dark, not much info. She reappeared to help in the Bio-Cyber War, but her activities are classified. There are gaps where she was presumed dead, as in for years."

"How did you find her?"

His eyes twinkled. "I followed her trail of bodies, learned her signature."

"What are her tells?"

He pressed his lips into a thin smile. "She's a sniper. Thousand meter shots are not unusual. She favors a .25-06 rifle. Sometimes it's suppressed to throw off detection."

"You do some sniping. Is that a normal sniper rifle?"

"Snipers pick the weapon that fits them and the job. They're tools. I favor some of the newer cartridges like the 6.5 Creedmoor."

"Colonel Nesbit explained that we were an advance team for a crew coming down under contract to eliminate someone attacking their client's operations. Is she part of that?"

"Though I haven't been able to track her to an attack, her signature is there. I'm sure of it," he declared. "Our best lead is to follow her. I'm sure she'll guide us to those attackers. As soon as we have anything, Nesbit will send down the crew."

Their food arrived and neither spoke further about the mission, though Rapha did check the camera view of Russell's house several times. On the walk back, Rapha was all eyes and ears. "Mexico has its dangers. Best to stay alert," he explained. At the hotel he told her to get some rest. "Have you done surveillance before?"

"Yeah, several times. I know what to bring and what to do."

"I'll forward all the information to you. You'll have it by morning. See you at zero six hundred."

* * *

Back on mission, nothing appeared to have changed. The house was still dark, the car was still in the driveway. Rapha settled back and began sending Judy all the information he had. *With her help we should be able to get the data we need or failing that, capture Russell for some intense questioning. I owe you for Nuevo Laredo.*

Chapter 40

Judy pulled up behind him at precisely zero-six-hundred. She brought him a thermos of hot coffee.

It had been a long night. Sniper training had inured him to patient waiting, but he longed for his bed. "Bless you, my child." After taking a sip of coffee, he pointed to the back of their tango's house before showing her the telephoto camera he'd set up. The output was a second screen on his laptop, the first being the view of the front of the house. "She's up. The bathroom light came on about twenty minutes ago. She's in the kitchen making breakfast. You can see her pass by the window."

"Is this her normal routine?" asked Judy, looking from the screen to the back of the house.

"As long as I've been watching, yes."

"There's another figure moving around. Is that Sabino?"

"Probably. As I said, they haven't done much more than stay in the house." *Strange that they haven't tried to elude him again. Why?*

They watched for twenty minutes. Rapha yawned. It had been a long night. When the movement alarm went off on the front view, all thoughts of weariness vanished.

"They're getting into the car." He turned to Judy. "We'll pick them up at the gate out of the community. I'll take the initial tail. We'll switch off so they don't spot us."

Fifteen minutes later, Russell's car approached the Deconcini International Port of Entry. Rapha tried to close the distance but the traffic was heavy, even at this early hour.

Jesus Christ, she's getting out of the car. In a panic, he watched her walk to the pedestrian gate. Her car drove away, Nick Sabino at the wheel. Sanchez tried to keep from screaming into his com set. "Judy, she's out of the car and walking to the border. I'm stuck in traffic and can't leave my car here. You park and try to catch up with her."

"Roger."

At his first opportunity, Sanchez got out of the line of traffic and parked. On foot he raced past startled vendors setting up their wares on the sidewalk for prospective buyers. He got in the line to pass through the Customs and Border Protection inspection gate. At least fifty people were ahead of him. *Jesus, where's Judy.* His heart thudding, he called her. "Where are you?"

"Just entering the turnstile. She went through about ten people ahead of me. I've got to quit talking. They don't allow cell phones at the check point. I'll call you when I'm through customs."

He didn't get a call before he entered. He turned his phone to silent mode. It didn't vibrate against his leg. As he exited, he turned it back on. It rang almost immediately.

"Bad news," exclaimed Judy in a frustrated voice. "Someone was waiting for her. I saw her climb into a white van and drive away. There was nothing I could do. The van was too far away to get a license plate, but I did get a picture. We might be able to enhance it and get the number."

His heart sank. *I am so FUCKED!* "Meet you at the hotel. We'll figure out what to do from there."

* * *

Nervously, Rapha dialed the satellite phone. A second failure at Nighthawk was not looked upon favorably. *This could mean my ass, or worse.*

"Did Judy Brown arrive?"

"Yes sir. She was at the hotel last night when I returned."

"You brought her up to speed?"

"Yes, sir."

"You have Russell under surveillance now?"

Sanchez sighed. "We lost her, sir."

The silence was worse than the yelling he expected. "Sanchez, you're a cunt hair from getting the privilege of personally reporting this to Los Xecas. Is Brown there?"

"She's conferencing this call, sir."

"Brown, what happened?"

"Sir, this was a well-planned and coordinated escape. Obviously she and Sabino knew they were being watched. She crossed the border on foot knowing we'd get hung up. Somebody was waiting for her. I did get a picture of the van that picked her up. Perhaps somebody back there can use it to find out more."

"Good job in a bad situation. Send it. I'm going to hold the troops here until you have something for me. No use having a whole team wandering around Nogales. These guys won't blend in well. What's next?"

Rapha found his voice. "We're watching the house. The camera showed Sabino's return. Either she'll come back or he'll lead us to her."

"Don't you fucking lose him, Sanchez. You'll never get the chance to talk to Los Xecas. Am I clear?"

"Crystal, sir." The call ended.

Rapha closed his eyes and hung his head. *Oh shit! I've never been on ice this thin.*

Chapter 41

Ilia had managed to isolate Don Zacaros' phone. It had taken a while, but now he had the voice signature. The drone tracked movement in and out of the house. They had a pretty good handle on this. Yes, Don Zacaros was planning a raid to take territory from the Sonora Cartel. They'd overheard him mention it. At the Hacienda, Sol and Dawn were on the monitors along with them. With the shifts split up, they'd been able to hone in on Zacaros' lieutenants and track them too.

Most of the vehicles coming and going from the house were large SUVs, though the occasional Humvee entered. Police cars and luxury cars also entered. None of them stayed for more than a few hours except a black Lexus which was there overnight. On one occasion they saw Don Zacaros leave the house and drive through town. The drone was able to keep up as he entered the harbor. He had a yacht. They kept logs of everything and were in constant contact with the Hacienda. The situation in Los Mochis was in *wait and see* mode.

"Sorry for the late night call," Ilia apologized. "Was Kiki able to slip away from her Bogey?"

Actually, two now," Sol revealed. "She pulled Houdini and lost them. From Sanchez's satellite call, she no longer under watchful eyes. Her plan delayed arrival of HK team until she reacquired."

"HK?" questioned Emilio.

"Hunter-Killer," explained Sol. "Sanchez and partner watching Nick. You have information for plans?"

"We don't know the Sinaloa Cartel route from Los Mochis to Sonora," Ilia answered. "It isn't firm yet, nor are we sure of their specific targets. They are waiting for something before final planning. We don't know what."

"Keep on it. Any hint they know about you?"

"As their plans gel, vigilance level goes up. So far we've seen no indication they know we're watching," Ilia explained. "We've been careful. Hopefully they don't even know we exist."

"Yeah, we watching too. Kiki at Bob's house in Casa Grande. Later in week she make way back to Hacienda with Bob's new toys."

"From what Kiki told me, I'm looking forward to seeing those. Dawn, are you holding up?" Ilia asked.

"Long hours and lots of irons in the fire right now, but yeah, I'm doing okay. Sol says I might get another field job when we get a break." An alarm blared. "What's going on, Ilia?"

"Intrusion alert. Look at your screen. We have unexpected visitors." On the front gate view police cars were pulled up, headlights on the gate, blue and red lights flashing. While they watched, a Humvee nosed up to the gates and pushed them open. Police with M-16s flooded into the courtyard. With a ram, they bashed down the front door. "Gotta go," Ilia shouted.

Quickly, he set the demolition charges. He and Emilio ran to the back door. Ilia's hand paused as he reached for the knob. Suddenly, the door flew open as it was kicked in. Two men pointed AK 47s at them.

"Don't resist, Emilio," Ilia ordered. Their hands went up in surrender. The men smiled, gesturing for their hands to go higher. Ilia heard a shuffle behind them. Black hoods were pulled over their heads, his hands were bound behind him. "We need to leave!" yelled Ilia. "Bombs!"

There was shouting as he was hustled out the back door. Hands under his arms dragged him around the house. The explosions shook the ground. Heat washed over him as he lost his footing. He was dragged and thrown into a vehicle. Emilio landed with a grunt beside him.

"No habla," shouted a voice. "You don't speak." To emphasize the point, a kick landed in his ribs.

They rolled back and forth like balls in an arcade game as the vehicle (Ilia thought it was a van) raced through the streets. Thirty minutes later the sound changed and the road became rough. *Dirt road.* When the vehicle stopped, with hoods still in place, they were hauled into a building. It smelled stale, with an undertone of rotting meat. Secured to chairs, they were left alone, at least Ilia heard no motion.

"Emilio, are you okay?" Ilia asked.

"Fuck no. I'm not injured, though. This is going to be bad, isn't it?"

"Yeah. It might have been better to go up with

the equipment." He hoped that the trackers embedded under the skin of their necks would bring help, but they were not long range. Help had to be within ten miles, and that wouldn't happen for at least eight hours, probably too late by then.

"The guys who took us were cops," Emilio exclaimed.

"Yeah, but it had to be the Mochis Cartel behind it."

"How did they find out about us?" Emilio cried.

"They either broke our encryption or someone ratted us out. The encryption was good, too good for this cartel to break."

"Who could it be?"

"I trust everyone on our team. That leaves Julio or Rosa–maybe both–but why?"

Why indeed.

* * *

He didn't think he'd slept, but the sound of the door banging open woke him. His hood was jerked away. The room was dim, no windows. In the glow of kerosene lanterns, Ilia saw they were in some sort of ranch building. Saddles were on stands, bridles on hooks. The floor was dirt. A chain hoist hung from an overhead beam. Below it, the ground was rust colored.

With hands and feet bound to the chair, his body ached from being in the same position too long. His throat was parched. He tried to swallow, but couldn't get enough saliva. At the sound of a groan, he turned to see Emilio in the same position.

A skeletal man with a pencil moustache wearing black trousers, highly polished cowboy boots and a black silk shirt approached. He stood in front of Ilia. With an Eastern European accent he said, "I will ask questions. You will answer. Whether those answers come soon or after much pain is up to you, but you will answer."

Meeting the man's cold stare, Ilia pressed his lips together, but inside he trembled.

The man's mouth became a thin smile, like a snake. "Ah so. We begin." He stepped to a small table with a briefcase on it. He opened it and studied the contents for a few seconds before selecting a knife, a filleting knife with a long thin blade. He turned. Ilia's eyes widened as they followed the point. "No, not you my friend." He nodded to two men who lifted Emilio from his chair. He struggled but to no avail. They hung his cuffs over a hook on the chain hoist. The rattling of the chain echoed around the room as Emilio was pulled up until his toes barely touched the floor. His shirt and pants were cut away.

Emilio glanced at Ilia, his eyes wide, his mouth agape. As he turned away, his mouth closed, his face hardened.

The thin man stood in front of Emilio, studying him like a puzzle. The knife twirled in his hand. He turned and stared at Ilia. "Who do you work for?" his voice quiet but with steel. Ilia said nothing. The man stepped to the hanging captive. He reached up and grasped his hair, holding his head steady. Swift as a snake, he stabbed the knife into Emilio's left eye and popped it out. Emilio screamed, his body shaking violently causing the chains to clank and the beam to creak.

The man walked to Ilia and held the eyeball to his face. "Who do you work for?"

Ilia turned his head toward Emilio, who watched him with his one eye, blood running from his empty socket. Ilia felt tears running down his cheeks as his vision blurred. He pressed his lips together.

The man placed the eyeball in Ilia's lap and returned to Emilio. Once again the knife twirled in his hand. He contemplated the hanging figure deciding what atrocity to inflict next. Over his shoulder he said to Ilia, "The eye was to let you know I am very serious. Your friend will now suffer pain that only you can stop. Who do you work for?"

Ilia pressed his lips tightly together and stared at the dirt floor, then glared at the man.

This time the knife traced a saucer-sized circle on Emilio's chest. Rivulets of blood ran down from the fresh cuts. He grunted, but the screaming started when the man reached into his pocket and pulled out pliers and began peeling off the skin. The circle of skin with Emilio's nipple landed in Ilia's lap with a plop. Hot blood soaked his pants. Ilia closed his eyes trying to shut out the horror.

"Who do you work for?"

With his eyes squeezed tightly closed, Ilia shook his head back and forth, back and forth.

"You will watch or I cut off your eyelids."

Ilia turned his head to face the horror of his friend being skinned alive. Screams interrupted by gasps for air penetrated his head as more parts were piled in Ilia's lap.

The silence when Emilio passed out caused the

tenseness to flow from Ilia. *This is worse than if I were being cut.*

Like the hiss of a snake the voice stabbed into him. "We let your friend rest and gather his strength. He will need it when we resume. It is your fault. You can stop this. If not, we will start on you."

The man and his companions left. Through the open door he saw that it was late afternoon. He looked at the pile of skin in his lap and heaved, vomiting to one side. He gasped for air and tentatively glanced at Emilio, afraid of what he'd see. The hanging figure looked like a freshly flayed deer carcass. Raw tissue bled, red streams running down his legs, dripping from his feet to soak into the dirt floor. *If help doesn't come soon, it won't matter.*

Chapter 42

Dawn's yell brought Sol, Zyra and Sasha running. "They've been hit!"

"What? Who?" Sol bellowed.

She pointed to the black screens of Ilia and Emilio's system running in parallel to theirs. "It's not a power failure. They have backup power. I haven't been able to contact them, just empty air."

"Roll video back hour," Sol instructed. "We see what this is."

They stood shoulder-to-shoulder watching the monitors. The first sign of trouble was the front gate camera showing police cars pulling up. Armed uniformed men piled out and lined up behind a black Humvee as it eased forward and broke open the gate.

The camera at the rear of the house showed two men with assault rifles at either side of the back door. One stepped forward and kicked it in. Ilia's voice came over the speaker.

"We've been hit! I'm setting the demolition charges. We'll try to slip out the back." A last view of the courtyard in front showed Ilia and Emilio with handcuffs and hoods being dragged away. The screens went blank. "The demolition charges," explained Sol.

"We have to get down there!" yelled Sasha.

Sol put his hand on her shoulder. "We do, but must be smart. You and Zyra leave soon as possible. Take one van. Pack what needed for major assault. We forward everything to you while you on road." He turned to Dawn. "Review communications. See if breach. Check video from Mochis for past day. Look for clues about who did this. I call Kiki."

Dawn's face registered shock. Sol took her hands in his. "Come on. We need you. Were any drones in air?"

She shook her head. "No, sir. We have a raven at Don Zacaros' house, but not in the air. The others were on the chargers. When the demolition charges blew, it knocked the relay to us off the air."

"Were we monitoring Don Zacaros' phone?"

"Yes."

"Review calls. See if he received messages about attack or where Ilia and Emilio are."

"Yes, sir."

He looked at Zyra and Sasha. "Be careful driving. We set you up with place to stay. Dawn and I keep Hacienda as control center until we set up in Mochis." He glanced at each of them. "Let's move people," he bellowed.

In his office, Sol called Kiki. He hated to give her bad news. He took a deep breath as she answered. "We got big problem in Mochis. Ilia and Emilio hit, taken prisoner."

"Shit! Who did it?"

"Dawn reviewing footage, but cops involved. I believe Mochis Cartel."

"How did they know we were there?"

"Either broke our encryption or we have leak. We need Bob and Kathy's help. You and Bob load motor home with gear you think needed. Drive down here, tow Bob's car. May need it. Lost van Ilia and Emilio use. We load Isolation Chamber into RV after you arrive. Bring the new toys. Motor home to be new command center in Mochis. We keep the main one here as long as possible.”

“Won’t the personal trackers tell us where Emilio and Ilia are,” Kiki asked.

“Short range. Without satellite, no long range tracking. Hookup lost when Ilia set off demolition charges. When set up there, we get drones up. Find them.”

“What about the existing drones?”

“Vulture and one raven on chargers. Gone in blast. No local central command, the remaining raven sit in tree in sleep mode.”

“It’s going to be rough for Ilia and Emilio, isn’t it?” her voice barely above a whisper.

“Yeah, time of essence. Hope we get there, save them. You brief Bob. We conference call as you drive down. Call me with questions and call when ready to leave. I relieve Dawn on the video and log review. Need to look at our encryption, ensure we are secure.”

Sol returned to the communications room. Dawn had views on all the monitors.

She glanced at him. “I’m running different sequences on each screen so it won’t take twenty-four hours to review.”

"Smart. Let me take over that. We need to know where leak happen. Look at encryption. Better you than me."

"It's really Ilia's area." She choked back a sob. "I'll do what I can."

"I check on Zyra and Sasha. Be back."

The van was parked in the courtyard, all doors open as the two women hauled gear to it. Sasha had tears streaking her face. Zyra's expression was stone. "We go in thirty minutes. Got some killing to do."

"We send you instructions and directions. When there, launch drones you have. Reestablish connection with us so we control drones, locate Ilia and Emilio. You do that?"

"I fly drones before."

"Tie us in. We do that. Do not attempt rescue yourselves." He pointed a finger at her "Need to repeat that?"

Her eyes narrowed. "Not easy with that one," Her head tilted toward Sasha. "When you leave to come down?"

"You set up first so we have easy transition of command. Things to do here, but maybe we ready to leave five hours after Kiki and Bob arrive. Call when you clear city and on highway."

"Da."

He walked over to Sasha. "We get Ilia back. Be careful. Don't need more casualties." Sol took a close look at Sasha as she wiped her cheeks and nodded. She was on the edge.

Back in the control room, Sol called Nick. "We need you here. Bob will have Kiki with him. Set house up so we control lights and things remotely. Use remote on dummies to make shadows. Put wig on one dummy so look like Kiki there. Dawn will run repeat loop on front camera so they not see you leave. I pick you up fifteen minutes after you call say you're ready. Bring gear for mission. You won't be back for while, maybe never."

Chapter 43

With a loaded duffle bag on each shoulder, Nick walked quickly down the driveway, tossed them into the van and climbed in beside Sol. As he pulled away he spoke over his com to Dawn, "Go ahead and put the camera at Nick's house back on live. Any conversation with the Nighthawk Security people indicating they know something's up?"

"No, they're quiet," answered Dawn.

"Need conference call to Kiki and Bob," instructed Sol. Minutes of silence passed.

"Done. Go ahead," said Dawn.

"Hey, Sol, what happened?" asked Bob.

"Ilia and Emilio taken prisoner in Mochis. Probably Don Zacaros. Zyra and Sasha driving down now. Kiki, Bob, Where you?"

"We just passed Picacho Peak. Should be at the Hacienda in two hours," Kiki said. "We loaded all the toys into the motor home."

"We're going down to Mochis, right?" asked Bob.

"We leave after you arrive and we pack everything."

"We should fly the drones over," interjected Bob. "Don't want them found if we're inspected."

"Good idea. Probably add an hour." Sol remarked. In his command voice, he continued, "We use motor home as new control center in Mochis. Locate Ilia and Emilio. Get them back. When you get to Hacienda, we load Isolation Chamber. Nick prep it to move." He glanced at Nick who nodded.

"How long ago did this happen?" asked Bob.

Sol glanced at his watch. "Three hours. We have record until demolition charges blew house."

Nick's face was a frozen mask as he digested this, picturing the situation Ilia and Emilio could be in. "What are our chances of getting them back?"

Sol frowned. "Less each hour. All I know for now."

* * *

At the Hacienda, Nick went directly to the interrogation room to begin prepping the chamber to install into the RV. If Ilia and Emilio were still alive, they'd need his skills as a doctor, so he added medical supplies to the growing pile of equipment. Interrogating those responsible would not be the distasteful chore he usually felt.

Sol's right. Every minute counts. If they'd started torturing Ilia and Emilio immediately, there might be nothing to treat. There was little subtlety with the cartels. They needed information, and they'd use whatever method worked on their captives for answers. What would they reveal? How long could they hold out? The Hacienda wouldn't be safe. *We're racing for our lives too. Without the link from Mochis, we're going in blind.* He heard the motor home pull into the courtyard.

Kiki ran out as it stopped. She wrapped her arms around him. "Something about combat makes me horny."

Nick glanced around to see if anyone had heard. "That will probably have to wait for a while."

He saw her laugh in an attempt to lighten the mood. "Shucks." She glanced around. "You got everything ready to load?"

"Just about." Bob came around the front of the RV. He shook Nick's hand. "You drive this thing to Mochis. It's like a boat!" He surveyed the courtyard. "So this is the Hacienda."

"Probably no time for a tour," Nick acknowledged. "We need to get loaded and on our way."

"Speaking of which," said Bob pulling out a portable control panel. Minutes later, the vulture drone settled next to the RV. The ravens followed.

Kiki bounded away. "Let's go into the command center. See what's new."

Something about crisis, combat and danger makes her come alive, Nick thought.

Sol and Dawn were huddled together. A Google Map of Los Mochis was on the wall-mounted monitor. Dawn tried to smile at them as they entered, but her face was drawn and tight. She pulled the view back showing one hundred miles of area. A green dot was on Highway 15. "That's Zyra and Sasha. They're about two hours away." She zoomed in. "We have two rooms reserved at the Hotel Zar Los Mochis. There's an RV park there too." A teardrop lit up on the map at the edge of the city.

"When should they be in range of the personal trackers?" asked Nick.

"They will need to get the drones in the air first," answered Dawn. "They should be able to do that within thirty miles of Mochis." More teardrops lit up. She pointed to one. "That's Don Zacaros' house. She pointed to another. That one not far from the hotel is where Ilia and Emilio had set up."

"Speaking of which," Bob said, "where are you on checking the security and encryption?"

"We're tight," answered Dawn. "I couldn't find evidence of a breach."

"A rat," Sol muttered, his voice icy. "Rosalinda Villa. Ilia, Emilio, Dawn and I knew the location. It has to be her. Have not called client. Don't know how deep betrayal goes."

"What'll we do about her?" Kiki's voice was cold and hard.

"She is for interrogation," Sol declared, looking at Nick.

He felt a strange twinge. *The problem with her is that Kiki and I knew her, worked with her. She doesn't know about the Isolation Chamber, but she will learn. What had turned her against them?*

We'll find out. There was something else that needed to be said. "Sol, you know no one can stand up to torture forever. Ilia or Emilio will break. The Hacienda isn't safe."

Sol frowned. "You right. Dawn and I start packing up here. We keep communication center as long possible. We use drones as perimeter alarms. Get out if–no, when have to. Our last mission whatever happens." He looked at Dawn who nodded back.

An hour later the RV was packed and ready to leave. Nick drove, Bob's car in tow. *This is Bob's first field mission–he should have company rather than drive alone.*

An hour north of Hermosillo Nick's phone rang. It was Sol. "Zyra and Sasha checked into hotel. Drones in air for quick look for tracker signals but will have to return soon for battery charges. We conference you in everything from them."

Nick turned to Bob. Possible? he mouthed. Bob nodded, pulling out his laptop. "Are we tapped into Zacaros' phone?"

"The raven at his house shut down. Low battery. With RV down there, we put up fresh drones. Dishes and antennas normal on it in RV park. We put new vulture drone overhead."

"I've got all our drones charging now," stated Bob.

"We'll be through Hermosillo in about an hour," Kiki noted.

"Yeah, we've got you on the map," Sasha said. "Drive carefully. Zacaros has to suspect somebody will be coming for his prisoners. He may have people watching."

"Yeah, if I were him, I'd try to set a trap," Kiki pointed out.

Nick glanced at Bob. *I'll have to keep an eye on him when the shooting starts.*

Chapter 44

"Sol, we intercepted a call from Don Zacaros about the raid," Dawn exclaimed. She put it on speakerphone.

"You have the spies at the ranch?" Don Zacaros' voice was a harsh caw.

"Sí, Don Zacaros. They are here."

"You have done nothing to them?"

"No. Only El Serpiente. He began interrogating one of them, as you instructed."

"Good. They have said nothing?"

"No, Patron. They are in the barn. One is tied to the chair. Fredo is guarding them. The one El Serpiente was questioning is passed out."

"Guard them closely. If they have compadres, there may be a rescue attempt. How many men are there with you?"

"Four men, five with El Serpiente."

"I will send more men. My source says these spies are part of a larger force."

"Sí, Patron. We will be ready." The call ended.

"You got that?" asked Sol. A chorus of ayes came back. "Clock ticking. We don't find them before reinforcements arrive, lots harder, more dangerous. Sasha, how long before you can put more drones up?"

"Full charge will be about two hours."

"Put another up now while others charge. Need to find them. We be online watching too."

Sol knew he should call Julio, but could he be trusted? It was Julio's contact who had set them up. *Did that betrayal include Julio? Why would he do that?*

"Sol, I got a faint blip from Sasha's drone." The excitement filled Dawn's voice as she pointed at the screen. "With only a partial charge, it's almost out of power so it's heading back to the hotel for a recharge.

"Not enough to get location?"

"No, but it was on the northern side of town. Zyra and Sasha can do a battery change rather than wait for a recharge. They have extra batteries. It should be back in the air within twenty minutes."

"Where motor home?"

She pointed to a map on another screen. "They're about an hour outside of Mochis."

"Get Kiki on phone."

Dawn hit a few keys on the keyboard.

"Hi, Sol. We heard. What do you want us to do?"

"First chance, stop and put drone in air. We got weak signal before drone return for fresh batteries. Signal on the north side of town. Maybe you pick something up."

"Roger that, boss."

Ten minutes later, Dawn let out a whoop. "We're up."

The map had the red dot of the RV from the phone triangulation and another blinking dot. "It's picked up the signal." She pointed.

"You getting this, Kiki?" Sol asked.

"Yeah. The signal's weak, hard to place. But we're moving down Highway 15 toward it. It should get stronger. We'll outrun the drone we have up, but we'll launch another in about ten miles."

"Zyra and Sasha will have other drone in air in five minutes. With this, can direct to that area. We can pinpoint."

Zyra's voice came in. "We have drone in air now. Flying north."

"Let us know when you get a ping on Ilia's tracker," Dawn said.

"Yah."

"We've stopped and launched another drone," said Kiki. "And it's already acquired the signal. We're going another five miles and pull off. We'll use the video feed to get a look at the area."

"We have signal. We do same," growled Zyra.

* * *

The view from Kiki's drone showed arid landscape with sparse trees and vegetation. Zyra's drone approached the same area as seen on another screen. A ranch house came into view. Ilia's locator dot was from a large building away from the main house.

"We have it!" cried Dawn."Now what?

"Nobody moving outside," Zyra noted. "Look empty."

"Go infrared," Sol instructed Zyra. "Two hours until dark. We wait?" he asked.

"Sasha want to go now. Me too." Zyra's voice was hard.

"I like dark better, but understand need for haste," expressed Sol. "Anybody else?"

"It'll take nearly an hour to get there and set up," noted Kiki, "I say we start now. We'll have to plan for more company too."

"We'll take control of both drones," Bob explained. "Zyra, how long before you're on that dirt road to the ranch house?"

"Thirty minutes to ready van and drive there."

"Pull off of the dirt road and hide the car," instructed Kiki.

"Not place to hide we see."

"Yeah," confirmed Kiki. "Okay, we'll park the RV at the highway back away from the turnoff and use Bob's car. I'll set up where I can cover the buildings and have line of sight on the road." She began looking at the terrain for her hide. *Not much here. It's pretty flat with little vegetation. I like the trees, but they're too close to the house, and I won't have a good view of the road.* She continued checking the area from the drone view.

"I found a place. I'll be four-hundred yards from the house and two hundred from the road. Not much cover, but it's the best available."

"Nick, after I'm set up, speed down the road and park about fifty yards from the house. I'll have your backs when they come out. Sasha, drive directly to the barn. Zyra, watch closely. There's another guard in there."

"Da."

Chapter 45

Sol watched the green dots of Zyra's van and Bob's car merge on the dirt road. The overhead showed the ranch grounds with the infrared hot spots of people. A pickup and a black car were parked outside. "We have four men coming out of the ranch house moving toward the building where Ilia and Emilio are." Bob's car pulled off the road and stopped three hundred yards from the house. "Kiki, are you in place?"

"Give me ten."

"Guys," Sol remarked, "in and out. Anyone comes down road, you are trapped."

"You're right," Kiki agreed. "Zyra, let Sasha and Nick handle things in the barn. We need a reception for any party crashers. After the baddies are down, park the van next to the barn so they can make a fast exit if needed."

"Yeah. We start before guys from house reach barn."

"I've got them. One guy dressed in black, the others look like muscle. I'm taking the muscle first. The man in black might be El Serpiente."

"Zyra how long?"

"Seconds."

"Roger," said Sol. "Infrared show two hot spots in outbuilding. Ilia's tracker shows a pulse. Not Emilio's. Nobody else is at ranch."

"Yet," commented Kiki. "Bob, any activity on the road?"

"It's clear. I'll move the vulture closer to the highway."

Kiki nestled in behind the butt-stock of the .25-06, the bipod giving her the stability she needed. "Firing," Kiki announced. "Go Go Go!"

On the screen, Sol watched one man go down. The others looked around, trying to figure what was happening. Two more went down quickly. The fourth man hit the ground and pulled out a pistol, firing from a prone position. It was ineffective–he was way out of range and didn't know where she was. As Zyra's van screeched to a halt in a cloud of dust, Kiki peppered the area around the shooter, forcing his head down. Zyra jumped out and ran to him, putting her knee in his back. Kiki shifted her sights to the barn door where the last guard was.

"We need him?" Zyra asked. Using his hair as a handle, she pulled his head up exposing his throat.

"Might want to ask him some questions," Sol answered. "Cuff him."

A head peered out of the barn door, then ducked back. Kiki counted to three and fired where the head had been. He peeked out again just as the bullet reached the door. The high speed twenty-five caliber bullet exploded within his skull, leaving a red mist in the air.

Zyra and Sasha ran to the barn. Nick jumped out of the van and followed. The man on the ground raised his head and Kiki put a round within a foot. He ducked down and lay still. "Still clear on the road?" Kiki asked.

"A black SUV just turned onto the ranch road," Bob cried.

"How long before he gets here?"

He's in no rush. Maybe five minutes."

Shit. She was going to need help. "Zyra, we need to set up a greeting for our party crashers.

Bring Bob's car."

Chapter 46

The fading light from outside and the golden light of the kerosene lanterns gave the inside of the room a dim glow. The scene was a horror show. Ilia had been hoisted up by the chain fall, small cuts all over his body seeping blood. To one side lay Emilio, looking more like processed meat than a human being. When Nick and Sasha entered, Ilia moaned. Sasha rushed to his side, tears rolling down her cheeks. For a moment, she was frozen, as if afraid to touch him.

Nick went to Emilio and felt for a pulse. Nothing. *Looking at the state of his body, that's no surprise. Nobody could survive that.* Sasha turned and looked at what was left of Emilio then glanced at Nick. He shook his head. It was only luck they hadn't stripped the skin from his neck, where the tracker was imbedded. He went to Ilia, gently pushing Sasha to one side. "With pain in her voice, she said, "He's lost a lot of blood."

Nick looked down at the blood-soaked ground, then at Sasha. *She's on the edge.* "Most of that isn't his. We need to get him to a hospital."

As they carried him out, Nick asked Sol, "What can you arrange for a hospital, knowing anything in this area will be a death sentence."

"I'm on it," came the immediate response.

As gently as possible, they lowered Ilia onto a stretcher and carried him to the van. They laid him on an air mattress. Nick went to the medical kit. "I'm going to put him on saline and start a transfusion as soon as we get him back to the RV. I have blood stored there for all of us. Sol, let me know what we can do."

"I have to call Julio for help," he explained. "No choice."

"I sure hope he wasn't behind this," Kiki growled.

"Me too," echoed Sol.

"Nick, we'll let you know when it's clear for you to leave," Kiki's voice came through his com.

"Sasha, I think we need to question the man in black laying in the drive. We need to confirm who was behind this. Find out then take care of him."

Nick flinched. He watched her walk toward the prone man, knowing there would be no pity from Sasha.

* * *

Sasha grabbed the man in black by his hair and dragged him inside. When he struggled, she gave him a vicious kick in the face, knocking him unconscious. He didn't move as she hung him from the hoist. The chain rattled as she raised him until his toes made light traces in the blood-soaked dirt. *This man is not a sicario. The inquisitor?*

A moan escaped from his split lip as his eyes opened. He squinted at her, trying to place where he was. Suddenly his eyes were the size of saucers. He struggled, moving like a worm on a hook.

She watched awareness come over him as he recognized what hanging from the hook meant, he screamed, bringing a smile to Sasha's lips. *Yes, he's the one who asked the questions.* Drawing her knife, she faced him. His total focus was on the tip of the blade as she wove a pattern in the air, back and forth in a figure eight. Slicing his shirt and tearing it away, she laughed at his heaving chest as he gasped.

"Who is your jefe?"

His eyes followed the blade as she moved it in front of his face. Before he could respond, her arm flashed faster than a cat's paw playing with a snake. She sliced off his ear. He stared at her, the knife so sharp he hadn't felt the cut. When the blood ran down his neck, he howled, eyes squeezed shut.

"Hey!" Sasha shouted. Her prisoner's eyes flew open. She placed the tip of the knife under his nose. "Su jefe?" His head was frozen in fear. Slowly the tip sliced upward, his nostril splitting, blood trailing down to his lips. He jerked, causing the blade to slice higher, more blood to flow. "Who is your boss?" He was frozen, dread painted on his face. "Okay, I see we must be more serious."

Her knife sliced downward, leaving a slit that began to ooze blood from his chin to his navel. She looked into his eyes and winked. "Don't move. I might cut something important." With little effort, the blade cut through the waistband of his pants and shorts. They fell away. With the sharp tip of the knife, she traced downward toward his groin leaving a red trail. He moaned.

"He will kill me," the man gasped.

Sasha laughed. "Slower than I will? You are already dead. Your choice is how long it will take and how painful it will be. Who is your jefe?" Her knife pricked his testicles. "Fast and painless or slow?"

"Don Zacaros," he wailed. "It is Don Zacaros."

She smiled. "That wasn't so hard, was it? I will keep my word." She sliced the femoral artery. "Adios, my friend. Vaya con El Diablo."

* * *

"Zyra, where are you?" Kiki asked. "You've dropped from my line of sight."

"Am in ditch one-hundred meters from road opposite side of you."

"We have to stop that SUV before it gets between us. I don't want us in each other's line of fire."

"Da. I understand."

"How long 'til we see him, Bob?"

"He'll be in your line of sight in two minutes. He's slowed, looking at my car."

"Zyra, I'll count down. I'm going to put everything into that car. We don't want them getting out. Anyone who comes out on your side is yours."

Kiki lay prone, feet spread as she pressed the butt-stock tightly into her shoulder. She was behind a slight rise, her scope covering the road, two hundred yards away. She put the selector on full-auto. The normal .308 caliber for the AR 10 would make full-auto fire wild and hard to hold on target. With its light recoil and being on the bipod, the .25-06 could hold well. Four thirty-round magazines lay to the left of the rifle. She intended to use every bullet. The SUV emerged from behind a tree and eased ten yards into the clear.

"Firing," she cried. She raked the side of the SUV front-to-back, shoulder high on the first pass, killing the driver and breaking out the darkened windows. Figures dived for the floor. The second pass was back-to-front, the path of bullet holes at seat height. One man stood and fired a pistol at her. Zyra's shot rang out and he was down. "Thanks," Kiki said as she switched magazines. The next line of bullet holes was at floor height, first front-to-back then back-to–front. She inserted another magazine and waited. Smoke rose from her heated barrel. At the sound of a moan, she repeated the floor height pass and the seat height pass. She inserted her last magazine.

"Last mag," she called.

"Da. Nothing on this side but holes. Car leaking red."

They waited. The only sound was dripping from underneath the SUV. A red stain spread across the hard-packed dirt.

"I check," purred Zyra.

Through her scope, Kiki watched for any signs of life.

"Just meat," stated Zyra.

"Anything else on the road, Bob?"

"No. The road is clear."

"Okay, Nick. You and Sasha can bring Emilio and Ilia out. Zyra and I will follow you."

Chapter 47

As the van raced toward the highway, Nick was on the phone to Sol. "Ilia needs a hospital. He's losing a lot of blood. Have you found one we can reach in time?"

"You know it was Zacaros?"

"Sasha questioned the interrogator at the ranch." Nick shuddered at the memory of how her questioning had gone.

"When Zacaros learns of rescue, he will check every hospital and doctor in area," Sol replied.

"He will find Ilia, and us, won't he?"

"Yes."

"I've got some supplies in the motor home, but only enough to keep him alive until he gets to a hospital. Guaymas is hours away."

"What about Emilio?" Sol asked.

"Emilio is gone. I'd like to have gotten the man who tortured him in my chamber, but Sasha took care of him." *Maybe she enjoyed getting the information too much.* "Ilia needs blood immediately. I don't have enough here. Can you get a medevac with an IV? It's the only way he'll survive."

"I will make call."

"Have them bring a body bag for Emilio. Wherever we move Ilia for help, Emilio's body has to go too. We have no place to put him."

"I call you fast as I can. Keep Ilia alive."

* * *

Sol dialed Julio's number. He was the only contact in Mexico who could help in time.

"We need help."

"I understand that your people in Los Mochis were taken. I am sorry, but for me to rescue them would expose me and those I am connected with to intense danger. My agents would be killed."

"It was your recommended contact that betrayed us. Are you in league with her?"

"Rosa? Are you sure?"

"She is the only one who knew where they

were. Are. You. With. Her?"

"No, my friend. She has betrayed me also, which means too much information about us has been passed on."

"We have recovered our people. One is dead, the other in need of a hospital. I repeat, we need help."

"I am sorry. I will scramble a helicopter to take him to a military hospital in Guaymas. The marines are still loyal. It is the only safe place."

Sol looked at the Google maps screen. "I will have them travel north on Highway 15. Let me know when the helicopter is in the air. Have it traveling down the highway. I'll give you the coordinates of where to meet them. I'll call you back." *Now we will see how good this Julio is.*

Sol called Nick. "Nick, at highway, pick up supplies you need from RV. Keep Ilia in van. Head north to Guaymas. Julio sending helicopter to pick him up."

"You trust him after this?" Nick questioned.

"No, but he only option. Motor home continues to hotel. Must not be identified with us."

"I'm going with Ilia."

"No. You needed in Mochis. This not over.

Sasha will insist on staying with Ilia. She will keep us updated. We clear?" His voice left no room for argument.

"Crystal," choked Nick.

* * *

Sol dialed Julio back. "I've arranged for man be transported north. Is helicopter in air?"

"It just lifted off. Do not worry. We will get your man to the hospital in time. He will be safe."

He better, thought Sol. "We setting up another headquarters in Mochis. Continue mission."

"Do I hear revenge in your voice?"

"Revenge clouds objective," Sol cited.

"And your objective is to deter Don Zacaros from his plan to move into Sonora Cartel territory. That aim hasn't changed. I have to assess what damage Rosa has done and make plans. I may need your help."

"What you tell her about us?"

"She knows only that your team needed a place to stay in Mochis. Rosa does know I am dealing with the cartels. She may have surmised something from that. Her position with Don Zacaros was to supply me with information of what he was doing. I now have to consider that much of what she told me wasn't true."

Sol decided to inform him about some of the data they had collected. "We have information his attack will happen. Have conversations confirming. If she tell you that, it is true. Why she tell you?"

"I am wondering about that. Perhaps she wanted me to expose my intents."

"This is last mission." There was silence. "Danger too great."

"Perhaps to me also."

Chapter 48

"Sasha," Nick called from the back of the van, "the rescue helicopter is in the air. Sol estimates it will be approaching in less than thirty minutes. Start watching for a place to pull off. We need to be away from the highway."

"This is mostly farmland," she replied over her shoulder. "You know wherever they take him I'm going."

Nick heard no room for argument in her voice. He didn't offer any. "I have to go back to Mochis after they pick you up."

He felt the van slow and turn. The road was dirt and rough. Ilia moaned. Sasha crept along to keep from jarring him as much as possible.

"I forward your coordinates to chopper," Sol said. "They say five minutes out. Sit with lights on.

They find you."

Nick heard the clatter of the helicopter before dust encircled the van. He slid the side door open. The Huey squatted fifty yards away, the rotors idling, a spotlight on them. Two men jumped out and approached the van with a stretcher. He helped them load Ilia into the helicopter, securing the stretcher to the floor. An IV unit with blood hung to one side. Carefully, one medic attached it to the port Nick had installed.

The medics returned with the body bag for Emilio. The younger one of the two medics vomited at the sight of the bloodied and shredded body. Nick helped them load Emilio's body into the body bag and then the helicopter. He backed up as the sound of the engines revved.

To the surprise of the medics, Sasha jumped into the open door. The looks she received from them weren't lost on Nick. *They should be careful. She has at least two guns and a knife hidden somewhere.* She looked back at Nick. He made a "call me" sign. She nodded.

Nick slid the van door closed and got into the driver's seat. Dust from the departing helicopter obscured the road for a few minutes. He sat with his hands on the steering wheel digesting the last few hours. Fatigue enveloped him. *Now the gloves come off.* "Everything okay?" asked Dawn over his com.

"Yeah, just letting things roll around in my head."

"Get back to the hotel. Kiki's cooked up some jambalaya for dinner."

"I'm not really hungry."

"I can imagine. The video of the scene was horrendous, but you have to eat to keep up your strength."

I know that. It's advice I give to my patients. Now I understand how hard that really is. "Is Sol there?"

"He needed a break. I'm on shift. Ha ha."

"Did he tell you of any plans?"

"Just what he told you–get to the hotel and set the RV up as a new communications center. We'll plan with what you learn."

"Have Sol call me when he returns."

"You call me when you get to the hotel."

"Will do."

* * *

The road stretched in front of Nick, his mind

frozen, not processing anything. He was on autopilot. Scenes of the carnage at the ranch played like a movie. The blood from Emilio's body and Ilia's leaking wounds had congealed in the back of the van. The air reeked of it and death. *God I need Kiki.*

"Nick, the Hotel Zar Los Mochis is coming up on the right," Dawn informed him.

"I see it. Thanks."

Nick drove to the RV park section of the hotel. Only a few of the slots were filled, so he had no problem spotting his motor home. As he parked next to Bob's car, Kiki came out of the RV. Nick stepped out of the van, his body stiffer than the trip justified.

Kiki threw her arms around him. "I'm glad you're here." She stepped back and scanned him from head to toe. "Are you all right?"

"I wasn't ready for the atrocity I saw inflicted on Emilio…." He hung his head and closed his eyes, forcing back tears. After several minutes, in a quiet voice, he said, "A rage filled me."

"Nick, it's okay." She put her hand on his arm. "It happens to me all the time. It'll pass."

He glanced at her sharply in disbelief. "Every

time I close my eyes I see Emilio and my imagination fills in the way he got there." Nick stared back at the van. "His body's gone, but he's still in there with me."

"Come inside." She pulled him up the two steps into the motor home.

He blinked in the sudden light. Bob was at the console he'd set up on the table, Zyra was behind him, looking at a monitor showing a large walled mansion. "Don Zacaros' house. I've got the large vulture drone in the air." He flipped a switch. "This is his phone."

Incomprehensible yelling came through the speaker. "Can you make that out?" asked Kiki.

My Spanish is pretty good," said Bob, "but this is hard. I think he just got the news about the ranch raid." The yelling slowed. "He's calling his lieutenants, ranting at them to search for us. The threats he's issuing won't figure well in his recruiting posters. Lucky there were no cameras at the ranch." They watched cars stream out of the courtyard. "He's calling Rosa. Wants her at the house, no doubt for more information. Does she know anything that can hurt us?"

"Don't think so," Sol said. "Ilia tell her only what she need to know. Julio maybe another matter. Don't know what he passed along to her."

"Any chance they can find us?" asked Kiki.

"I hope not," Nick murmured.

Chapter 49

Kiki and Nick had one of the two rooms at the hotel. Kiki guided Nick to the bed. He sat heavily, staring at the wall. Gently, she undressed him before getting him under the covers. His eyes closed in exhaustion and shock. A moment of sadness filled her at what he'd been through. Though a battlefield medic, the purposeful cruelty had shocked him. He needed rest, more than merely a good night's sleep. His compassion drew her to him, but sometimes that got in the way of her purpose. Yet he had strength she admired. Her mind prickled. *Oh no! Not now.* The Director!

"Your team did an admirable job at the ranch, Katherine. You have provided me with a banquet of hatred and fear from Don Zacaros and his men. He is so angry. Yet another flavor I like.

Very tangy from him."

"Always your caterer, aren't we?"

"Not at all, but you are the ones I enjoy talking with. In addition to Don Zacaros, be cautious of Julio Cardenas."

"Did he conspire with Rosalinda?"

"No, but your knowledge of his past makes you a threat to him. The awareness of his plans that your team has makes all of you a threat. Rosalinda Villa has her own agenda with regards to Julio. She considers him her true enemy. By helping your team, she was getting closer to him until she could exact her revenge. You were only a means to an end. Be very careful for you are beset by enemies from all sides. Please stay alive. I do enjoy speaking with you. Tata.

She sat quietly, digesting what The Director had told her. One last glance at Nick who was snoring quietly. *I hope it's a dreamless sleep.* She stood and quietly closed the door behind her, leaving their room to return to the motor home.

Bob and Zyra were still huddled over the monitors watching Don Zacaros' mansion. "Anything new?" Voices from phone calls were background noise.

"It's probably a good thing we left no survivors at the ranch. The revenge Don Zacaros would wreak on them would be horrible. These people are such savages it's hard to conceive they are even human."

"I'm not sure they are," murmured Kiki.

Zyra glanced over her shoulder. "How is Nick?"

"He's tired, physically and mentally. He's a doctor, and helping people is his lifework. He tries to stay away from the brutality of this life."

Zyra grunted. "Not easy with us."

"Sometimes, he's my conscience. I need that." Kiki felt a tear roll down her cheek. *He pulled me from a path to madness once.*

"Would make my life complicated," Zyra growled, then laughed. "Men are difficult, women easy."

Kiki leaned forward. "Who's on at the Hacienda?"

"It's me, Dawn," came the answer. "I've been following while Sol tries to keep things together with our boss."

"Any problems there?" Kiki asked.

"Sol's keeping that information to himself for now. I get the feeling Julio is worried about

Rosalinda Villa. That worries Sol too. I do know he is adamant that this is our last mission, at least for a while."

Thank God for that. When things get this complicated, it's a downhill path could only have one result. "Anything going on with our Bogeys?"

"They still have your house staked out. No communication with Nighthawk."

"Three days of nothing and they may get curious," Kiki muttered. "Should we consider something to keep them interested?"

"Good idea," came Sol's voice. "We stage one. I got word from boss that Ilia in the naval hospital in Guaymas. Guards on door. Sasha with him."

"Are the guards to protect them or keep them there?" wondered Kiki aloud.

"Probably both," admitted Sol. "First one problem before another. We sit on Don Zacaros communications. We know he is planning attack on Sonora Cartel. Search for us may delay a few days, but we need details."

"I have the computer tracking key words," offered Bob. "We'll take shifts to monitor twenty-four/seven."

"We from here too," offered Sol. "With all of

us, won't be too bad."

There was a beep and a phone conversation started. On the screen the trigger word *Fantasmas* showed. "This is the work of the *Fantasmas*. The attack has their method."

"Who knows about them?" It was Don Zacaros' voice.

"We have people in Nogales who know of them."

"Talk to them. I will speak with Rosalinda. She knew of the two we captured. Perhaps they were *Fantasmas*. She may know more."

When that call ended, Don Zacaros immediately called Rosa. "I need you here. We have questions about the two men we captured."

"Sí, Patron. I will be there tomorrow."

"You will be here in thirty minutes."

"Sí, Patron." The call ended.

"I sure would like to be a fly on the wall for that conversation," remarked Bob.

"Can you tap into the phones and use them like microphones?" asked, Kiki.

"This isn't a *Mission Impossible* episode," Bob chuckled. "We're not that good. At least not yet."

Kiki stepped back. "Great. I'm going to check on Nick and catch some shuteye." *No Director or dreams, I hope.*

Chapter 50

Rapha's phone woke him from a pleasant slumber. The heavy curtains didn't completely shut out the daylight, but the room was dim. He'd volunteered for the night shift staking out Katherine Russell's house. "Hello," he answered groggily.

"Anything happening at Russell's house?" The Colonel's voice rasped.

"No, sir. It's been quiet. People move around inside. Lights and the television go on and off, but no one's left the house."

"It's been several days since anyone stuck their head out. Have you seen Russell return since she crossed the border?"

"No, sir. We did see Sabino go into the house a few days ago, but nothing since."

"They knew we were watching their house, so he's laying low or given us the slip again. If there's no person visible, you better check. I mean more than shadows passing by a shuttered window. You got me?"

"Yes, sir."

"In the meantime, Russell is in the wind, and that worries me. I'm sure she's not taking a vacation. We need to find her." The call ended without a goodbye.

Shit! He and Judy would have to come up with some ruse to check the house. Sabino might know his face, so it would have to be Judy. He called her and explained the situation.

"One of the silhouettes does appear to be a woman, but I can't tell if it's Russell. If she's in that house, she slipped past us," offered Judy. "Not impossible, but we've been careful. She would have had to sneak in a side window. I'll start reviewing the tapes."

* * *

"Kiki, we had some activity on the Nighthawk line," Dawn explained. "They're starting to suspect you're not there, so Sol is going to deliver some groceries to the house."

"That'll keep them occupied for a while," Kiki confirmed. "But eventually they'll figure it out."

"We do the same thing as when Nick left," Sol said. "We intercept signal and run front camera on loop so Dawn enter the house unrecorded. She answer door when I show up with groceries. We do same when I return to pick her up. Bob, you run patches on front camera from there?"

"Sure. There'll be a flicker when we enter the patch, but unless our Bogeys are techs, they'll never notice. Just to confuse them, I'll put some other flickers on the signal."

* * *

Judy watched a figure move by the kitchen window shade. She focused. Out of the corner of her eye she saw the front camera screen flicker. A car with the banner reading *Carnecia Nogales* on the side stopped at the curb. A man in a white shirt and tan slacks got out of the car. He retrieved two plastic grocery bags from the trunk before walking to the door. He rang the bell. The door opened wide enough for the bags to be passed inside, but gave no clear view of who opened the door. All Judy could see was the silhouette of a woman taking the bags. The door closed and the man returned to his car. She called Rapha.

"Check your computer screen. Someone made a delivery to the house." He grunted. The call had awakened him again, but this was news he needed to hear.

"Give me a few minutes. I gotta boot up."

She heard water running, or was he peeing?

He came back on a few minutes later.

"Did you wash your hands?"

"Fuck you."

"Aren't we a bit testy this afternoon? Was that Russell?"

"I think so. No clear view, though. Who else would it be?"

"Yeah, okay. Whoever it was is putting groceries away in the kitchen. It would be nice if they'd open the curtains. I'll keep watching."

Rapha called Nighthawk. "Colonel, there was a grocery delivery to the house today. We think it was Russell who answered the door. She's still at the house." He hoped he sounded surer than he felt.

"Good. Our client got word of some trouble in Los Mochis with another of their partners, the Mochis Cartel. Something went down, but it's not clear what. I'm meeting with them in a couple of hours. If Russell makes a move, let me know."

"Sir, we've been watching for a while. Why don't we go in and take her?"

"Sanchez, we need information. She won't be taken alive, so no information. Keep watching and see if she leads us to others."

"I'd like to be able to monitor any calls she makes, but without her cell number, we can't. Brown says that we'd have to triangulate from three towers focused on that house, then look at any calls made or received from that location. We need better technology."

"I'll see what I can do."

"Sir, send me the details about what happened in Los Mochis when you get them. I know her signs. If it was her partners involved in Los Mochis, I might be able to tell."

"It could also be a rival gang. They're always trying to expand and take over operations from each other. It's a constant state of war. Let me see if I can link you into the meeting."

"Sir, do you want the video of the grocery delivery?"

"Send it. We've got techniques to enhance the clarity. Call me with any changes."

"Roger that, sir," he said to a dead line. He wanted to capture her so badly and exact revenge. *Perhaps it wasn't the Fantasmas in Mochis, but it feels like it to me.* She had duped him in Nuevo Laredo. *Is she fucking me again?*

Two hours later Rapha's phone rang, waking him for the third time.

"Sanchez, you're on speaker. I'm in a meeting with CIA AD Dick Forester and David Kennedy. Since you know the most about Katherine Russell, listen to what happened in Los Mochis. We want your opinion as to whether it is her group who attacked the Mochis Cartel."

"Roger, sir."

"What happened," began David Kennedy, "is that the Mochis Cartel captured men they claim were spies. One was Mexican, the other not. Not Anglo either, maybe Mediterranean. We're looking for an ID on him now. During the questioning, the Mexican died. Someone staged a raid and rescued the survivor who was wounded. They removed the body of the other man, as well. All of the men at this ranch where they were being interrogated were killed. The setup looks like a sniper gave cover for the attack of three or four others. During the rescue, another cartel vehicle approached the area. All five of those individuals were killed before they could exit the SUV. The estimate is that over one-hundred shots were fired. It had to be a mounted machinegun that hit the SUV."

"What caliber was used?" asked Rapha.

"We had one of our men go to the site to investigate. Four men at the ranch were shot with a small caliber weapon, perhaps 5.56 mm. One man was hung from a chain hoist and carved up. Those in the SUV were shot with something smaller than thirty caliber, maybe 6.5 mm or smaller. Could be a 249 Gulf. Whatever was used had the power to punch completely through the vehicle."

Shit! "It was an AR 10 in .25-06, Katherine Russell's signature weapon," affirmed Rapha. "We have her under surveillance here in Nogales, but someone on her team could have done it." *She can't be in two places at once.* He felt his sphincter pucker. *Maybe she's not here.*

Chapter 51

Rosalinda Villa basked on a lounge chair in the sun beside the pebble-bottomed pool. Water burbled down a rock fountain to one side. Though appearing calm and serene, inside she was fuming. She looked up at the sound of footsteps.

"You look so comfortable, my dear," Don Zacaros said, his shade falling across her face.

She frowned. *After the way you grilled me last night, about the two renters. I placed them at the request of Julio Cardenas. Now you call me your dear? If I hadn't alerted you to Julio Cardenas being behind it, you'd have had no interest. Once again your rash action has caused me problems.* Repeatedly she'd told him she knew only that Cardenas wanted her to help. She knew nothing else about them. It was obvious that one was not Mexicano. She had not been able to place his accent. The other was Mexican, and she suspected from Sinaloa.

"Your attack on the two men was premature," she snapped. "They were able to blow up their equipment and now we don't know what they were after."

"My men are going through the wreckage. We'll find out about them. They had driver's licenses. The one named Ilia was ex-Mossad. My American contact recognized the name. That is all we could find, but I have other contacts. The other hombre was from Los Mochis. We are questioning his friends and family now. We will learn more."

"Your questioning of the two resulted in nothing. And now you've lost them and your interrogator. He was killed in the same way he asked questions." With a smug expression on her face, she added, "I wouldn't be surprised if he told them everything, especially that you were behind the raid." *I have to be careful. If I goad him too much, he'll turn on me.*

Don Zacaros reddened. "El Serpiente told me in his last call that one of the men was dead, the other near death. He won't last long. I have alerted all of the hospitals and doctors. If he shows up we'll have him back. If he doesn't show up, I am positive he is dead. We are going through the debris of their van now. There is more to discover."

The smile on his face showed no humor. "The rescue of them was military precision. They had heavy weapons, and my men tell me there were at least twenty men involved. My gringo friends sent an investigator to look over the site. We will get help from them to see what happened and who was responsible. The army of attackers has to be hiding somewhere. We will find them."

"You also placed me in danger," Rosa snarled. "Julio Cardenas is no fool. This attack could have been staged to look like a police action. Instead your men barged in with no attempt to disguise who they were. Cardenas has men on the police force. He will know it was you, and he will quickly figure out I betrayed him. Now I have no place to go."

"Ah, Bonita, you can stay here. You are a wonderful addition to my pool." He swung his arms wide at the expanse of the yard. "I am sorry if I was hard on you last night. I was upset at the incompetence of my men. It is lucky for those at the ranch that they all died in the raid."

Rosa sighed. "I cannot stay here forever, and Cardenas has a long memory. When I first returned to Mexico, he nearly killed me before I convinced him I had been forced to attack his gang's headquarters in California. Convincing him was muy dificil, especially when all I wanted to do was kill him for what his men did to me and my sister. That is what makes this betrayal so satisfying. I still want to be the one to cut his throat."

"And you will, Chiquita. You need not worry about him for long." Don Zacaros smiled, his white teeth peeking through his heavy moustache. "As soon as we strengthen our position in Sonora, we will remove those who support him and this presidente. In the end, he will go."

"When is this attack in Sonora to take place?"

"I am calling a meeting tomorrow. My men tell me Eduardo Robledo, the head of the Sonora Cartel, was taken by someone three weeks ago. He has disappeared."

I haven't heard anything about that. Who did that?" *This information adds a new spice to the mix.*

"We thought Los Xecas kidnapped him, but there's been no ransom demand. My men suspect the *Fantasmas*. Now a new head, Pablo Escobedo, is moving in as Sonora's new boss. Perhaps it was him, but that is not important right now. Escobedo is still consolidating power. They are in a weak position. We need to hit them soon."

"I want to be in on the planning," Rosa gave him a half smile. *He'll make a botch-up of it on his own.*

"No, Bonita. I will meet with my men on my boat where no one can spy. You would be seasick like the last time we sailed together."

She paled at the memory. "You must tell me of the plans. Can I conference in on a cell phone?"

"We can do that. You will hear what we plan. Your ideas are useful."

* * *

Kiki and Nick entered the RV bringing coyoté pastries and fresh coffee from the restaurant. "Sorry we couldn't deliver any to you, Sol," Kiki laughed.

"Thank you for thought."

Sol and Bob were watching and listening, Sol at the Hacienda, Bob in the RV in Los Mochis. Bob reached for a pastry. Zyra was asleep in the hotel room.

"Nick, Kiki, is that Rosalinda Villa by the pool?" Sol asked.

They both leaned over Bob to get close to the monitor. "I can zoom in." he said. The image of the woman on the lounge chair grew but was blurred. He pushed more keys and the picture became clear. The shadow of the man standing beside her fell across her face.

"He's making a call," Bob exclaimed. He turned on the speaker.

"Carlos, call your lieutenants. Tell them to meet me on the boat at ten-o'clock. We have a planning meeting."

"Sí, Patron." The call ended.

"Hm," grunted Sol. "Game is starting. Well, is the woman her?"

They looked at each other. "I think so," said Kiki. "We were together several years ago and she's changed." Nick shrugged.

"Keep close watch on Don's house. If he pulls enough men for meeting, we can hit it. Take her. She full of information, I'm sure."

Kiki glanced at Nick, a grimace on his face.

"I've never interrogated someone I knew before.

I don't know how I'd feel about it."

Kiki put her hand on his shoulder. "Nick, she's the reason Emilio was tortured to death and Ilia is in the hospital. She is the enemy."

"I understand, but it's someone we know."

"Nick," Sol's voice was soft, "she would see us all killed."

"She doesn't know Kiki and I are involved."

Kiki studied him. "Do you think that would change anything?"

"Maybe. We did save her and her sister."

"Yes, from Julio Cardenas and his men. Why would she be working for him now?"

"Not important here," Sol ordered. "Not enough people for attack. Dawn and I will come there. With Nighthawk intensifying search, we will have to leave Nogales anyway. Now is good time."

"How is Ilia doing?" Nick asked.

"The boss say he and Sasha safe at hospital. Doctors say transfusion you gave saved life. Blood they giving him will result in rapid recovery. Cuts hit nothing vital. Blood loss was problem. Interrogator wanted him to last."

"Bastard!" exclaimed Kiki. "I'm glad Sasha took care of him."

Nick's face was expressionless as he pushed aside the vision of the man hanging from the hoist. "How's Sasha doing?"

"Didn't talk to her. Call later. See what she says."

"I don't like the idea of our people in someone else's hands." Kiki announced.

"Also me, but he is boss. Been straight with us."

"So far," she quipped.

"Yes, so far. No choice. Without him, Ilia would be dead."

"Okay," Kiki grudgingly admitted. *But we'll be watching him.* "We need to get Sasha's take."

Chapter 52

Sol's heart beat faster as he dialed Julio's number. He desperately wanted an update on Ilia.

"Hola, my friend. We got your man in a Marine hospital safe and under guard. It was a very quiet operation. Only his doctor, his nurse and the guards know he is there. None of them know anything else about him."

"That is good. Thank you for saving life, getting him to safe place."

"His sister is staying in the room with him. She is most impressive and very beautiful."

"Be careful with her. She is a member of my team. She has skills."

"Yes, I'm sure you don't want anything to happen to her."

"It's not her I worry about. How is my man?"

"His doctor tells me the cuts were not serious, but with so many, he lost a lot of blood. One hour longer, and it would have been too late. He is getting transfusions now. He is also on antibiotics. Who knows what was on the knives that were used. We will see how he improves over the next few days."

"That's good to hear. We have all been worried," Sol said, hoping he could believe Julio.

"What have you found out about Don Zacaros' plans?"

Ah, here it is. With Ilia and Sasha in his hands, he has leverage. "We are watching and waiting. As soon as we uncover what he is going to do, we can make plans and take appropriate measures. There is a problem though. Without my man and his sister, we are undermanned." Though true, it was the best he could come up with to get them back.

"Perhaps I can supply you with some people I trust. I would not like to see you do anything without enough people."

But you will force us if necessary. Unknown people on my team. I think not. "Thank you for your concern and your offer. We will be careful. Until we know of his plans, I do not know what response is needed, nor how many people are required. *The fewer people who know about us, the safer we are.* I will call you tomorrow to learn more of his condition."

* * *

Sol immediately called Sasha. "Give me update."

"Ilia's body improves quickly with the transfusions," she whispered. "He still has shock from torture of Emilio and himself. He speaks but I can tell he's not fully recovered."

"Is his mind getting better? How long before he can work with us?"

"Right after we got here, he didn't speak. Now he does, and he recognizes me, so yes, he is improving. The cuts and the stitches make him stiff, so I want to get him moving. When I was in school, I took courses in sports medicine and therapy, so I know it is important to get him out of bed and moving. Tomorrow I want to take him for a walk outside, but the guards have kept us in the room so far."

"You are not allowed to go out?"

"Not yet. I am not sure whether they are to protect us or keep us here. The room has medical equipment and one small window but no television. Meals are brought to us, so we're isolated."

"That's probably a good thing. If you are found, you are dead and not quickly."

"Very few know we are here."

Sol detected the nervousness in Sasha's voice, though she was trying to sound strong. "Ya, probably safer. Do you know where you are?"

"We are on a military base. I can hear soldiers drilling. It is very humid and smells of the sea, but I do not know our exact location. The flight on the helicopter was less than an hour."

"Julio tells me you in Guaymas on naval base. I am assured it is secure."

"It feels safe like a jail cell. What is happening in Los Mochis? Have you taken revenge on those responsible?"

"We work on it. You were first to find out Don Zacaros behind capture and torture of Ilia and death of Emilio. He says it over phone while we listen. Rosalinda Villa betrayed them."

"I knew it," she exclaimed. "She was the only one who could have leaked their location. Does our boss know of this?"

"He sound surprised about Rosalinda. Nick and

Kiki knew her from Bio-Cyber war. She fought with them against Julio. They not understand her alliance. Her betrayal worries Nick. She know much about Julio and his operations, but not about us, only that Julio wanted Ilia and Emilio in Los Mochis."

"So she didn't know why Ilia and Emilio were there?"

"Don Zacaros was supposed to find out from them. She and Don Zacaros will pay either by us or by Julio."

Sasha's voice was icy. "I want in. Revenge is Ilia's and mine."

"I understand. You took retribution against El Serpiente."

Her laugh was without humor. "I gave him what he gave to Ilia and Emilio. I only wish I'd had more time. I could have made his life longer and more unpleasant."

"When you think Ilia able to move?"

"The doctor says a week, but if I can get him up, maybe in a day or so. His mind will mend faster once he is walking. The question is how do we get out of here?"

"I work on that."

Chapter 53

The ringing satellite phone woke Rapha. *Why does Colonel Nesbit always have to call when I'm asleep?*

"Sanchez, we're close to getting things on track with Los Xecas without my having to turn you over to them. Expect a call. They want to meet and hear you tell your side of what happened in Nuevo Laredo."

"That's good news, sir."

"I'm sure they'll want to talk to Katherine Russell. She is still there, right?"

"Judy and I have been on watch constantly. She hasn't left the house."

"I sent the team down. They'll be there in five hours. They will sit in on the meeting, and I want to conference in. Call me afterward."

"Roger, sir. I'll set things up from this end."

* * *

After monitoring things in Los Mochis last night, Dawn hated to wake Sol, but this was important. She knocked on his door. "Sol, we may have a problem. Our Bogeys are meeting with Los Xecas about the attack in Nuevo Laredo."

"Moment I be there. Kiki and Nick on line too."

With Sol sitting beside Dawn in the communications room, Kiki and Nick were on the phone as she played the recording of the call from Nesbit to Raphael Sanchez.

"Shit," exclaimed Kiki. "We knew it couldn't last. We have bugs in his room don't we?"

"If they meet in his room, we'll hear it," Dawn confirmed. "If they conference with Nesbit, we'll get that too."

"Los Xecas will go into house," Sol declared. "What will they do when find it empty?"

"I sure wouldn't want to be in Sanchez's shoes then," laughed Kiki. "Way too many people will want a piece of his ass."

"Sol, Nogales is about to get too hot," Nick suggested. "I think you and Dawn should get out now."

"We know this coming, so we moved everything into box truck. It now looks like a Bimbo Bread van but will be mobile command center. We leave after midnight. Hacienda will be relay station as long as is possible. Hate to leave anything, but in choice between people and equipment, people win. You monitor everything from there while we on road. With no problems, we there by noon tomorrow. This last mission as team in Mexico. We all make exfil plans. Be thinking. We talk when I get there."

* * *

Despite her objections at not accompanying him to Los Mochis, Sol dropped Dawn off near the border just after midnight. She would walk across. Kathy was waiting to pick her up and take her back to the Casa Grande house. It was the safest thing for her. He was sorry to see her go. They'd grown close over the last few weeks, but this mission could be fatal and he cared for her. He swore to her he'd see her again.

* * *

The roads were nearly empty at that hour, only heavy haulers. After Hermosillo he popped his first amphetamine. Falling asleep would be bad. As he passed Guaymas, he was tempted to try to see Ilia and Sasha or at least call. Instead, he took the bypass and stayed off the phone. The less anyone knew of his movements, the better. The rest of the drive to Los Mochis was uneventful. Bob had rented another space in the Zar Los Mochis RV park for the box truck and another room at the hotel, this one a suite.

Before taking time out to rest, Sol called them together. He was winding down from the upper, but he wanted to get things done before he crashed.

"Share your plans to leave or not. Secrecy has benefits, but may need to help each other. I return to the U.S. Pick up Dawn. She with Kathy. From there we'll go to Israel."

Zyra smiled at them. "Sasha, Ilia and I travel across Mexico to Gulf. We talk of this before. Will book passage on freighter to Haifa. Contacts from a past contract will help."

"Bob, I assume you will return to Casa Grande?" Sol asked.

"As long as we can stay in Nick's house, we will. All of you know where to find us." He glanced at Sol. "Perhaps we can travel together."

"Good for both of us. He looked at Kiki. "What

about you and Nick?"

"We have a boat in Puerto Peñasco we sail on occasionally. Three times in the past we've used it to disappear. Our destination this time depends on the wind, but I'm leaning toward Australia or New Zealand. A vacation from this life for sure."

"Sanchez is getting another call, not from Nighthawk," Bob announced.

Chapter 54

Rapha stopped at the gate into Russell's community. The guard waddled out of the shack and approached the window. Pointing to the sign on the side of the van, Rapha said, "Flowers for Katherine Russell." The guard looked at his clipboard. "Ah yes, her husband called a few minutes ago to let you in." He raised the symbolic barricade that would not stop anybody. Rapha slowly drove toward her house.

An hour ago, his hotel room had been crowded with the five Los Xecas and four members of the new Nighthawk Security team, headed by Craig Jeffers. With some nervousness, Rapha reviewed what had happened in Nuevo Laredo.

"I was following Katherine Russell. She is a

target we have been after for a couple of years. Colonel Nesbit also wanted me to meet with Los Xecas about an alliance." He glanced at Chuche Cortez, the leader of the Xecas sicarios. "We had a tracker on Russell's car that I followed from Nogales. In Laredo, I had a room in the same hotel she was in. When I found her room, I bugged it so I could listen. I heard no other voices in the room. It was my plan to take her when she left the hotel."

"Why didn't you take her in her room?" asked Jeffers.

"I knew she was armed. It could have been a mess. I wanted to listen to find out what she was up to." Jeffers nodded agreement. "Before sunup, I got an alert she was moving, so I followed that tracker across the border to the fence outside your headquarters." He glanced at the sicarios. "She wasn't there. The tracker was used to lure me to your area. How it got there, I don't know. If somebody carried it, I did not see them. From across the river in Laredo, she shot your lieutenant. She then fired marker rounds around me, making it look like I had killed him. I never fired a shot."

"That is more than 700 meters," remarked Chuche.

"She is that good," commented Rapha. "In Afghanistan, she had the reputation of the best sniper in the military." He continued. "Your men fired at me thinking I was the assassin. I fled and Colonel Nesbit arranged an extraction for me."

Chuche laughed. "Probably good. I am not sure my men would have just taken you prisoner. So we need to talk to this asesina Katherine Russell. She is at her house?"

"We have had the house under constant surveillance." Rapha brought up condensed footage of the surveillance showing shadows on the curtains, lights going on and off, then Nick and Katherine in the backyard. He skipped forward to show the silhouetted figure in the doorway accepting the groceries delivered to the house. "She moves about but has not come out. We suspect she knows we are watching."

"We go in one hour," stated Chuche. His tone of voice leaving no room for argument, even from Jeffers.

Mentally, Rapha rubbed his hands together. At last that bitch will get what's coming to her.

* * *

He pulled into Russell's driveway, stopping

behind her car. Two of the Los Xecas soldiers got out with a large bouquet of flowers and walked to the door. One of the Los Xecas men remained in the van while three of the Nighthawk team went through the gate into the back yard. The rest of those involved were watching from his hotel room. From the driver's seat, Rapha watched, anticipating the sound of gunfire.

Nothing. Five minutes passed, then ten minutes more. The men emerged shaking their heads.

"Nobody home," grunted Craig, the leader of the Nighthawk team. He squeezed his six foot-four frame into the passenger seat of the van. The scar down the right side of Jeffer's face was white. Rapha cringed. The rumor at Nighthawk was that's what happened when he was mad, really pissed.

"You saw the footage. Nobody left the house," Rapha stammered.

"They had it set up. It's a smart house, so they could turn lights off and on remotely. They could move things to look like people's shadows."

Rapha's heart was pounding so hard he thought it would burst. This was the end. He'd never leave Mexico alive. And it might not be Russell who killed him.

"We'll go back to your room and review all of the footage. They got out somehow. Call Brown to meet us. No use watching an empty house. Somehow I doubt they'll return. The place was cleaned out. I'll call Colonel Nesbit with a report."

Back in the hotel room, Los Xecas were on the phone to report back to their boss. Craig Jeffers called Nesbit. Rapha sweated. "Cue it up," Craig snapped at Rapha, distain in his voice. "Nesbit is having our in-house experts go over all the video at headquarters. While we're watching, Sanchez you're gonna tell me everything you know about Katherine Russell. Start with her last tour in Afghanistan." The scar was white again. A shiver ran up Rapha's spine. Jeffers would kill him in a second if Nesbit ordered him to.

Hours later, Rapha was telling them about seeing her in the plaza, when the phone rang. "We've found out what she did," Nesbit stated without preamble. "Take a look at the video before the grocery delivery. There's a break where footage from the front camera was looped. During that break, somebody entered the house."

"How did they do that?" Rapha asked.

"They accessed the signal from the camera and

overwrote," JJ, the IT guy with the Nighthawk team, stated. "That means they've also had access to our phone signals."

"That's what the team here thinks," Nesbit confirmed. "When the car drove up with the grocery delivery, the figure in the door was silhouetted. We enhanced it. That wasn't Russell. Later, there's another break. We assume it was to pick up whoever was at the house. Russell was already gone."

"Sir, we…," Rapha stammered.

"Shut up, Sanchez," Nesbit snapped. "It would easy to blame you, but this isn't entirely your fault. Russell and her team have been two steps ahead of us all along. I've got security going through our protocols to see if we've been hacked. Jeffers, I want a sweep for bugs."

"Yes, sir!"

"Meanwhile, JJ, start an electronic search for encrypted messages in Nogales. We don't need to break any encryption, just find and isolate those signals. We may be able to triangulate on their location."

"Yes, sir," JJ answered.

"I want them found," Nesbit thundered. "Is that

clear?"

"Crystal," replied Sanchez and Jeffers simultaneously.

"From the reports out of Los Mochis and your assessment of the attack against the Mochis Cartel, Sanchez, prepare for a trip to Los Mochis. I'm convinced the *Fantasmas* are there. Be ready to leave tomorrow."

"Yes, sir," Jeffers said.

"We have assets in Los Mochis," offered the head of the Los Xecas team. "We can help. Also we have technology. We will find them."

Chapter 55

"Looks like you got out of Nogales just in time," Bob announced as the team gathered around him in the RV to listen to the conversation from Raphael Sanchez's hotel room. "We're busted." He glanced at the others seated in the motor home. "Worse, they'll know more about our technology when they find the bugs. And believe me, they will find them."

"Yeah. Glad I left and sent Dawn across border to Kathy," Sol muttered.

"As we speak, the Nighthawk guys are scanning the Nogales area," said Bob. "I can shut down the Hacienda, but that will leave us blind to Nogales."

"Without bugs and monitors, we blind now," stated Sol. "Shut down. May find Hacienda anyway. Doesn't matter. We not go back there."

"We made a big splash here in Los Mochis," asserted Kiki. "They'll be coming."

Sol nodded before giving his attention to Bob. "Can you do better encryption? They look for signals."

"I'll write software that will bury it in typical messages. We'll piggyback on those. I'm pretty sure their search will be for encryption. If they start looking at messages with more bytes than are seen in the message, we'll be busted again, but it may buy us some time."

"Good idea," commended Sol. "Can you do the same with drones?"

"Whew! This is going to be a long night. With the drone information, we'll use a varying frequency change. Any signal they see will be so short they won't be able to lock onto it. I'll see what I can do."

"Also, we use box truck as command center. Motor home secondary center. Give us more space and backup."

Bob smiled. "That's pretty easy. We were already set up when you were in Nogales."

"Speaking of drones," remarked Kiki, "what's

the latest on Don Zacaros?"

"Meeting on boat in two nights," responded Zyra, her voice nearly a growl. "We not have Simtex too bad. Sink boat."

"Could we bug boat or use drone?" Sol wondered aloud.

Bob shook his head. "We could put bugs on it, but the signal relay over distance is the problem. Depending on how far he goes, our drones could be too far out to sea. Not good."

"We could hit his house and capture Rosalinda when he pulls the guards out," Kiki suggested. "We'd be able to plant bugs in his house while we're there."

Sol crossed his arms, deep in thought. "Yeah, but when we do, the clock starts. Attack bring Los Xecas and Nighthawk Securities to Mochis fast. Dangerous and risky."

"What about Ilia and Sasha?" Nick, directing his question to Sol. "No matter how secure Julio says the base is, they will be found."

Sol stared back, then shifted his glance to Bob. "Any idea of Don Zacaros' timeline?"

"Nothing for sure, but I'd say within the next week. Activity is ramping up."

"We hit them," Sol announced, his decision made. "Maybe get enough info from Rosa to make plans. He turned to Bob. "You good with safes?"

Bob eyes narrowed. "The modern electronic ones, pretty good. I have some tools for them. The old-fashioned dial, not so good. Why?"

"Don Zacaros keep lot of cash at house. We hit that while there. With kidnapping and robbery, they not look for bugs we plant."

Brilliant, thought Kiki, her admiration for Sol going up a notch. *With the vulture drone overhead watching and acting as a repeater, we'll know everything going on. We'll learn of Don Zacaros' attack plans. We might not even need to kidnap Rosa. Except for the revenge factor. I might be willing to let that go, but Sasha and Ilia are another matter.*

Kiki's mouth twisted into a half-smile. "Sol, why are we on Don Zacaros' timeline?" Silence filled the RV as all heads turned toward her. She held up a matchbook from the Jakarta Club in Hermosillo. "If this were found at my hide, along with cigarette butts, the logical conclusion would be that one of the attackers was in this club. Hermosillo is in Sonora."

"Shit! Great idea!" Sol exclaimed. "Don Zacaros believe this Sonora Cartel hit. He have to hit back–soon, with his temper. Must send message he is not weak."

"Yeah, and with our last attack, the clock is ticking for Nighthawk to come to Los Mochis. We can't wait for Don Zacaros to act. Let's push him." Kiki beamed.

"Where did you get that?" asked Nick, pointing at the matchbook.

"It was on the ground in the next camper slot. I picked up some butts too."

"Everyone get rest. We need rest." Sol's phone rang. He glanced at the caller ID. "Hello, Sasha."

"Sol, Ilia improves, but I am not sure when we'll be able to leave. May not depend on his health."

"Is he able to travel?" asked Nick.

"He says so. Doctors say not a good idea."

"Think Julio would hold you to pressure us?" Kiki asked, looking at Sol. "I don't relish the idea of trying to pull off a rescue from the Mexican Navy," she declared.

"Not come to that," assured Sol. "Sasha, I get back to you shortly."

* * *

In the box truck, Sol dialed Julio's number.

"Ah, Sol, I was about to call you with news of your man. He is recovering well, though I am told he needs more time in the hospital."

"I need him for this mission. Is vital. We have doctor on team can take care of him, so must move him here." There was a long pause.

"I can arrange to have him flown tonight to the place we picked him up. I will call you when the helicopter is ready to leave."

"Thank you."

"What have you found out about Zacaros' attack?"

"My man you have is technical expert. Need him for more details. Not know enough, only attack in planning stages. I worry that with my people there, someone find out. Bad for us, bad for you."

Again there was a pause. "True. I have word that Los Xecas are working with Americans hunting for those who have attacked their operation."

"Thank you for information. We be careful. Leave phone plugged in. We send you new software, better encryption. Increased security."

"Yes, I would be at great risk if my activities became known. We must take all precautions."

"With us also." *Being intermediary between bad guys and bad guys isn't comfortable position.*

* * *

Seeing only swirling dust as Nick looked out of the windows, the clatter of helicopter rotors rattled the van. The van's side door slid open and Sasha helped Ilia inside. She strapped him into the seat like a housewife belting in her kids. She slid the door closed with a slam. Nick glanced out as the noise from the helicopter rose. He noted it had the same tail number as the one that picked up Ilia and Sasha before.

Shielding her eyes from the dust, Sasha climbed into the passenger seat and smiled at Nick. "Good to see you."

"Good to see you. And you, Ilia," he called over his shoulder, "How are you doing?"

"I feel strong, but everything hurts."

In the rear-view mirror, Nick saw him smile. "Yeah, I bet. With all the cuts, you'll be taking it easy for a while. We don't want you pulling any stitches. Did they send meds?"

Sasha dug into her tote and pulled out a baggie

with pill bottles inside. "We are good there. What's happening with the ones responsible?"

Nick drove slowly over the bumpy dirt road. "First, everyone is now here in Los Mochis. We had to leave Nogales. Nighthawk teamed up with Los Xecas and sent a team to our house. We were able to overhear the report made to Colonel Nesbit. Irate would be too light a word. They're hunting us. Your capture and our rescue drew their attention, so Los Mochis is on the map for them."

"Are they on the way?" asked Sasha.

"Not yet. Nighthawk comes with their client's hi-tech from the USA. Ilia needs to take a close look at our security. Their tech went up a few notches." He glanced at Ilia in the back seat whose eyes were alert. Nick could tell he was listening to every word.

As he hit the highway, he accelerated. "They will find our bugs, and they're looking at their own security. Probably find the monitor for the satellite calls."

Ilia grunted. "Okay, I will change our frequency coding."

"Bob's doing that, but you should look over what he's done. We can't afford a single mistake.

Second, we plan to hit Don Zacaros' house." Sasha stared at him; her mouth open in surprise. "We need information on his plans to attack the Sonora Cartel, so we'll bug the place. Also Rosalinda Villa is there. We want her."

Sasha's eyes glinted. "I want her," she said, her voice almost a growl.

A shiver ran down Nick's back as he remembered what Sasha had done to the interrogator at the ranch. Through the rearview mirror, he glanced at Ilia again. "Don Zacaros has been holding his planning meeting on his boat, Good for privacy, bad for us. Even if we bugged it, he might sail out of range of our reception."

Ilia nodded. "I will think about that."

"Things are moving fast now. I'm sorry we're piling all of this on you so soon," Nick apologized.

"It was boring in the hospital. No television, no books." Ilia smiled. "Not even tech manuals."

"I guarantee life will be a lot more exciting with us."

Ilia laughed, then grimaced. "It always seems to be so."

Chapter 56

Kiki peeked out from her hide at Don Zacaros' well-lit mansion. On the overhead view from the drone, they had watched him leave in a caravan of vehicles late in the afternoon. Salsa music drifted across the open ground. Two guards patrolled the front of the rectangular house. There were two more men in the back. The IR sensor on the vulture drone showed three more people inside. Don Zacaros needed most of his men and guards for his planning session. He'd left this skeleton crew to guard his money and Rosa. The odds were six against seven—not too bad, except Bob was hanging back in his car for now. Ilia manned the control center. He wasn't ready for field work. Kiki wore a helmet with a heads-up display from the drone and communications with everyone on her team. She could toggle it to give her night vision or infrared views.

Her hide was two hundred yards away in a hedge that surrounded the well-manicured grassy expanse all the way to the house. The approach over open ground for the rest of the team meant that first she had to knock out the guards in front. And anybody who came out of the house, without raising the alarm. Sasha and Zyra would deal with the ones in back, then enter at the same time as Sol and Nick came in the front.

As soon as the house was secured, Bob would enter and deal with the safe. They'd grab cash and Rosa and be off. That was the plan.

Again, Kiki had chosen the 300 Blackout with its own night vision scope. The range was short, and the rifle could be effectively silenced. The two guards in front walked from opposite corners of the house, crossing at the front door and proceeding to the end. They'd turn and repeat. Both were armed with AK style assault rifles, pistols at their waists. She had timed their complete cycle–seven minutes. The time to hit them was as they were approaching the corners. She could take one while the other's back was to him, and he was far enough away that the sound of the bullet striking flesh would take him a few seconds to identify. When he turned to see what had happened, she'd take him. Piece of cake. The assault would start when the second man fell, and Zyra and Sasha had the back secured. "Everybody in position?"

"Sol and Nick good"

"Zyra, Sasha good."

Just as she was waiting for the men to cross, another man came out of the house. "Hold! Zyra, Sasha, the boss is checking on the sentries. He'll probably check those in the back too. Wait until he goes back inside. Let me know."

"Da."

The man shared a cigarette with the sentries then returned to the house. "He may be coming out in a few minutes. He's done with the ones in front."

"He talks to them now. I could take them."

"No. Three is too many at one time. Wait until he goes inside."

"Da. He enters now."

"The two in front are crossing now, two minutes." With her crosshairs on the man on her left, she counted off the seconds. "Now." The rifle emitted a soft pop and the man went down. The clatter of his falling rifle caused the other man to turn. Her crosshairs were on his head. Another soft pop and he collapsed. "Front clear." The front door opened. "Hold! The boss must have heard the sound of the rifles hitting the ground."

The stocky man ran to the guard on the left, drawing a pistol. One glance and he turned to look across the grassy expanse, pistol sweeping the yard.

Kiki's shot took him in the chest, followed by another to the head as he lay on the ground. "Clear. Go Go Go!" She toggled her heads-up display to see the view from the vulture drone overhead. Zyra and Sasha were just entering the house. Two bodies were sprawled on the ground. She expanded the overhead view to see if an alarm had been tripped that would bring in more troops. The road was quiet. "Inside clear," came Nick's message. "Two men down. Rosa tased. I'm injecting her now."

"Bob, come in. Electronic safe," announced Sol. "Bring toys."

Bob ran past Kiki with a small tool box and several duffle bags.

"Sasha and me come out," informed Zyra. "We bring woman then watch road if opening safe sets off alarm."

Kiki continued to sweep the grounds in case they'd missed anybody. On infrared there were no hot spots, nobody else. Her heads-up showed the road still clear. No alarm yet. It was the arrogance of Don Zacaros and the cartel that allowed them to make this raid. That would change after tonight. She heard Sol ask Bob, "Can you open it?"

"We'll see," he answered. "The program has to run through. Hah, got it." She heard a gasp. "There must be millions in here," Bob exclaimed.

"Take bundles of hundreds. We take what we carry and get out," Sol ordered.

Fifteen minutes later the three emerged dragging the duffle bags. Sol had a canister like an oxygen tank strapped over one shoulder. In the distance she heard sirens. "Let's go. Pick up the pace. The safe must have been alarmed."

"Bring the van here," ordered Sol.

"No," shouted Kiki. "Security cameras are covering the grounds for sure. And keep the masks on." As they passed her, she checked that cigarette butts and the matchbook cover were on the ground along with brass casings. Usually she cleaned up her hide and policed her brass, but that's not what a sicario would do. They'd all been careful not to leave fingerprints on their ammo, loading the clips with gloves on. The absence of fingerprints would be suspicious, but better than their own.

Her heads-up of the drone view showed flashing lights, many flashing lights ten blocks away. She ran to the car and jumped in with Bob and Zyra. "There had to be an alarm, the police were alerted somehow."

Bob put on his night vision goggles and floored it. "We can check the signal log from the drone later. It doesn't matter right now." They drove without headlights for several blocks.

"It's okay," Kiki said, still wearing her heads-up. "All the cop cars drove into the estate. You can turn the lights on and slow down. The drone will keep watch on them until we get back to the hotel."

Through the drone camera she watched six uniformed men enter the house, guns drawn. The rest fanned out across the grounds. Two checked her kills. In back, one man checked out the two bodies. Ten minutes later, one man exited the house with a phone to his ear. He appeared to be yelling into the phone, his arms waving in the air. Los Mochis was about to get hot.

Chapter 57

In the back of the RV where the interrogation room had been set up, Kiki stared at the unconscious Rosalinda Villa, naked and in the Isolation. "She didn't see you, did she?"

"No, we kept our masks on, and I didn't speak." Nick turned to face Kiki. "You know she helped save your life in California?"

With a sad look on her face, Kiki sighed. "Of course I remember. That's why this will be so hard, but we have to know what's in her head. And now more than the mission depends on her information. Our lives do. After the hit tonight, Nighthawk will be here looking for us."

Nick didn't like being reminded. "How long do you think before they get here?"

"Unless our attempt to make this look like a

robbery or a Sonora hit works, two days at the most. Probably more like tomorrow."

"We did spray-paint a Los Xecas symbol on the wall," he remarked, smiling.

She chuckled, shaking her head. "Yeah but Nighthawk is working with Los Xecas. It'll take about five minutes to check that out." She glanced back at Rosa, then at Nick. "You need any more help?"

"I can take it from here."

"Let me know if I can do anything."

* * *

She left the back room of the RV to sit across from Ilia at the table where the flat screen and speakers were connected to the command center in the box truck. He was monitoring the feeds coming from the bugs at Don Zacaros' house and the vulture drone. Sasha and Zyra were in the RV overhead bed peeking over the rail. Bob and Sol were in the box truck listening and watching on parallel channels.

"Zacaros just arrived," exclaimed Ilia as loud shouting came over the speaker.

"That is one really pissed off man," laughed Bob. "Glad I'm not in the room with him." The ranting continued without a break for another twenty minutes.

"He yells at dead men," joked Zyra. "No answers for him."

"He's blames Los Xecas," exclaimed Sol, "wants war with them." The explanation of what he was going to do to them went on for ten more minutes. On the view from the drone overhead, they saw someone run into the house. The ranting stopped.

"Wait, the police captain has the cigarette butts and the matchbook cover," Ilia pointed out. "He's calling his lieutenants," They watched the huddle in the yard part as Don Zacaros joined the group. One officer handed him the items he'd found. Don Zacaros stared at them for a few minutes, then turned and hurried back into the house, jabbing buttons on his phone as he walked.

"He's calling another meeting at the house," Ilia said. "Sounds like the schedule for the attack on the Sonora Cartel just got pushed up."

Nick appeared from the back of the RV. "Kiki, I need your help." She rose and followed him into the interrogation room.

* * *

With the door closed he faced her. "I'm not sure how to get into her mind, but I had an idea. She wasn't religious when we worked with her, and without any religious jewelry I think she's still not. What we know about her came from our time together in California."

Kiki nodded. "She believes I was killed in the attack in Casa Grande." She saw a grim smile on Nick's face.

"That's why you have to be the voice in her head."

Kiki took in a quick breath. She'd never been the interrogator before. "Nick, I don't know how to do this." Nick was the one skilled in directing the conversations to get the answers they needed from those in the Isolation Chamber. He put his hand on her shoulder.

"You've been with me many times. We'll work together. I'll control the meds and write out the script if you need it. You talk to her. Make her believe she's talking to your spirit and that she's dead."

Nick sat in the chair with the laptop and the monitors showing her pulse rate, blood pressure, breathing, brainwave activity. It was the complete status of Rosa. As Kiki slowly eased herself into the other chair, he said, "I'm going to introduce the stimulants and reduce the sedatives. But first we have to administer the curarine. We don't want her thrashing around." He added it to the IV drip portal. They both watched her breathing slow. "Now some more stimulant." They watched her pulse rate increase. He played off the curarine and the stimulant making sure she wouldn't smother, because her chest would become paralyzed.

"She's waking up. Now some psychedelics." Focused on the monitor, they saw a spike in the EEG. "She's awake." Her breathing increased, as did her pulse rate and blood pressure. Still there was no sound from her.

Through her headset, Nick instructed Kiki, "Talk to her."

"Wake up, Rosa,"

"Who is that? Where am I?"

"It's Kiki. You remember me from California. We attacked the gangs together. You helped Nick save me after we rescued you from those men in the mountains."

"Kiki? You are Kiki? You can't be…. The gangs killed you in Arizona," her voice rose. "We went to the memorial service." She was quiet. "But somehow you came back and killed Sean Gallen."

"That was not me. It was Tama. You remember her?"

"Yes, the young girl."

"She became the sniper after Gallen killed me."

"Then you're dead?" her voice a whisper.

"I am, and so are you."

"This is death?"

Kiki looked at Nick. He pinched his arm. She understood. *"Do you feel anything? See anything? Do you hear anything with your ears?"* There was silence. On the monitor they watched a jump in brain activity as she tried to move. *"You cannot move because you have no body."*

"I thought I would be burning in hell for the things I did."

"So you believe in heaven and hell? Do you believe in God?"

"I believe in hell. When I was little, my mother took me to church. Once I believed in God, but the things I've seen God wouldn't let happen. My sister, her daughter," she sobbed. On the monitor, her blood pressure rose.

"What did you do that should put you in Hell?"

"I killed men in California, and I liked it because I hated. I have helped kill men in Mexico, seen them tortured. I have watched young girls and boys sold as slaves," her voice was a wail. "And most of all, I hate Julio Cardenas. Thinking of him burns my soul. I tried to kill him in California. But you stopped me. Why?"

Nick increased the sedative slightly.

"He had to stay alive to take the Mexicans from California back to Mexico."

"He ran from you."

"Yes, he did. You worked with him, didn't you?"

"I needed a ruse to get close to him. I didn't want to just kill him, I wanted to destroy him. Death is too quick," she said with acid bitterness in her voice. "He raped me, my sister and gave us to his men like toys. His men killed my niece. She was only two years old!" she sobbed.

"Tell me what happened at Don Zacaros' house."

"People burst in wearing masks. They killed Alejandro and shot me with something. I fell, unable to move, then everything went black."

"You were working with Don Zacaros to attack the Sonora Cartel, not Julio Cardenas."

"Julio wants to manage all the cartels, but Sonora was his main one, where his roots began. Once Don Zacaros had taken over that, we would destroy Cardenas and all those with him."

"Don Zacaros was your man?"

"I could control him. He was in love with me."

Kiki glanced at Nick, shrugged and continued.

"How were you going to attack?"

"Eduardo Robledo, the head of the Sonora Cartel disappeared. Pablo Escobedo, his number two, is the new head of Sonora. He has not the loyalty of everybody and is slow in cleaning up opposition. Don Zacaros has a small army that will hit their headquarters."

"How is he going to move an army into Nogales unnoticed?"

"He is going to move them to Puerto Libertad on his boat, then by bus north past Puerto Lobos and take the back road to Caborca. He will return to Los Mochis with the boat. Some sicarios will take the cartel headquarters in Caborca while the bus continues on to Nogales for the main attack." There was fierceness in her voice. "Julio will lose his control of the Sonora Cartel. It will be the beginning of his downfall."

"Why this elaborate trip? Why not load the bus in Los Mochis?"

"The plan depends on surprise, and the chance of detection is too great. The Sonora Cartel would be warned. Puerto Libertad is small but has docking facilities for the Don's boat. They will be in Sonora and there are no inspection stations on Highway 3 to Puerto Lobos, so the chances of being stopped are small. The unpaved road to Caborca is seldom traveled."

Kiki could hear the pride in Rosa's voice. *"This was your idea, wasn't it?"*

"Without me prodding Don Zacaros, nothing would happen except that Julio Cardenas would control all the cartels in Mexico."

"When was this attack to take place?"

"Next week, but after this assault on his home, I don't know what will happen."

Nick whispered, "I'm going to tell Sol what we've found out. You get more information about the size of the forces and how they are armed." He rose and patted her shoulder, whispering, "You're doing a great job."

* * *

"Kiki's doing the interrogation," Nick said,

sliding into the seat at the table across from Ilia. Sol's face was on the split screen. He was in the parallel system in the box truck. Nick sighed. "They're going by boat to Puerto Lobos then by bus to Caborca. Part of the sicarios will take the Caborca branch of the Sonora Cartel while the rest go into Nogales."

"Don Zacaros had used his phone to bring Rosa into the planning session," stated Ilia. "We have the recording, and it confirms what you just told us."

"By the way, Sol, what was the tank you brought out of Don Zacaros' house?" Nick asked.

"Fentanyl gas. It may come in handy."

Nick grunted, remembering something about that gas. "Isn't that what the Russians used against the Chechens when they tried to rescue the hostages from the movie house?"

Sol smirked. "Yeah, but got dosage wrong. Killed everybody." He shook his head in disgust as he continued. "Leave to idiot Russians to kill all hostages. Some rescue, huh?"

"I think Don Zacaros is so pissed about our attack, they're going to leave as soon as he can get everything loaded," Ilia said.

"Sounds like tomorrow to me. The day after at

the latest," confirmed Bob.

"Are you done with her?" asked Sasha from the upper bunk, nodding toward the back room.

Nick looked up as she leaned out. Her eyes blazed. He flinched at the thought of what she would do. "Kiki's getting details."

He turned back to Sol. "We should make plans. If we're going to hit them on the road, we should start tonight."

Sol's mouth twisted. "Yeah, right. We must be gone from Mochis tomorrow. Nighthawk Security and Los Xecas will hear of attack. They scramble."

Ilia had the Google maps view of Puerto Lobos and the road to Caborca up on the screen. They all studied it for possible sites for an attack.

"Kiki makes ambush plans." Sol announced.

Chapter 58

Gathered in Sanchez's hotel room, the members of the Nighthawk Securities and the three sicarios watched as Rapha answered his phone. He looked at the caller ID and paled as he said, "Sanchez."

"Nesbit here. Our client has reports of another hit on one of their partners," he announced. "This is the second incident in Los Mochis. The first was a raid by police on a house where they captured two people, spies they think." The house blew up before any evidence could be recovered. The captives were subsequently rescued in a military-style attack. The second confrontation in Los Mochis was a kidnapping and robbery. Again, it was a military style operation with a sniper giving cover while a team hit the target."

"That has to be Russell and the *Fantasmas*, sir," exclaimed Rapha. "It's their signature."

"We're not sure," Nesbit sighed. "That is the *Fantasmas'* MO, but there was some evidence that it was a rival gang, either Los Xecas or the Sonora Cartel. Los Xecas have a lot of ex-military. They could have carried this out."

"There are Los Xecas sicarios here with us now. I'll ask." He turned to the sicarios. "Did Los Xecas attack the Mochis Cartel?" The men looked at each other. The leader picked up his phone. "He's checking now, sir. Do you have more information about the attack?"

"They had a sniper cover the front. The hide was found with evidence. That tells me this sniper wasn't military trained. The two guards in the rear were shot and then their throats were slit. That's the same MO as our targets. Cameras at the site caught the action. Two attackers front, two at the rear plus the sniper."

"Throats slit! That's the *Fantasmas*," Rapha insisted.

"They also had an expert who opened the safe." Nesbit laughed. "Estimates are that four million in cash was taken. Wouldn't mind getting my hands on that. Don Zacaros was about to make a deposit in an offshore account. In addition, they kidnapped one woman after immobilizing her. The cameras picked up two of the attackers dragging her out. That's not their usual style."

"Sir, this has Katherine Russell written all over it," Rapha interjected. "The kidnapped woman will be interrogated. Getting information is something they have been quite successful at. In her and Sabino's bios, interrogation was the reason they teamed up with the FBI during the Bio-Cyber war. There were no specifics about how they do such successful questioning. A lot of missing information about them."

Nesbit sounded frustrated. "I tried to find out about them too. Somebody buried that data deep," he admitted, anger in his voice. "Sanchez, I'm not sure this woman they kidnapped knows anything useful. They may ask for a ransom. Reports are that she was a favorite of Don Zacaros."

"A ransom would be out of character for our targets." Rapha glanced at Chuche Cortez, the leader of the Los Xecas team who was shaking his head. "Sir, the Los Xecas say it wasn't them who carried out the attack. What about the Sonora

Cartel?"

Nesbit sighed. "That remains a possibility. It's also possible this attack is an up and coming gang."

"I find it interesting there were so few guards at the house," said Jeffers.

"Don Zacaros was holding a planning session on his boat. He took most of the guards with him."

"So whoever hit him had been watching for a while," Jeffers interjected. "They knew he and his men would be gone. How could they have that information?"

"Good question," observed Nesbit. "I'll check with our client to see if they have any satellite coverage of that area. We can check back to see if anyone set up an observation stakeout."

"Whether they do or not, sir, we should move our team to Los Mochis ASAP," Jeffers declared.

"I agree. I'll see if the client can task a satellite to cover that area and get you access to the security camera footage from the estate."

Craig Jeffers looked at the other Nighthawk members. "What were they planning, sir?"

"I'll check with the client. I'm not sure how important that is."

"Sir, past assaults by the *Fantasmas* have been

concentrated on kidnapping groups and those waging attacks on other gangs," offered Rapha. "If the Mochis Cartel was planning an attack on another cartel, it would point to Katherine Russell." *Why couldn't Nesbit see that Russell and her gang were behind this?*

"You believe the stolen money was to divert attention, and the kidnapping is to gain information?"

"Yes sir, absolutely. The *Fantasmas* are planning something more than a robbery and kidnapping. If we move to Los Mochis immediately, we may be able to catch them before anything worse happens."

"They could also use the stolen money to disappear. I concur. Saddle up and let me know when you're there. I'll get what I can from the client and let you know about the satellite coverage."

* * *

Chuche Cortez had listened to the conversation between Raphael Sanchez and his boss with interest. He became convinced that Sanchez did not attack the Los Xecas communication center in Nuevo Laredo. He was also convinced the

Fantasmas had been responsible. That they were waging war against cartels involved in kidnapping, one of Los Xecas main businesses. But their attacks had occurred in Sonora and perhaps now Sineloa. Eventually they would expand eastward and become Los Xecas's problem. Except they had already attacked in Nuevo Laredo.

"Raphael, the normal *Fantasmas* assault is a team attack with a sniper giving cover to those carrying out the attack, correct?" questioned Chuche.

"That's what I've seen. Yes. It sounds like the Los Mochis attack is theirs. Katherine Russell is their sniper. She was the top sniper in the American military several years ago." Rapha related the story about Russell and her family. "The first time she disappeared, she and Nick Sabino flew a helicopter from a boat in the Caribbean. They took a captive with them. The helicopter was lost, presumed downed at sea. The captive was Julio Cardenas."

"I recognize that name," Chuche said. "Julio Cardenas led the most powerful cartel in Mexico seven years ago until he disappeared. A few weeks later he was back and became more powerful. Sounds like the helicopter did not go down. When he tried to take back Southern California for Mexico during the Bio-Cyber War in America, he failed, but it made him very popular. He has been very quiet these last years, and his large cartel broke up into the many cartels of today. Los Xecas would like to be part of this hunt for the *Fantasmas,* but for now we will give you the control. I will contact our men in Los Mochis for any information."

"Thank you, Chuche. We leave tonight."

* * *

Once outside the hotel, Chuche and his men went to La Roca restaurant. In the back room, he called his boss and explained what was happening.

"Keep an eye on this gringo Nighthawk team," Juan Soto admonished.

"I have more thoughts about this as an opportunity," offered Chuche. "If we let the *Fantasmas* succeed in attacking Don Zacaros, it will weaken him. We could move in on the Mochis Cartel and take over the western importation of drug manufacturing components. From there we could move north and take the Sonora Cartel. Los Xecas would be the biggest cartel ever."

Juan Soto laughed. "I like the way you think.

The complication is the American CIA. They are partnered with both Mochis and Sonora. That is the client of Nighthawk Securities. We want to be allied with them, not oppose them. We will talk it over and let you know."

Chapter 59

Kiki stepped out of the back room of the RV. "Nick, I need help putting her to sleep." He immediately stood and joined her at the Isolation Chamber. She watched him increase the sedative drip, decrease the amphetamine and curarine. On the monitor, they watched Rosa's respiration, heart rate and brainwave activity slow.

"Did you find out anything else of interest?"

"More than I wanted. I'll tell everybody about the plans when we join the team." Her eyes filled with tears. "Oh, Nick, she thought she was talking to a dead me. After I supposedly died and we left Arizona, she continued to fight the gangs. Her sister was killed by men working for Julio Cardenas."Kiki sat and covered her face with her hands. Minutes passed. "After Cardenas returned to Mexico, he became too powerful for her to attack, so she pretended to become his ally, always looking for the chance to kill him. She wants it to be slow, make him suffer. Revealing his role in trying to control the cartels is not enough. She has to be the one to execute him. Her bitterness and hatred are powerful."

With her eyes glistening, she looked at Nick. "If she had known I was alive and part of an operation with you, she wouldn't have informed on Ilia and Emilio. I'm sure of it."

Nick grimaced. "Shit! Sasha won't understand that right now. She's more bitter than Ilia."

"I know, she's full of revenge, blinded to anything else."

Tears rolled down Kiki's cheeks. "I'm not sure giving Rosa to Sasha won't be a blessing. None of the others we interrogated were able to come back to reality." She looked at Nick. "Do you think she can come back?"

"I've never felt the need to bring anybody back. I don't know. I'll have to think about how to do that."

* * *

"You are done with the traitor woman?" demanded Zyra. Kiki nodded. "Good, we take her." Sasha and Zyra exchanged looks.

"Not now and not here," asserted Kiki.

"Why?" Sasha asked, her normally cheery voice hard and cold.

"We have to be on the road within a few hours. Killing her, disposing of her body will take too much time. We'll leave her in the Isolation Chamber, right?" She looked at Nick.

"She'll keep in there."

"Did you find out any details from her regarding the attack plans?"

Kiki nodded as she slid into the seat at the table. "She is the one behind this plan. It's too bad we can't turn her because she controls Don Zacaros." She stared at Nick, then related Zacaros' plan.

"That's what we got from our telephone tap," Bob confirmed. From the box truck, he had the map of the Mexican coast on their screen and the one on the RV table. "Take a look, Kiki. What comes to mind?"

Kiki studied it for a few minutes, crossed her arms and sat back. "It would be wonderful if we could hit the boat, but we haven't the means to put that together in time. The thing to do is attack them while they're all together on the bus." She glanced at Nick. "Puerto Libertad is a city with a lot of people. Not good. The chance of civilian casualties is too great." Her finger traced a path up Highway 3. "Too much traffic on this road." At Puerto Lobos she followed the dirt road to Caborca. "This is the road, and the best place is where it passes close to this mountain." She circled a spot on the road about thirty miles from Caborca. The circle appeared on the touch screen. "It's isolated with good views of the road for miles. We'll set up the ambush here. I'll build my hide on this hill. We'll stop the bus here." She marked an X. "It's three-hundred yards of clear range for me. We'll set up two other hides on the other side of the road here and here." Two more Xs marked spots on the map. "The bus becomes a trap."

Zyra wore a big smile. "I like."

"How long will the boat trip last?" Kiki asked Ilia and Bob.

In the box truck, Bob expanded the view to show the coast of Mexico from Los Mochis to Puerto Lobos. He traced a path offshore. "If he cruises at twenty knots, sixteen hours. If he pushes the boat to thirty knots, twelve hours. Bad weather and currents will extend that. The Sea of Cortez has big currents."

"How long will it take us to drive it?" Sol asked.

Bob traced the road from Los Mochis past Puerto Libertad and Puerto Lobos and onto the road to Caborca. "Eight hours-thirty minutes if we push it."

"Any idea how long before Don Zacaros will leave?" Sol asked.

Nobody answered. "We got his phone and his number two man, José Gomez's phone tapped. They're still trying to reach everybody. I don't think they'll be ready until tomorrow after twelve o'clock."

Sol sighed. "That's good news. It give us time. I'm beat. Ilia, you, Sasha and Bob take shifts listening. Everybody get some rest. Before you drop off to sleep, have everything packed and ready to go."

* * *

Kiki sat on the bed in their hotel room, her head in her hands. "Nick, I don't think I can let Sasha kill Rosa."

"I understand how you feel, babe." He walked

370

over to her and wrapped his arms around her, holding her tightly for a few minutes. He pulled away. "Listen, while we're on the road tomorrow, I'll try to bring her back. You explain to Sasha and Zyra what happened to her. Once they understand, they may not want to kill her."

"And if they don't understand?" her voice was very quiet.

"One step at a time. Let's see if I can bring her back."

Kiki felt her mind prickle. One glance at Nick and she knew he felt it too.

"Oh boohoo. Regret is a sour flavor, not one I like."

"You never have regrets, do you?" Her rebuke was sharp.

"Never. It is a wasted emotion. Julio Cardenas is in league with the President of Mexico to control the cartels. Rather than make them adhere to the law, he is ignoring the law to unite them under his regime. He will change the law. They will become a super cartel under his leadership."

"It will save lives and reduce violence," Nick said.

"It will reduce my meal ticket. Violence, fear and hatred are my favorite flavors.

"I can't feel badly for you. It is human suffering you're feeding on," Kiki sneered.

"More availability of drugs will increase human suffering unless aid and treatment programs are increased. That is something governments do not do. Abandon this undertaking. You are moving into a very dangerous situation. I do not see how you will get out of it alive.

"We've been in dangerous situations before and survived," she snapped.

"Yes, you have, but never with four opponents trying to kill you at the same time. This may be farewell. I have truly enjoyed our time together. I wish you luck. You will need it. Tata"

"Wait, you said four opponents. Who are they?" But the voice was gone.

Chapter 60

Kiki sat at the table in the motor home thinking about what Rosa had told her. She now understood more about the exhaustion and distaste Nick felt over these interrogations. It was the ultimate deception, and in this case it was a former friend and ally.

"We have schedule, maybe." Zyra shouted from the computer monitor. "This Don Zacaros will sail tonight at midnight. Weather bad now but to improve by then." She looked up from the monitor. "We know time."

"Good news that," exclaimed Sol from the command center box truck. "All day to prepare. Nick, Kiki, take motor home. Bob, drive your car.

Ilia, Sasha and Zyra take van. I drive box truck. Time to set up ambush. Kiki, you think yes?"

She was glad to focus on something besides Rosa. "We don't want all the vehicles at the site," she glanced at the team. All eyes were on her. "Let's put the RV in a park in Caborca. It's only thirty miles. We'll pick it up afterward before we split up. Bob should drive it back to Arizona. We'll take his car and leave it in Puerto Peñasco. He and Kathy can get it later."

"What about traitor woman? There is time to deal with her now," Zyra pointed out.

Kiki stared at Zyra. "I questioned her further. She is not to blame, and more importantly, her true target is Julio Cardenas."

"Julio Cardenas our boss?" Zyra asked.

"Yeah. There are questions about his concern for us," Kiki divulged. "Nick and I saved his life years ago, then we fought against him in the Bio-Cyber War. Rosalinda Villa was with us. When the gangs came after us, I had to die. It was the only way to protect everyone we loved. Until recently, Julio Cardenas and Rosa believed I was dead and Nick had disappeared. We were instrumental in his failure to make Southern California an extension of

Mexico, so. I doubt Julio has much love for us."

"But he knew you with our team," Sol interjected. "He approve you."

Kiki wore a wry smile. "Possibly he had additional plans for us when we were hired. We understand the role he is playing in these attacks on the cartels, information that could get him killed." She looked at Sasha and Zyra. "All of us know."

"Interesting history," noted Ilia, "but what does that have to do with Rosa?"

"If I can bring her back," Nick started, "and I think I can, she will become a tool. She can control Don Zacaros, who is in love with her. This plan to attack the Sonora Cartel was hers. Once she realizes that Kiki and I are here, she will side with us as she did in California."

Kiki hoped that was true but kept her doubts to herself. "Through her we gain control of the Mochis Cartel and have an agent watching Julio Cardenas. If he turns on us, we'll know."

"And if you cannot bring her back she is mine." Sasha said, a deadly tone to her voice.

Nick frowned. "She is yours, but only her body will be left. Her mind will be gone. I will start now. We'll know if this is possible in a few hours."

* * *

Nick took a long look at the Isolation Chamber. Could he do this? Will it make things worse? He let out a deep sigh. There were many firsts here. He decreased the sedative, increased the amphetamines, and added the curarine. The monitor showed she was coming out of deep sleep. His plan was to hold her in a dream state.

"Rosa, can you hear me?"

"Yes." Her voice sounded dreamy and detached. "Who are you?"

"This is Nick from the war. Do you remember me?"

"Yes, Nick from California. I remember. You saved my sister and me."

"Yes, it's me. You've been dreaming."

"I am not dead?"

"No. You dreamed of Kiki. Do you remember?"

"Yes."

"You believed Kiki was dead, but she isn't."

"But I saw her body. Sean Gallen shot her."

"We had to fake her death or the gangs would kill everyone we knew. We had to flee the country to get away."

"She's alive? Where is she?"

"She is here."

"Where am I?"

"We are in Mochis."

"It was you who took me from Don Zacaros' house. He will find me, and he will kill you."

"We are well hidden. Would you like to see Kiki?"

"Yes."

"I want you to go back to sleep. When you wake, she will be here with us." Nick increased the sedative slightly and stopped the amphetamines. He turned off the lights as he stepped out of the room. "Kiki, I need you."

"She's in a light sleep," he explained. "She will suffer two shocks. One is being alive. I've laid the groundwork for that. The other is that you're alive. I want to go slowly. It will take an hour to purge the drugs from her system."

Together they watched the monitors. When her breathing and heart rate were normal, they opened the lid of the Isolation Chamber. Rosa looked to be asleep. Nick disconnected the IVs and the sensor pads. They eased her out, dried her off and wrapped her in a large fleece robe.

"She should wake up in a few minutes," Nick

said. They sat her in a chair. She stirred, her eyelids fluttering.

"Rosa, wake up. It's Kiki and Nick." She looked around, trying to focus in the dim light. At last her gaze fixed on Kiki.

"You are alive," her words slurred. "I dreamed that you and I were dead. Am I still dreaming?"

"No, you're awake," Kiki put her hand on Rosa's shoulder.

"Where am I? The last thing I remember was people breaking into Don Zacaros' house and shooting me. The pain was horrible, then everything went black."

"You're with Nick and me." Rosa's eyes darted to Nick.

"Where are we? What's going to happen now?"

"We are part of a group that included Ilia and Emilio, the two men you rented a house to and then betrayed to Don Zacaros."

Rosa winced. "I didn't know you were with them. Was it you who rescued them?"

"Yes, we did, though Emilio was dead," Nick explained.

"I am sorry. Were they spying on Don Zacaros?"

It was obvious that her mind was clearing quickly.

"Yes. Our group has been called the *Fantasmas*."

She sucked in a breath. "You are attacking other cartels. Don Zacaros believed those men were spying on him, that they were enemies."

"The *Fantasmas* have been trying to reduce the violence in Mexico that kills and enslaves so many innocents. Don Zacaros and the other cartels are responsible for that."

"But you are with Julio Cardenas?"

Kiki nodded. "We all are," she declared softly.

"You battle the cartels with Julio Cardenas for Mexico?"

"Yes," Kiki answered.

"I don't understand." She looked from Nick to Kiki. "He wants control over all the cartels."

"We have been hired, and Julio is our boss," Kiki continued. "We are trying to save lives."

Rosa's gaze locked on Kiki. "But I don't think it is possible to remove the violence. It would be like trying to teach cocks not to fight. It is the nature of the cartels to battle. To not fight is a sign of weakness, and the weak are devoured by the strong.

That is the way of the world, not just Mexico."

"Perhaps with a strong enough leader that can change," Nick offered. "We believe that Julio Cardenas and the President of Mexico are trying to change the cartels to legitimate businesses and convince them that fighting is not profitable."

"He will legalize drugs?"

"That movement is already moving ahead," Nick stated. "It is one step to saving Mexico from gang rule. What the United States does about it is a concern. They will threaten to cut off aid, withhold money, bribe or remove politicians, maybe even try for a resolution in the United Nations. The sad fact is that the hunger for drugs in the United States is destroying Mexico. The U.S. government is trying to battle drugs on foreign soil instead of treating it in their own country. Some do not want to see drugs legalized."

She shook her head. "That is true of many in Mexico. Already the legalization of marijuana has cut into the profits. That is why the focus is changing to other drugs and kidnapping and human trafficking. But Julio Cardenas cannot be trusted. He is evil."

"That may be true, but we will see," remarked

Nick. "He holds a secret position within the government, Minister of Cartels."

"The question now is what to do with you," Kiki interjected.

Rosa turned to face Kiki. "What is your mission? Why were you in Los Mochis?"

"We know Don Zacaros is planning an attack on the Sonora Cartel. It will result in many deaths of innocents. We are going to stop it."

"And if I oppose you in supporting Julio?"

"The man who was captured and tortured by Don Zacaros wants us to give you to him," Kiki snapped.

"I am sorry for your friend. If I had known he was with you, but also with Julio Cardenas I would do the same. Cardenas and his men raped me and killed my sister. I have sworn to kill him."

"Will you betray us to Don Zacaros?" inquired Nick.

Rosa's expression hardened. "I fight against Julio Cardenas."

"I will talk to Ilia," Kiki rose. "Try to dissuade him from killing you."

"We're taking you with us for now," Nick said. "Can we trust you not to escape?" Her eyes burned.

"Okay, so be it." He secured her hands and feet with cable ties to the chair. "If you yell, I'll tape your mouth."

Chapter 61

Julio glanced at the caller ID on his phone. Don Zacaros. "Hola, Don Zacaros."

"Bad news, Julio. My home was attacked last night. My money was stolen and my amiga was kidnapped. You promised me security."

"This is the first I heard of it," Julio said, trying to sound surprised. "Do you know who it was?"

"They tried to make it look like Los Xecas, but I think it was those bastards, the Sonora Cartel," Zacaros snarled.

Julio held the phone away from his ear. Don Zacaros was known for his short temper. "How many attackers?"

"My cameras showed five, but there was at least one more. All my guards were killed." Again his voice went up a notch.

"How can this be? With all of your guards, five or six people attacked, and none of them were killed. How is this possible?"

"I was on my boat," Zacaros screamed. "Most of my sicarios were with me."

"I see. And who is your amiga that was taken?"

"Rosalinda Villa. She was taken. If it was Los Xecas, they would be demanding a ransom. There has been no word."

Shit! The Fantasmas had taken Rosa prisoner. She was his spy and his lover. They knew she'd betrayed them to Don Zacaros He had to talk to Sol about getting her back before they exacted revenge on her. He needed to steer this conversation away from her. "How much money did they steal?"

"We're still counting, but more than three million U.S. dollars," answered Don Zacaros.

"What are you going to do?" Julio asked in a calm voice. *How stupid to keep that much cash at the house. That raid had been quite profitable for the Fantasmas.*

"I am preparing to attack the Sonora Cartel. They did this."

"I would ask you to wait to see what I can find out. Perhaps it was the *Fantasmas*." A successful attack by the Mochis Cartel would hurt his allies, the Sonora Cartel.

"They are in Nogales and Sonora, not in Sineloa," sneered Don Zacaros.

"Let me check into it. I will let you know."

"Call me later today. I need answers." He hung up.

So the Fantasmas kidnapped Rosa. He wanted her. She was beautiful and smart. After the fiasco in California, she had come to him proclaiming her love and wanting to work with him. With her at his side, he could go far. Was she still alive? Had they interrogated her? He shuddered at the thought. Of course they had. Katherine and Nick, and now the rest of the Fantasmas knew who he was and what he was doing. Perhaps they were more of a liability than an asset.

He called Sol. "Hello, my friend. I just received a call from Don Zacaros about an attack on his house. I assume you were responsible."

"Hello, Julio. Yes. Needed information."

"You took money and Rosalinda Villa?"

"We did."

"Have you questioned her?"

"Yes."

"What have you learned?"

"Don Zacaros plans to attack Sonora Cartel in two days. We make plans to stop him."

"And Rosa, how is she?"

"These interrogations do not go well for the victims."

"That is too bad. I was fond of her. She was useful. What will happen to her?"

"It will be quick, that I can promise."

"I would like to know what your plans are."

"Julio, I think it best if we not share those. Nighthawk Securities is contracted to CIA to hunt us. No doubt when they hear of attack, they will come to Los Mochis. We leave evidence to divert blame to others, but was shallow thing. Not buy us much time. Nighthawk with CIA able to break our codes. They find us. This our last job for you for now, maybe long time. No more communication is best, could expose you too."

"When I hear about your success in stopping the attack, I will send payment as usual. Added to your take from Don Zacaros it will be quite a payday. I guess it could be called severance pay. Thank you, my friend. Perhaps when things calm down, we can do business again."

"Adios, Julio."

The bitterness about Rosa stung. *At least I won't have to worry about her revealing secrets. The Fantasmas are another matter, particularly Katherine and Nick. I truly admire Katherine, but she and Nick are liabilities. I didn't get to my position by leaving loose ends.* He picked up the phone again.

"Rudolpho, do you know who this is?"

"Sí. I recognize your voice. We have not spoken for a long time."

"Los Xecas understands the advantage of organizing business in Mexico. I applaud your methods, though of the violence and kidnapping I do not approve."

"We know this and have restricted that business to land east of Sonora."

"I know you are working with the gringos, Nighthawk Securities. I would like to speak to them. Who would be my contact?"

Chapter 62

By early afternoon the *Fantasmas* were on Highway 15 headed north from Los Mochis. In Puerto Libertad, Ilia put magnetic stick-on logos on his van disguising it as a *Comisión Federal Electricidad* vehicle. He placed a monitor camera on a power pole overlooking the port. With it, they could watch the docks, showing them Don Zacaros' arrival. By late afternoon they were at Puerto Lobos. This late in the day, there was little traffic. Once on the road to Caborca, they were alone and surrounded by darkness. They turned onto a dirt trail that the Google Maps showed went behind the hill Kiki planned to use for her set-up. The road where the sicario bus would pass was three-hundred yards away. The four vehicles formed a circle like the wagon trains of old. As a precaution, camo netting covered them. The desert radiated the heat away, and the temperature was dropping rapidly. No campfire, no lights that might be spotted either by satellite or drone. The Milky Way blazed across the black sky. Seated around the ice chest, they finalized plans.

"Early morning, I drive motor home to Caborca." Sol pointed to the map on his laptop. "I take room at Motel Eternia, less than hour away. I park motor home there. Bob, follow in car. Give me ride back. Kiki, what setup?"

She looked at each of them. She had been turning plans over in her head on how to stop the sicarios yet keep everybody safe. They were outnumbered fifty to eight, so they had to keep the sicarios contained. She pointed up the hill behind her. "I will build my hide near the top of this hill, which will give me a clear view in every direction. Ilia, you'll park the van five hundred yards back down the road toward Puerto Lobos. Use the jack to look like a flat tire. They won't stop for you. You'll be the first to see them, and you'll control our drone."

She turned toward the other two women. "Zyra

and Sasha will park Sol's box truck on the road below this hill. Raise the hood like you're having engine trouble. The bus won't be able to get around you, so it will have to stop," she pointed back over the hill. "Give the impression you are desperate touristas." She laughed envisioning their playacting as helpless. "The driver will get out to help the two attractive women, but more importantly to get the truck moved so he can get by it. He'll close the bus door to keep the air conditioning inside. When he approaches you," Kiki focused on Zyra, "take him out. I'll keep everybody else on the bus with the Barrett. A fifty caliber is intimidating. After the first shots, they will all hit the floor." She chuckled. "I want their heads down, and a fifty caliber hole will get their attention. The Barrett gives me coverage for more than a mile along the road in case we need it."

She glanced at Bob. "You're inside the box truck with our electronics checking for signals, jamming the phones and watching the road with the drone along with Ilia." She paused. "Should we put up more than one drone?"

"I think the large vulture will give us all the coverage we need," said Bob.

Kiki nodded. "I'll fire a few more shots into the bus door so they keep it closed. We don't want anybody to try to escape. The shots into the driver's seat will move them away from the front. With their heads down, Zyra, you and Sasha take the gas canister to the bus and start feeding gas through one of the bullet holes in the door." The tall black woman looked puzzled so Kiki added, "I want to use the gas on them first. The fentanyl gas should knock them all out. Safer for us." Zyra gave her a brilliant smile. Sasha nodded her approval.

"While you're doing that, I'll put rounds through the bus engine, to make sure it doesn't move. I want the air conditioner off too so there's no ventilation."

"What's to keep them from knocking out the windows?" asked Nick.

"I'll cover the side of the bus toward me, you and Sol to cover the other side. Get spots with some cover about two hundred yards out and about a hundred yards apart, one of you toward the front, the other toward the rear of the bus. That should keep you out of my line of fire. Use the camo netting to stay hidden. If anyone attempts to knock out a window, take them out. Shoot through the side of the bus rather than the windows. The safety glass windows shouldn't shatter, but holes in the metal will be smaller and better. We want that bus closed up as much as possible so it will fill with gas." She looked at each of their faces to see that they understood what she'd said.

"After the gas is feeding in, I'll switch to the .25-06. Smaller holes and lower recoil. Zyra and Sasha will use the box truck for cover. The sicarios may try to rush the door. Anyone that I don't get, shoot them. After the gas takes effect, Zyra and Sasha can go onboard and finish the task. We want everybody to stay in that bus and not try to escape."

Zyra clapped her hands. "I like this plan."

"Why won't they be shooting back at us?" asked Sol.

"There may be a few handguns on board, but all of the heavy stuff is stored in the luggage compartment below," answered Ilia. "Don Zacaros was quite emphatic about nothing obvious in the bus in case they get stopped."

"No one leave alive," Zyra laughed.

"And afterward?" Sol asked.

Kiki looked at each of them. "Ilia, Zyra and Sasha drive back down the road to Puerto Lobos,

Guaymas and then away wherever you want. Take a duffle bag of money. Sol and Bob take the box truck to Caborca to pick up the motor home and then onto the States. Take a duffle bag of money with you too. Split it however you want. Nick and I head to Puerto Peñasco. Sol knows how to get in touch with us."

Sol nodded agreement. "Ilia, what's your estimate of the boat arrival in Puerto Libertad?"

On the laptop, he brought up the view from the camera at the port. "The weather report called for winds and there they are." He pointed at the monitor. In the moonlight, a gray mist whipped across the water. "That scud blown from the wave tops means that the wind is still blowing hard which has slowed them down. I guess they will arrive late afternoon. Once the boat docks, they load their gear onto the bus. I figure it'll be about an hour before their bus arrives here. We'll have a drone up as soon as the bus leaves so we can see them coming."

"Is a good plan," exclaimed Sol, "simple and straightforward. Now what can go wrong?"

"What if someone shows up on the road?" Bob asked.

"I'll fire a few shots to discourage them," Kiki stated. "If anyone makes it off the bus, we have to concentrate fire on them. No one can be allowed to escape. It the gas doesn't work, we'll all have to riddle the bus and go onboard to clean out the mess. That's the dangerous event. If it comes to that, I'll put rounds into every seat front to back. You and Nick do the same from your side."

"What if Don Zacaros has a follower car to see that everything is going according to his plan?" asked Bob. "They could be outside of our jamming radius and call him when our attack starts."

"No help can arrive in time to save them," Sol said. "If we are fast."

Kiki felt good about the plan. It had been accepted and they'd tried to find any faults.

"What about the traitor woman?" asked Zyra.

Kiki pressed her lips together for a few seconds. "Nick succeeded in bringing her back. We're both convinced Rosa's focus is on killing our boss, Julio Cardenas. To explain more about what happened, during the Bio-Cyber War, Julio Cardenas led an army of Mexicans to support the gangs who had taken over California. Sean Gallen promised Southern California would become a part of

Mexico in exchange for his help." She looked at Nick.

"Kiki and I were part of a resistance effort," Nick explained, "to delay the unification under the gangs until the United States had recovered enough to return and take California back. It was a rough time with the smallpox pandemic and the collapse of the electrical grid killing millions. She and I were an army of two until we were able to recruit from the survivors. Kiki was seriously wounded and had to get to help. During our flight, we rescued Rosa, her sister and young niece from gang members."

Kiki grimaced at the memory of her near-death trip. "Julio Cardenas and his army enslaved any survivors they didn't kill. He raped Rosa and her sister before giving them to his men. After Nick and the kids rescued them, Rosa became part of our team fighting the gangs in California. We were effective and Gallen put a bounty on me. To protect our friends and family, we faked my death and disappeared. Though Rosa and the others believed I was dead and Nick was gone, they continued to fight until the liberation.

"Even after he fled back to Mexico, Cardenas

wasn't done with them. He wanted to kill the resistance fighters. His men captured Rosa's sister and niece, torturing them to death trying to find out her whereabouts. Rosa has sworn to kill him. In Los Mochis, we got in the way of that. She didn't know about Nick and me, only that Julio had her set Ilia and Emilio up to spy on Don Zacaros. She needed Zacaros to get to Julio. I leave it up to you." She looked at Ilia. "What do you want to do with her?"

"This woman does what I would do," asserted Zyra.

"Do you trust her?" asked Ilia.

Kiki stared hard at him. "I trust her to do what she has sworn to do. She will not keep our secrets."

"I do not want to kill her," stated Sasha.

"She is your problem," Ilia stated.

Kiki and Nick exchanged glances. "Okay, she goes with us when we split up. Whatever we decide won't have any effect then."

"Let's get some sleep," ordered Sol. "Tomorrow will be a long and eventful day."

Chapter 63

"We arrived in Los Mochis at noon, sir," Rapha reported to Colonel Nesbit. "Our headquarters is in the Hotel La Jolla, top floor."

"What have you found?" Nesbit sounded anxious over the speakerphone.

"We're searching for signals or encoded messages." He glanced at JJ who was intently watching a laptop monitor. "Several of those are coming from Don Zacaros' house. Looks like he's been bugged. Thus far, no control signals." JJ nodded. "The Predator we borrowed from DEA shows very little activity at his house. Frankly, sir, these guys, the *Fantasmas*, have gone silent or maybe just gone." Rapha looked at the Nighthawk Security team and Los Xecas sicarios spread throughout the suite. Their eyes were focused on him.

"Sanchez, I got an interesting tip," reported Nesbit. "I'm not sure who it was from, but the message was that Don Zacaros is planning an attack on the Sonora Cartel and the *Fantasmas* are going to stop it."

"How big is the force Don Zacaros is sending?" asked Jeffers.

"It'll be a bus load, so probably fifty or more," answered Nesbit.

Jeffers laughed. "I don't care how good the *Fantasmas* are, they can't take on that large a group in a fight. How are the cartel sicarios traveling?"

"My source says they're going by boat up the coast. Once in Sonora, they'll move by bus."

"When is this attack to take place?" Rapha asked.

"My source didn't give me a firm date. You need to confirm that Don Zacaros is still in Los Mochis. If not, the trip may have started. Range your drone along the route to Nogales. Look for anything out of the ordinary."

"The best way to stop them is sink the boat," remarked Jeffers. "It's what I'd do. Could

Katherine Russell and her group be planning that?"

"If they had explosives, they could rent a ponga and ram the boat, but they've never used explosives in the past. They may not have had time to get them," pointed out Sanchez. "The next best thing to do is hit the bus, ambush them."

"Yeah, this whole thing is moving fast," observed Nesbit.

"I'll check with Los Xecas about Don Zacaros' whereabouts," offered Rapha. "Sir, the drone has about six more hours flight time before it has to return for refuel. We'll start looking."

"Let me know what you find."

"Roger that, sir."

Rapha looked at the Nighthawk team and the three Los Xecas to assure himself they'd understood the information and instructions. Chuche Cortez immediately rose from his chair. "I will check with my contacts here in Mochis about Don Zacaros," he announced as he left the room.

"What are you seeing at Don Zacaros' house?" Rapha asked.

An aerial view of the house appeared on the screen. "Four guards are visible. That's not many guards," noted Craig Jeffers, "especially since they've already been hit. What's the infrared show inside?" Another view showed four heat sources inside. "Okay, my guess is he isn't there. What's his vehicle?"

Judy looked up from her tablet. "According to the info I've been able to find, he usually rides in a black Hummer."

"Start a search for that," commanded Jeffers. "We got anything on his phone?"

"Not yet, sir," responded Brenda. "If we had a number, we could call and trace from there."

Jeffers looked at the two sicarios and raised an eyebrow. One of the men walked out of the room.

* * *

Chuche had returned to the Los Xecas' hotel room and was on the phone. "According to our sources here, we're pretty sure Don Zacaros is on his boat. This sounds like a good time to go after his operation. How many men do we have in Los Mochis?" He looked up as his second in command, Jesus, entered. "Twenty may be enough since he took most of his sicarios with him on this cruise. Let's pull them together." Jesus signaled. Chuche muted the phone.

"The gringos want a phone number for Don

Zacaros." Chuche asked the man on the phone who told him the number. Jesus shut the door as he left to return to the Nighthawk suite. "Let me know when you have the men assembled," Chuche said. "As soon as the gringos leave, we'll hit Zacaros' headquarters.

* * *

Jesus wrote the number down for Craig Jeffers. He glanced at it and handed it to Brenda. She punched in the numbers. "Went straight to voicemail. He's either on the phone or out of range."

Chuche entered the suite. "Don Zacaros is on his boat with many of his men," he announced.

"His attack against the Sonora Cartel has begun," Rapha declared. "He's moving his men by boat. I'm not sure why. It seems like an unnecessary complication."

"Moving by boat limits his exposure," offered Jeffers. "The question then becomes where will they put in?"

JJ brought up a map of the Mexican coast. "Looks like he could put in at Guaymas, San Carlos, Puerto Libertad, Puerto Lobos or Puerto Peñasco. All of them are accessible to Nogales."

"Zoom in," commanded Jeffers. "Guaymas is big enough but what does it gain him? The same for San Carlos. Both of those ports require miles of road travel and he's still in Sineloa which means they'll have to go through check points. Their chance of someone noticing is slight, but it exists. His destination has to be farther north." He pointed to the map. "Puerto Libertad looks possible. Puerto Lobos doesn't have a dock that can handle a large boat. Puerto Peñasco has the facilities, but it is farther to Nogales."

Jeffers picked up his satellite phone. Their drone was a Predator on loan from DEA controlled by a pilot in the U.S. Jeffers was in contact with the pilot. "Can you move the drone over Puerto Libertad?"

"It'll take about three hours to get there," came the response.

"Do it."

"It's on the way," sir.

"How long a drive is it from here?" asked Rapha.

"More than eight hours," replied Jeffers, looking at the map. "Any idea when Don Zacaros left?" He looked at Chuche.

"He left at midnight."

Jeffers stared at JJ who was studying the map. "Twelve to sixteen hours travel time by boat," he answered the unasked question. "If they left at midnight, they should be arriving in four hours."

"All right, people, saddle up. We're going to be late to the party."

* * *

Jeffers called Nesbit from their Humvee. "We're on the road now, sir," he reported. "Los Xecas report that Don Zacaros is already moving his men north by boat. Our drone showed his Hummer parked at the docks."

"So he's moving them by boat," Nesbit said. "Are the sicarios with you?"

"No, sir. They said they had other business in Mochis. It's just the Nighthawks team."

"That should be enough, but be careful. These *Fantasmas* are professionals."

"So are we," said Jeffers, smugness in his voice. "We can handle them, sir." Jeffers glanced at the others in the Hummer, who nodded agreement.

"Do you know where the boat is going to dock?" asked Nesbit.

"We've studied the coast, and believe he will

put in at Puerto Libertad. It is the logical place to bus them into Nogales. Our best guess is that the *Fantasmas* will hit the bus. It's the most vulnerable target. It has to be on the road to Nogales, but we're not sure where. I'm studying the maps of the area to find a likely place. I've dispatched our drone to that area, so we'll know more when it arrives on station." He sighed. "As it stands, if the destination is Puerto Libertad, the bus will be loaded and on its way before we get there. The drone will give us the route, but we'll have to catch up."

"Shit!" Nesbit screamed. "Keep me informed. I'll try to get you help."

Chapter 64

From the table in the box truck, Ilia declared, "The boat is nearing the dock. The water's pretty rough–probably not a fun trip." They all gathered to look at the screen. As they watched the men come off the boat, many of them staggered. "Not a lot of sea legs there," remarked Ilia. The men formed a relay line to unload crates from the boat and stash them in the cargo area of the bus. After forty-five minutes they began filing on board.

"Clock ticking," confirmed Sol. "Get in position. An hour before show time. Ilia, get drone in air. Can you use directional antenna aimed at ground?"

"Yeah, and a rotating control frequency. It won't be seen from above. Hard to detect, impossible to lock onto besides."

"Must assume Nighthawk in Los Mochis. Now on hunt for us," Sol said. "If they know Don Zacaros' plans, they figure out ours. Probably have U.S. assistance, a UMV. Cover everything with the camo netting. This drone will have camera, IR and radio monitor. We switch to lo-tech." He handed out walkie-talkies. "Range of one mile. Stay off air. Only use when necessary. Let's go, people."

* * *

Kiki was on the top of the hill behind a pile of rocks. Her view was perfect. She set the Barrett up on the bipod and checked the scope. From her bag she pulled out five magazines, placing them beside the gun. She'd probably only need one, but didn't want to dig for more. Next to the Barrett, she set up the AR 10 with ten magazines beside it. She cleared loose stones and rocks before laying down her pad with the two guns side-by-side. The camo netting was draped over the pile of rocks in front of her, extending above her and secured by a few more rocks behind her. It was a good hide. The netting would knock down her ejections so she wouldn't have to search for them later if the case catchers missed any. An added plus was the shade the camo gave her. She was invisible, a part of the hill.

Through her scope she watched Sol and Nick find small hollows that gave them cover on the opposite side of the road. She flipped down her heads-up display showing them from overhead. Once their camo was in place, they blended beautifully into the ground. On the road, Zyra and Sasha had the box truck stopped to one side, but not far enough that the bus would be able to pass. The hood was up and the two women sat on the ground beside the truck in the long shadow as the sun lowered into the west.

The aerial view from their drone showed nothing on the road but Ilia's van and the box truck. There was no sign of those lying in wait. "All good," she said. There were clicks of acknowledgement. *Now for the wait.* She was used to waiting. *Not so for the rest.*

She allowed herself to daydream about being back on their boat. She and Nick had been hunted before. The trimaran had been home to them as they sailed around the Caribbean for several years until those seeking them either forgot or died off. It was rigged so that it only took the two of them to sail it. Those were carefree days. Nick had played traveling doctor when they stopped at small islands, giving free medical care to those who couldn't afford the trips to other islands and their clinics.

Bob's voice came over the walkie-talkie. "I'm picking up a signal. There's another drone in the area."

Kiki wanted to ask for more information, but her signal might reveal her position. She rolled over, pulled out her mini-binoculars and began searching the sky through the netting. If it was overhead, it was too high for her to pick out. That could mean a Predator. Was it armed? She doubted the DEA would send an armed drone into Mexico. But the CIA? Worrying wouldn't change a thing. She focused on the mission.

Bob's voice came over the com again. "The signals are high frequency. The radiation detection is probably the same. Still, best not to chatter. Good call on our drone antenna, Sol. There's no signal emanating above our drone. Ilia, you've set the drone on automatic so we don't send to it?"

"It's programmed on a figure eight repeating pattern. If I hit it with a laser, I can change programs."

"Good. Our drone is just another buzzard

looking for dinner. Their UMV may have IR capability, but as hot as the ground is, it won't pick out anything."

"Tally ho," said Ilia.

Kiki's heads-up aerial view showed the bus several miles away, a dust cloud boiling behind it. She watched as it headed down the road for them. Kiki began her breathing exercises. It calmed her mind and gave her a steely focus.

The bus slowed as it passed Ilia's van. It drew up behind the box truck and stopped. As predicted, the driver got out and stared at Sasha and Zyra who stood and waved at him. Another man started to get out of the bus, but the driver waved him back as he pushed the door closed to keep in the air conditioning, keep out the desert heat. Kiki sighted on the bus door.

Chapter 65

Craig Jeffers turned the laptop around so Rapha could see the screen while he drove their SUV toward Puerto Libertad. "The drone found nothing along Highway 3," he explained. "It's fairly well traveled, so an ambush could have complications. But when we brought the drone back to Puerto Lobos, we noticed a dirt road that goes to Caborca. There are two vehicles stopped on that road, a van and a box truck. I think we've found them."

"Can you get a closer view?" Rapha asked.

Jeffers relayed the request to the drone pilot.

The pilot explained, "We're at maximum magnification now. If I drop the Predator down, it'll become visible. There would have to be an emergency to violate the altitude restrictions."

"Okay, hold altitude and circle," Jeffers

snapped, not happy with the restriction. "Are you picking up any radio traffic?"

"No, sir. No cell or radio. There is an occasional CB signal, but that's what the cops use in Mexico."

"What's the normal range of CB units?" Rapha asked.

"Ten miles, usually," answered Jeffers. *What were CB signals doing out there in the middle of nowhere? Somebody else was using a CB.* "Good catch, Rapha."

"Sir, I have three hours before bingo fuel. We'll have to bring it back to Ft Huachuca," the drone pilot advised.

"Is this drone armed?" Rapha asked.

"Sir, we do not put armed drones over Mexico."

Jeffers frowned. "Keep the drone on site as long as you can. Feed me the videos." He turned toward Sanchez. Speed it up. If we're late getting to the party, they'll be in the wind,"

He called Colonel Nesbit to report the situation. "We're still several hours out. Don Zacaros' bus left Puerto Libertad thirty minutes ago."

"Shit!" Nesbit's voice was tense.

"Sir, I'm forwarding the drone camera view to you. These two vehicles," he circled them with his finger, leaving a trace on the laptop screen, "are suspect. The bus will get to them in forty minutes. If the attack happens in less than ninety minutes, we're going to miss them."

"Goddamnit!" Nesbit shouted at no one. "Let me see if there's something I can do. I'll call you back."

They were behind a huge truck loaded with produce barely doing fifty miles-an-hour. Jeffers felt his face flush. "Get around this bastard!" he shouted at Rapha.

"When I can, sir."

At last the truck driver signaled with his left-turn signal that it was clear to pass. Rapha floored it and they shot past. Outside the SUV, the desert flashed by as Craig Jeffers urged them to go even faster. His phone rang. He looked at the caller ID. Nesbit.

"Craig Jeffers here."

"Jeffers, getting there before Katherine Russell and her group take on the bus isn't critical. Sure, our client's partners will sustain another hit, but they'll live with it. Getting her is key. Keep a watch when she leaves and follow her with the drone. I'll try to get you a chopper."

"Roger that, sir."

Jeffers watched the ambush site trying to pick out where people were. Their camo was good, but he knew how to spot it. As a sniper, Russell would be where she had the best field of fire. The box truck was obviously to stop the bus. It would be the killing site, so that's where he started his search. Two figures were sitting in the shade of the truck.

As the image focused on the two, he could see two women. Neither had weapons visible. Distractions. If he was going to set this up, he'd have the main shooter on the hill. That would be Russell. Carefully, he inspected. Yeah, he could see her camo. It was a good blend and only his trained eye picked it out.

There had to be at least one more shooter on the other side of the road where the bus would stop to prevent people from bailing out. Yard-by-yard he scanned the ground. He was able to identify two more spots he was sure had snipers. Okay, he had the setup. It was exactly the method he'd use. *Goddamn, she is good.* He felt admiration for Russell. This was professionally done.

"Move back toward the van with the flat tire on the way in," he ordered the drone pilot. That van could be coincidence, but he didn't believe that. It was there to alert them to the start of the trap and keep civilians away. A single man appeared to be laboring to change a tire on the rusty van. *Good disguise. A well-planned military style operation. Admirable.*

Knowing what was going to happen, Jeffers was eager to see it unfold. The dust cloud of the approaching bus caused a shiver of anticipation. He watched the bus slow and swerve around the van. His heart beat faster and his finger twitched as he watched the bus stop behind the box truck. The two women, wearing typical tourista garb of shorts and halter tops, were now standing on the bumper bent over the engine. *Yeah, a distraction.* The bus driver got out, turned and said something to the passengers and pushed the door almost closed. The two women stepped down and turned as he approached their hands up in a helpless gesture. The women pointed at the engine. The driver bent over to look into the engine compartment. Fascinated, Jeffers watched the tall black woman step behind him, grab his hair with her right hand, slide a short knife from her waistband and cut his throat with her left. *Quick and efficient.*

At that moment, dust rose from the top of the hill as a large caliber weapon fired. *That's Russell.* The door to the bus slammed closed. Another shot from the hill, probably through the door to discourage anybody from being near it. *What are they going to do? Blow it up, riddle it with bullets? This is like watching a movie.*

"Sir," radioed the drone operator, "telephone signals are being jammed."

Jeffers began to laugh. *They haven't missed anything yet.* He leaned close to the screen as the two women dragged what looked like a welding tank to the front of the bus. They ran a hose through the hole made by the rifle and opened a valve. They ran back to the box truck, went inside and reappeared with rifles.

His attention was drawn to the parked van as a man stepped away and retrieved what appeared to be a large bird that had landed a few yards away. *Shit! Nice drone. We never noticed it.* Once the bird was stored, the van approached the rear of the bus. The driver got out holding a rifle. Two more shots from the hill struck the engine compartment of the bus. If the motor had been running, it wasn't now. One of the passengers tried to kick out a window on the side away from the hill. A shot from one of the two snipers on that side dropped him back inside. The door started to open, but a shot from the sniper on the hill stopped him. *Not as much dust. Russell had changed to a smaller caliber rifle. It's what I'd do. Much more controllable with sustained fire. She was good, WAY good.*

The two snipers on the opposite side of the bus began firing under the bus. *Someone's trying to escape through the emergency hatch in the floor.* The shots must have discouraged them. Fifteen minutes later, things seemed quiet. The two women donned gasmasks and entered the bus. Another fifteen minutes and they emerged, both bloody. The whole ambush had taken less than forty minutes. He had no doubt that everyone on that bus was dead. And in the fashion of the *Fantasmas,* probably with their throats slit.

His phone rang. Reluctantly, he glanced away from the laptop screen and at the caller display: Nesbit. "Yes, sir. Did you catch everything?"

"God damn, they were fast! I don't know what was in the tank, but there wasn't another shot fired. You stay with Russell."

"Aye, sir." On the screen, the two women

stripped down, throwing their bloody clothes into the bus. At the van they pulled out clean clothes and climbed in. The two snipers rose from the desert. One headed for the box truck. Another man came out of the back of it, closed the rollup door and climbed into the cab. The truck headed down the road toward Caborca.

"Sir, the jamming stopped." relayed the drone pilot.

"Yeah, figured that. We're on the sniper on the hill. She's our tango." he told the drone pilot. "She'll appear in a few minutes. Don't lose her."

He'd seen six people. The other man headed around the hill as Katherine Russell emerged from her camo. She was smaller than he'd imagined. She cased her two rifles and headed down the back side. Together, she and the man, probably Nick Sabino, pulled the camo from a blue Toyota.

"Sir, twenty minutes to bingo fuel. After that, I'll have to fly it back for refuel."

"Roger that. Stay as long as you can." *Shit, we're forty minutes away.* Jeffers watched the screen as Nick Sabino, pulled another woman from the car, her hands bound behind her back. After Russell stowed her gear in the back seat, she talked to the woman for a few minutes, drew a pistol and freed her hands. The woman squatted behind the pile of camo. Bathroom break for …a prisoner? *I guess that's better than messing up the seat.* Russell tied her hands again and put her back in the car. Sabino took the wheel, Russell in the shotgun seat. The car bumped down the trail and onto the road following the van toward Puerto Lobos. Operation over, they were splitting up.

"Keep the drone on that blue car," instructed Jeffers to the pilot.

"Roger, sir."

When they hit Highway 3, the car turned north. *Shit.* He turned to Rapha. "We're sixty miles away—might not catch them before they get to the border at Lukeville, and it will be dark in thirty minutes."

"Can't go any faster, sir. The traffic and the road are bad."

Jeffers phone rang.

"Sergeant Jeffers, where are you?" Nesbit demanded, his voice nearly a growl with anger.

"On Highway 3, sixty miles from the turnoff to Puerto Lobos. You watched the ambush take place?"

"Dammed efficient job. Wish they worked for

us. Your chopper should be there in fifteen. Give me coordinates when you get to a spot for pickup."

"Roger that, sir."

The SUV slowed as Rapha spotted the ranch road that Jeffers called out from the Google maps screen. Jeffers called his CO back with the coordinates. Within ten minutes, dust enveloped them as the helicopter landed. Jeffers was still on the phone to Nesbit. "The chopper's here, sir. We'll be on the way in under five, might catch them just after dark. We're going to lose the drone for a while–refuel."

"It's okay, there aren't many places to turn off of the highway. Take her alive if you can, but it's not a priority. Understood? Have Brown continue following with the Humvee. The rest of the team goes with you."

"Roger, sir." He looked back at Judy Brown who nodded that she understood. A smile crossed Jeffers normally dour face as he followed JJ, Rapha, Boz and Brenda to the chopper. The helicopter was a much better gun platform. *Take her from the air? That would be like picking up a rattlesnake. If only I had my M249 with me.*

Chapter 66

"What'll we do with Rosa after we get to Peñasco?" Nick asked as they drove north on Highway 3.

"She chose not to stay with the bus." Kiki looked over her shoulder at the woman handcuffed in the back seat. "Can't say I blame her. Probably a lot of ghosts roaming around. When Don Zacaros finds out his plans are gone, he'll be furious. He might not treat her well."

"We can turn her loose just as we sail out. There's not a lot to do to the boat to get her ready to sail, so the stop in Peñasco will be short. We'll sail over to San Filipe on the Baja and really outfit her for a longer voyage. We'll provision there. The farther we are from here, the better."

Kiki sighed. "I have to say, I'll be glad to be back on the boat. Being on the water always feels like a sanctuary for us."

"Any idea where you want to go?" Nick asked.

Kiki's eyes slid toward the back seat telling Nick she didn't want to reveal more to Rosa. "Away from here."

The sun was setting to the west behind the dunes, obscuring the ocean and the beach. *A couple of hours and we'll be out of here.* She remembered their last voyage and the peace of mind it brought. Loud banging shocked her out of her reverie. Bullets struck the car in a staccato rhythm. *Shit! They've found us.* Nick braked hard and swerved to the left as the Blackhawk helicopter passed to their right and began to settle onto the highway, blocking it. The car skidded, nearly flipping before making a turn onto a dirt road heading through the dunes and toward the beach.

"Brace yourselves!" Nick shouted as he floored it. Smoke was coming from the front and the engine was making knocking noises. Bullets made puffs in the sand around them as he swerved from side to side.

Despite being thrown around as if she were on a

roller coaster, Kiki reached over the seat and opened the case for her Barrett. She grabbed a magazine and snapped it into place. The gun was big, the car was small. Everything felt awkward. The bumps from the dirt track that was barely a road smacked her head into the roof several times. Rosa screamed and dove for the floor, trying to make herself small. More bullets struck the car, shattering the side windows, crazing the windshield. Something tugged at her shirt. *Shit! That was close!* She glanced at Nick. He hadn't been hit.

Rosa was shrieking in panic from her fetal position on the floor. After a half-mile, the car bogged down in the soft sand, stuck. Nick could coax nothing else from it. Smoke enveloped them.

In less than a second, Kiki jumped out of the car, raised her earplugs from around her neck and inserted them. She dragged the rifle out and ran around the car, putting it between her and where the helicopter was last seen. Flipping the bipod legs down, she settled them on the hood. Through the smoke from the engine, she saw the helicopter rise three-hundred yards away, slide toward them sideways, allowing three soldiers to shoot through the doorway. Bullets ricocheted off the roof, whined overhead and kicked up sand around them. It was nearly dark, visibility difficult. Kiki jacked a round into the chamber, turned on the night vision and took aim. Her first shot hit one of the shooters in the doorway of the helicopter, knocking him backward in a mist of blood. The other two ducked back to either side for cover. *That won't protect you.*

Her second shot splattered the copilot and hit the pilot. He wasn't dead…yet, and managed to set the copter to auto gyrate to the ground behind a dune. *That's going to be hard landing, probably won't kill them, though.* "Nick, get out!" she yelled. "We have to make a run for it." She reached inside and hauled the still screaming Rosa out of the back seat of the car. Kiki slapped her. With eyes the size of silver dollars, she stared at Kiki. "Shut up and listen. You might live." Swiftly, she cut the ties from her wrists. "Find a spot away from here." Kiki pointed toward the highway. "Bury yourself in the sand until this is over." She shoved Rosa away, causing her to stumble.

The Barrett was too heavy to run with and not best for shooting people. She pulled out the AR 10.

Nick had the 300 Blackout. Both had Berettas. "Nick, we need to get to the beach. We can run faster there than in this sand. We'll be exposed, but so will they." As they ran through the dunes, a high-pitched scream came from the helicopter. *Someone was wounded and not dead.*

Nick yelled over his shoulder, "I think that chopper had the same tail number as the one that dropped off Ilia and Sasha." The rattle of automatic fire made his words hard to understand. She ducked behind a dune. Nick stumbled and went down.

Kiki immediately recognized the sound of a bullet impacting flesh! *Shit! Shit! Shit! Nick was hit.* Crouched over, she ran to him and pulled him behind cover. In the dark she ran her hands over his body. His chest was sticky with blood welling up from a hole in the lower right side. *Liver. The damn shot hit his liver.* Another bullet whizzed overhead. The shooters had them located. She and Nick had to move, but dragging him would be too slow. She'd have to slow the shooters down instead. She took two quick shots.

Bent over, Kiki ran east, away from Nick and the beach. She turned on her night vision sight on the .25-06, settled behind a dune and scanned the area. One soldier was three hundred yards away darting from dune to dune. As he stood to run for the next cover, she fired. *A head shot. He won't bother us again.* Her shot had given away her position. Bullets sought her out as she ran for another dune farther away from Nick. Like angry hornets, bullets whined around her and kicked up puffs of sand. Again she peeked over the top. This guy was fast! He was closer, a lot closer. The man was huge, easily over six feet-four. She saw him dip down behind a dune. She waited. He had low-crawled to within one-hundred feet before she got her shot. He was looking for her, just his head showing. Her bullet entered just above the night vision lens on his helmet. *Two down, one to go, I hope.*

Shots rang out from Nick's direction. She spun and ran toward him, heedless of being a target. Nick was where she had left him but on his side, his rifle pointed toward another figure fifty feet away on the ground groaning. With her rifle on the man, she called out to Nick. "Are you okay?"

"Not really. Losing a lot of blood."

"Let me check on the other guy." She walked over, her rifle never wavering. He was curled up, his back to her. He'd taken a shot to the leg that put him on the ground. Another shot went through his groin below his body armor and into his guts. Blood was pumping out and soaking into the sand. *He'll be gone in minutes.* "Who are you?"

"Raphael Sanchez," he groaned.

"You're our Bogey. Why have you been following me?"

He mumbled. She couldn't hear and leaned closer, her rifle pressed against his head. "You killed my brother, Miguel," he gasped. "And now you've killed me." He struggled to roll over. "But I kill you."

She saw the grenade and sprang backward. Not fast enough, not far enough. The concussion and the shrapnel hit at the same time, knocking consciousness away. When she came to, her ears were ringing, and she could barely see. Blood was running into her eyes. Her body armor had protected her chest, but one arm felt shredded. Wiping the blood away, she tried to stand, failed and tried again. One leg worked, but not well. The other hung loosely, blood streaming from it onto the sand. Using her rifle as a crutch, she hobbled over to Nick. "I don't think we're going to make it.

You're bleeding out and so am I. I don't want to die in the sand. Can you make the beach?"

"No."

Kiki plopped down beside him and lay back in the sand. "Okay, the dunes aren't so bad." She wiped her eyes again and tried to look at the stars, but her eyes wouldn't focus. "Shit, Nick. I really wanted to see the ocean, sail away." She reached across with her good arm and took his hand. His breath rattled out. "I'm sorry, Nick. I wasn't good enough."

A shadow passed in front of her. *Did I miss a soldier?* She tried to reach for her Berretta, but that arm wouldn't work.

"Let me help you." The woman's voice was husky and deep. Kiki wiped her eyes again trying to see the woman as she squatted down. She took Kiki's good arm and pulled it over her shoulder. Standing up, she raised Kiki to a stand. The pain forced a scream to erupt from Kiki. "Let's go to the beach," the woman said calmly.

"No, I don't want to leave Nick." She looked back toward him. With blurred vision, she thought she saw a man pick him up. Her head spun as a wave of dizziness surged up. "Who are you?"

"I'm Leticia Gardner, and I'm going to take you to get help."

"Unless you have a trauma center on the beach, we'll never make it."

"I have a water ambulance, and it's better than any you've ever known."

Kiki let that pass. "Nick too?" She tried to focus on the man carrying him. He wasn't large, but carried Nick as if he were a feather. She squinted. The man looked familiar, but with bad eyes in the dim light, she could barely see more than shadow and darker shadow. Seconds or hours later she saw the white line of surf. Leticia helped her wade out into the bath-temperature water until it was above her knees. Floating in the water was a huge black shape. They stopped beside it.

"Sit here." Leticia gently turned her, helping her down onto a soft seat inside an opening in the dark shape. "Now lay back."

She sank into a soft bed and kept sinking down until it closed over her. Darkness and peace welled up, pushing the pain away. She drifted into oblivion.

* * *

Leticia stepped back from the whale-sized fish

that held Kiki. She turned and watched the man gently place Nick into another one. The bed absorbed him, enclosing him like a cocoon. "Our med-cells will keep them until we're able to do whatever patching is needed."

He smiled. "I'm glad we got here in time. These two are special to me. They were with me in Medina when I was resurrected. Nick and Kiki have been instrumental in President Carson's plan to bring peace to the world. We've worked together in the past to eradicate those opposing that peace. Get them well. There is more work for them to do."

"Mohammed, I'm taking them to your home to recuperate first, then I'll decide whether to take them to Ocealla. We've let no surface people into our cities–yet." Leticia laughed. "If they go to Ocealla, you are assuming they will want to leave. They may want to join us underwater in Homakuwa."

"I have been in their heads. I think they like the land too much, but we will see."

"You are making progress in creating a more tolerant human civilization. Someday we will be able to return to the surface world."

"You will, and Homakuwa is vital to human

survival. Thank you, Leticia."

"Are you sure you don't want to return with us?"

"I have another recruit to rescue."

She turned, stepped into the maw of the giant fish and sat in a chair beside the heap that contained Kiki. The chair formed around her. A bubble enclosed her and Kiki, and both fish wiggled until they were loose from the sand. She watched the Prophet walk back over the dunes. She waved to his back. Quietly, the fish wiggled themselves free of the shore, turned and swam away, submerging.

* * *

Rosa heard the crunch of footsteps on the sand. She tried to be perfectly still, holding her breath, but fear caused her to quake.

"Rosalinda Villa, you can come out now. No one is going to hurt you."

Cautiously she raised her head. A man stood over her. He reached down for her hand. She was not afraid and grasped it. A tingle passed through her as he helped her to her feet. "Come with me. We have work to do and your job is what has been your goal."

She looked up into his face. His eyes glowed

blue and drew her in. The world disappeared, and she was flying through space. Serenity enveloped her like sinking into a warm bath. Stars zipped past in streaks. "Where are we going?" she asked, but the words formed in her mind. Ahead, the stars became so dense that they were a cloud. At the center was a black circle. Their speed increased until they came to the circle. Everything stopped. They hung is featureless darkness. A soft glow grew around them. Peace and understanding flooded into her. This place was what everybody sought. "Who are you?"

"I am Mohammed al Jar. Some call me the Prophet, but I am merely an envoy from God. We must return."

"But I want to stay."

"You will return but now is not your time."

Her eyes flew open. She was back in the dunes holding the Prophet's hands.

"Come. We have things to do."

Chapter 67

"I'm at the site now, sir," Judy Brown radioed to Colonel Nesbit. "I've been calling, but no signals from anybody." She wore a helmet-cam sending what she saw back to Colonel Nesbit. "The pilot and co are both dead. Looks like the co was hit first by a fifty. Killed instantly, the pilot was hit by the same shot–bled out but managed to get the bird on the ground first. Hard landing."

"Will we need a truck to get the helicopter out?"

"I don't see any damage to it except for a couple of holes and minor damage to the landing gear. The chopper needs to be checked out, but my guess is it's flyable."

"What about our people?" Nesbit sounded weary with a ray of hope in his voice.

Judy couldn't believe the carnage at the crash site. She was glad she hadn't eaten in the last few hours. "JJ was hit by the fifty. Sorta blew him apart." She moved the cam around showing the blood coated interior of the chopper, pieces of what she didn't want to identify stuck to the walls and scattered across the floor. A figure wrapped in a blanket, flat on the floor with feet elevated moaned. "Bullet passed through him and took Brenda's arm off. Somebody managed to get a tourniquet on her. She's alive, but barely. Stable for now. They gave her first aid treatment for shock. No sign of Jeffers, Boz or Rapha."

"Jesus, I can't believe this. They were one of our best teams. They must have gone after the tangos."

"Yes, sir. My thoughts too." She moved away from the bloodbath of the helicopter, glad to be moving but on high alert. "Three sets of tracks moving toward the car, first together, then looks like they split up. I'm following the set that goes directly toward the vehicle."

She wanted to tiptoe, afraid Russell would target her, but she couldn't see anybody. "Sir, is our drone back? This would be a lot easier if I didn't have to be so cautious."

"Yeah, it's refueled and back. The IR is showing no heat sources."

Judy breathed a sigh of relief. "That's good news/bad news, sir. I'm at the car now." She panned the cam around. "Lots of bullet hits, no blood, no bodies. Two cases from a fifty and the Barrett here, obviously too big and heavy to hump around in a hurry. This was where the shooter was when the chopper got hit."

"Goddamn that Katherine Russell was good. Why couldn't we recruit her?" Nesbit grumbled.

"Two sets of tracks going toward the beach, another set heading east toward the highway. I'm assuming that Russell and Sabino are sticking together, so I'm following their tracks toward the beach." She paused studying the ground as she walked. "Okay, brass. Looks like .25-06. Shooter was here. One set of tracks splits away going east through the dunes away from the beach. No sign of our guys, so I'm going to range back toward the chopper to see if they are there."

"You getting this?" Nesbit asked of Julio. They were conferenced together, both audio and video. He still didn't know this guy's full name, but whoever he was, he'd had enough pull to get them the chopper.

"Yes, thank you."

Judy's voice came on. "Okay, sir. I found Boz." She focused the cam on the body. "Head shot. Never knew what hit him. I'm swinging around to find the Sarge's and Rapha's tracks." Static filled the airways as she moved away. "More tracks, sir. Somebody was crawling east away from the beach, probably trying to flank them. The shooter must have been close for them to be crawling. Aw shit. Here's Sergeant Jeffers." Again she focused on the body and the single hole through his helmet. "Another head shot. If this was all Katherine Russell, she was good, really good." She gulped. "Hope she's not still around hidden under the sand where IR wouldn't spot her."

"It's okay, Judy. The IR detector is good. It'd see a heat source unless it was buried deep. Nobody else is alive there."

"That'll make this go a lot faster." She wanted to be away from this slaughterhouse. The image of another Russell head shot caused a shiver to crawl up her spine. *How could one woman do this?* "Sorry about our guys. I found where Russell was when she shot Jeffers. Shit, he got close. Her tracks go back toward the beach. I'm moving that way."

She slogged through the powdery sand. She gasped. "Damn. I found Rapha. Looks like he got hit at least two times, one a body shot under the armor, the other in the leg, but it was a grenade that killed him." She leaned close to give Nesbit a clear view. "Blew him in half." She panned the cam. "His guts are scattered." Judy swallowed, forcing the rising bile back down. She knew these people. "He must have had it on top of himself."

She stood and backed away from the ruin of Raphael Sanchez. "Lots of blood in two more places, not Rapha's. That has to be Sabino and Russell's blood. Rapha hit them, and judging by the amount, hurt them badly." Any satisfaction she would feel was overshadowed by the deaths of her fellow soldiers. "Found the .25-06 and a 300 Blackout but no bodies. They left their weapons behind. I'd say both Russell and Sabino were seriously wounded. Maybe Rapha used the grenade to get her in a suicide hit." *That's serious dedication. Don't know if I could do that.*

"There're more than two sets of tracks leading toward the beach. They had help."

"Shit! Who the hell could have helped them?" exclaimed Nesbit. "The other *Fantasmas* went in different directions from the ambush site."

"I'm following the tracks to the beach. There're two heavy trails of blood, so both are bleeding out. One set of tracks is deep. I'd say whoever made those was carrying one of the wounded. The other sets look like one person helping another who can barely walk. Lots of foot dragging. All the tracks go to the water's edge." Judy bent down to examine the wet sand. "Something big and heavy was here, like a boat. Not a Zodiac, heavier than that. It's either a catamaran or two boats, though the tide is coming in, so it's hard to tell. Sir, we're talking a lot of blood. I see no sign of a helicopter landing. Unless they got immediate attention, they will be DOA somewhere."

"What about the other woman who was in the car?" Julio asked.

"There are two sets of tracks from the beach to the wounded, then the four sets going back to the beach. Another set of tracks goes from the beach back to the dunes. Maybe whoever left the beach went to her."

"No sign of another vehicle?" asked Nesbit.

"Not in the dunes, sir. Sand's too soft for anything but a tracked vehicle. I'm back at their car, and I see a set of plastic cuffs that were cut off. I'm following the tracks that lead east. Okay, looks like somebody was hiding under the sand. One set of tracks from the beach come here. Then two sets leave. They go east toward the highway. Must have been another vehicle that picked them up. Gone now."

"Okay, Judy. See that Brenda is okay. Get that mess cleaned up. Julio, can you get a medivac in for Brenda?"

"Yes, but it will take a while. The helicopter that's there was the closest one. I'll have an ambulance leave Puerto Peñasco immediately. It will take about thirty minutes."

"Sir, we've got some plasma in the med kit. I'll start an IV. Buy her a little time and help with shock."

"After you do what you can for her, search the car. It may have some clues about the other members of the *Fantasmas*. We might get an idea of who helped them."

"Roger that, sir."

* * *

"Julio, I still don't know your full name. What should I call you? Nesbit asked."

"Call me Julio."

"Can you arrange for a pilot to fly your chopper back?"

"Yes," Julio said. "I'll do that. Also, I'll start running checks of medical facilities in the area for gunshot patients." There was a pause. "Most importantly, I need to know that Katherine Russell is dead."

"We all need to know that," Nesbit's voice had a tremble.

"Call me with any further information," said Julio. "I particularly want to know about the woman prisoner."

"I have your number. I'll call you with any update." He ended the call.

While Colonel Nesbit had been on this call, he'd run programs on this guy's phone to find out information, get an identity. Every avenue he tried was blocked. His people could break the security, but that would take time. Whoever he was, someone had set up some really strong firewalls. He did not like working with unknown people, particularly when it got his people killed. His phone rang. It was Judy.

"Sir, there is a duffle bag full of money in the car." She focused the cam on it.

"Wow! How much do you think?"

"No time to count it, but I'd guess at least a million bucks."

"Tuck that away in the SUV and bring it back. We'll use it for our casualties and their families."

"Yes, sir."

"I know this site has been hard to inspect."

"Yes, sir. These were my friends. I really hope Katherine Russell is gone."

"Me too, Brown. Me too. I'm sending another team down to help, but they won't be there until tomorrow. Stay safe." *Was Katherine Russell dead or alive?* The question nagged at him. She was too dangerous not to know that answer. She'd killed two Blackhawk personnel in the past and four more today plus the pilot and copilot. The bus had been a slaughterhouse. This hunt gave her another reason for revenge. A shiver ran down his back.

"YUM!"

Author's Notes

As an author, I enjoy picking topics that are apropos to things happening in the world. Many times I try to put a message into the story to make readers think. The *Evolution River Series* is my idea of where evolution is taking the human species. This novel disregards whether humans are the product of Devine Intervention or evolution. It is about evolution in the future. *Sea Species* addresses where the genetic age will take the human species. This age has already started and cannot be stopped. The changes to life are as unimaginable as were the changes happening after the electronic age. They couldn't be foreseen. *The Envoy* is a tale of earthly disaster and how the human race survives with the help of a new species and a new prophet. In this novel, the new species adapts itself to move beyond Earth. *The Genesis* takes the reader to the ends of evolution. What are those? GOTTA READ THE BOOKS.

In the Dead Series, I created a heroine who is a brilliant warrior, tough and cold when needed. *Dead & Dead for Real* is about terror attacks within the United States. While writing the book, I believed that was my fiction. Later I discovered it wasn't mine and it wasn't fiction. *Dead Reckoning* is about the new warfare, where land captured or troops killed are not the objective. The destruction of your enemy's economy wins wars. In *DR,* the weapons are biological and cyber attacks against the infrastructure of the U.S. Both are way too real. Enemy troops never have to physically invade. If that doesn't scare you, it should. Pay attention to what COVID has done to the economy. *Dead Again* is about the battle to recover from economic devastation and rebuilding the nation. *Risen from the Dead* introduces a new prophet on earth (ties into *The Envoy),* and delves into the evils that President Eisenhower warned us about the Military Industrial Complex. The book describes the United States' return as a world power when it becomes the global supplier of clean energy instead of weapons. *Dead Prey* was fun because I researched the dire state of Mexico where lawlessness plays a huge part. Soon after I began writing, the Presidente announced he would not fight the cartels but work with them. Of course, I introduced the Air America history from Viet Nam. Don't know that? Look it up. The corruption from illegal drugs rises to the top echelons of government, and not only in Mexico. I end the novel with no winners, so there has to be more to the story. What happens when the war against drugs really takes place on our shores? Maybe it's time to end this war that has been going on far longer than any other the United States has ever fought.

I tied the Dead Series into the Evolution River Series with several passages, which necessitated the 3rd edition of *Sea Species*. There are main characters common to both. *Dead Prey* ties in even more closely. Where does the Dead Series go from here? I'm not sure yet, but I'm not ready to let go of Kiki and Nick. I'm too close to them. There will be more.